'Kindly keep your opinions to yourself. I shall take no notice of them.'

'Oh, I think you must,' he answered cheerfully. 'They are so sensible, you see.'

For a moment this outrageous statement threatened to rob Sophie of the power of speech. Then she found her voice.

'How true! What could be more reasonable than a demand to become your spy and put my life and that of my son in danger? Why, such suggestions must be commonplace in genteel circles!'

Hatton's eyes twinkled as he looked at her. 'So the kitten has claws? Well done, Mistress Firle!'

'Don't try to patronise me!' she snapped.

'I shouldn't dream of it. I am accustomed to respect my colleagues...' Hatton was grinning at her.

Dear Reader

The Regency period is a favourite with authors and readers, perhaps because it produced a most attractive air of confidence in men and women alike. This makes it fun to write about and strikes a chord with readers today. The stories may be set two hundred years ago, but human beings do not change.

The heroes may seem cold and ruthless and a law unto themselves, but they are always men of honour and susceptible to love like other men. And although in those days women had few rights, many had great strength of character—and the heroine of this book, Sophie Firle, is one of them. I hope that you'll enjoy this story as the young widow struggles against all the odds for the survival of herself and her son—with a bit of help from an attractive stranger, Mr Hatton…

This book is the first in a new trilogy linked to the Wentworth saga—*The Love Child*, *The Merry Gentleman* and *The Passionate Friends*, all previously published by Mills & Boon®. The children of the characters in the original trilogy are now grown up and have their own lives to lead. Don't worry if you didn't read that trilogy—each book tells its own fascinating story and can be read independently of the others.

Best wishes

Meg Alexander

THE GENTLEMAN'S DEMAND

Meg Alexander

MILLS & BOON®

First published in Great Britain 2001
Large Print edition 2002
Harlequin Mills & Boon Limited,
Eton House, 18-24 Paradise Road, Richmond, Surrey TW9 1SR

© Meg Alexander 2001

ISBN 0 263 17208 2

Set in Times Roman 15 on 16 pt.
42-0502-80145

Printed and bound in Great Britain
by Antony Rowe Ltd, Chippenham, Wiltshire

THE GENTLEMAN'S DEMAND

Meg Alexander

Chapter One

1810

In the gathering dusk of a winter afternoon the long low parlour was filled with shadows. A few logs smouldered on the hearth, puffing out occasional gusts of acrid smoke. Neither of the occupants of the room appeared to notice. Then the man began to cough.

'For God's sake send for candles, girl!' he snapped. 'And send for someone to tend this fire before we choke to death.'

Such a fate might be better than further hours of argument, Sophie thought wearily. She kept that sentiment to herself as she rose to ring the bell.

'The wind must have changed direction,' she said quietly. 'We've always had a problem with this chimney…'

'Would that it were your only problem!' The man fell silent as a servant entered the room. It was but a momentary respite. As the door closed behind the boy he picked up the lighted candelabra and carried it over to his daughter's side, setting it on the table by her chair.

'Just look at you!' he snarled. 'To think that any child of mine should be living under these conditions! I shouldn't have known you for the girl you were six years ago.'

'What did you expect?' Sophie cried in desperation. 'Have you no mercy, Father? It's but a month since I was widowed…'

For a moment there was silence. Then, with a visible effort to control his anger, Edward Leighton spoke in a softer tone.

'Forgive me for distressing you, my dear, but I can't see your loss as anything but a blessing. You are still young, and you have your life before you. Come home with me and make a fresh start. We shall find some way of glossing over your absence for these past years. A single mistake may be forgiven, serious though it was…'

'A serious mistake?' Sophie gave a bitter laugh. 'Father, you haven't changed. How lightly you dismiss my marriage…'

His face darkened. 'I never took it lightly. It was the worst blow of my life. I gave you too much freedom, Sophie. When you eloped you ruined all my hopes for you, and with such a man! You could scarce have chosen worse.'

'Stop!' she cried. 'You shan't disgrace Richard's memory.'

'Others did so long ago. You won't pretend that he was aught but a penniless nobody, possessed of neither character nor probity?'

Sophie's eyes flashed fire. 'How dare you say such things? You didn't know him.'

Her father gave an ironic laugh. 'I decided to forgo that honour. Others were not so fortunate. Why was he dismissed from the Revenue Service? Can you tell me that? I heard some talk of corruption.'

Sophie rose to her feet and eyed him with disdain. 'I never believed those lies. There was a plot against him.'

'Others believed it. The evidence was strong, and the authorities were in no doubt. You knew better, I suppose?'

'I refused to listen to rumour, or to believe those trumped-up charges.'

'Still as headstrong as ever, Sophie?' Edward Leighton sighed. 'I must admire your loyalty, even though it is misplaced.'

'You'll never understand, so there is no point in speaking of these things.'

'Very well. I haven't come to quarrel with you. My dear, nothing will restore your husband to you, but life must go on. It is early to speak of it, but in time you will remarry... With rest and an easier life you will regain your looks, and then we'll see. William, you know, has never married, and he is of a forgiving disposition.'

Sophie stared at him. 'So that's it!' she said slowly. 'I might have known that there would be some reason for your sudden change of heart. It wasn't concern for me that brought you here. Unwed, I am of use to you again.'

Her father was quick to rebut the charge. 'You are grown so hard,' he complained. 'Must you pick me up on every word? Your mother and I are thinking only of your happiness.'

'And that of Sir William Curtis too, no doubt. I'm sorry, but I don't believe you. You've always coveted his fortune and his lands.'

'Was it so wrong to want the best for you? I could never understand why you took against him.'

'A man with the reputation of a lecher? Father, you were blinded by his wealth.'

'No man is perfect, Sophie, as you must have learned by now. All this high-minded disregard for comfort and position proves to me that you are still a foolish girl. It is not the way of the world.'

Sophie did not answer him.

'There is no hurry for you to wed again,' he said in a coaxing tone. 'We shall not rush you into making a decision. William has shown great forbearance. He has forgiven you your—'

'My silly misdemeanour in marrying another man? How noble of him. I wonder, will he accept my son as well?'

Edward Leighton's face grew dark. 'Don't be a fool!' he snapped. 'I'm not suggesting that you bring the boy.'

Sophie looked at him in disbelief. 'What are you saying? You can't mean it! Christopher is your grandson.'

'No!' he cried. 'I'll have no whelp of Firle's beneath my roof. You must send him for adoption…'

It was enough. Sophie rose to her feet. 'I always thought you hard,' she said. 'But this is unbelievable!'

'You may believe it, my girl. Was I ever hard with you? I gave you everything—'

'Everything but understanding, Father—'

'Pah! A child should be dutiful and obedient to the wishes of its parents. You had no experience of the world. At seventeen, how could you decide where your best interests lay?'

'Not with Sir William, certainly…'

'Firle was a better choice? In my view he was lucky not to be transported.' A bitter laugh preceded his next words. 'You don't agree? Tell me, then, where did he find the money to buy this place? It is a well-known hostelry. Have you any idea how much it must have cost?'

Sophie shook her head and turned away. It was a subject which had often troubled her. 'He had friends…' she whispered.

'That, at least, is true, but who were they? Did you ever meet them?'

Her silence gave him his answer.

'I see that you did not. You didn't think to ask? Well, after all, it was not a woman's place to do so. I don't blame you for your ignorance, but you must face the truth. The man you married was a handsome weakling, seduced by the opportunity to make easy money.' Squire Leighton looked at his daughter and sighed. 'You aren't the first woman to be deceived by such a creature, and you won't be the last, more's the pity.'

Sophie began to tremble, but she faced him squarely. 'You shan't say those things of Richard—' She could not go on.

'Stuff! What do you know of men and their desires? Firle was on the make, my dear. His prayers were answered when an heiress fell into his lap. He must have thought that I'd forgive you once you were safely wed.'

'I know better!' Sophie was on her feet, her cheeks aflame. 'He wouldn't have touched a farthing of your money, and nor would I, even had you offered it.'

'There was no danger of that.'

'No, you made that all too clear. You cut me off completely, Father. In these last six years I haven't heard a word from you. I wrote to Mama, but I had no reply. Did you forbid her to answer me?'

'I did.' Edward Leighton looked about him in disgust. 'Would you have had her visit you here, in a common alehouse? How pleasant it would have

been for her to see her daughter mixing with all
and sundry!'

'I'm not ashamed of it. It is an honest living.'

'Bought with the proceeds of corruption?'

Sophie controlled her anger with an effort. Then,
as the gusting wind sent rain lashing against the
window-panes, she changed the subject.

'The storm grows worse,' she observed quietly.
'Will you stay here tonight?'

'I must leave within the hour. Sophie, you
haven't answered me. Come home to us. One mistake may be forgiven. It will soon be forgotten—'

'As I must forget my son?'

'I meant what I said.' Her father's lips tightened.
'I won't house that reminder of your folly.'

'Then there's no more to be said. I thank you,
Father, but I can't accept your offer.' Sophie
glanced through the window. 'Won't you stay?' she
asked again. 'You won't wish to travel in this
weather.'

'I'll be the judge of that. I may tell you that
nothing would persuade me to remain beneath your
roof. Of all the wicked, ungrateful girls...'

'I'm sorry you feel like that.'

'I do, and I wash my hands of you. You've made
your bed. Now you must lie in it. It will break your
mother's heart, but you must make no attempt to
get in touch with her. From now on I have no
daughter, and nor has she.' He pushed past her and

stormed out of the room, calling for his carriage as he did so.

Sophie stood by the fire, listening to the bustle as his horses were put to. She felt sick at heart as the carriage rolled away, but he was asking the impossible. Nothing would have persuaded her to part with her son. Christopher was her life.

There had been no question of her falling in with his demands, but the stormy interview had shaken her to the core. The shock of seeing her father had unnerved her, but a feeling of desolation was soon followed by anger. Then that too faded, giving way to despair. What was she to do?

On the day that Richard died she'd closed the inn, wanting only to be left alone. A dreadful lethargy had possessed her, and when her servants began to drift away she'd made no effort to stop them, knowing that she could not find their wages. Richard had left her penniless. It was but one more blow to add to those she had already suffered.

She felt very cold. Shivering, she moved closer to the glowing fire, standing before it with a hand on either side of the mantelshelf. At least her father's visit had succeeded in shaking her out of the apathy which seemed to have paralysed her will.

On the day of the tragedy she'd felt that she could not go on, struggling against the fates which seemed to delight in dealing her so many cruel blows. Had it not been for Kit...

Her lips curved in a faint smile. Thank God he was so young. He, at least, had been untouched by what had happened.

She glanced at the clock. Kit had been sleeping for an hour. He wouldn't wake just yet. Meantime, she must try to think of some solution to her problems.

Perhaps she could sell the inn. Then she'd be able to move from this isolated spot and make a new life for herself and her son in one of the larger coastal towns.

Absorbed in planning for the future she stood on tiptoe, studying her reflection in the mirror above the mantelshelf.

It wasn't surprising that her looks had shocked her father, she decided. Grief had taken its toll upon her face, and the grey eyes looked enormous against the ivory pallor of her skin. She twisted a lock of hair between her fingers. It felt lank. She couldn't remember when she had last washed it and the heavy mass of auburn curls no longer shone.

She wrinkled her nose. The smell from the burning logs was worse than ever. Then she gave a cry of terror. This was the smell of burning cloth. Glancing down, she saw that her skirts were badly singed and yellow tongues of flame were beginning to race upwards. She stepped back quickly, but it was too late. She was already ablaze.

Screaming, she beat wildly at her skirts, but to no avail.

Then she was enveloped in folds of heavy cloth and thrown roughly to the ground. Strong hands beat none too gently at her garments as she was rolled back and forth.

Frantic with terror, Sophie struggled to free herself, but she was powerless in the iron grip of her rescuer.

'Lie still!' a deep voice ordered roughly. 'And for God's sake stop that squawking.'

Sophie had little option. The unceremonious handling of her person had left her breathless, but at last she managed to push away the cloth which covered her head. Then her eyes fell upon a kneeling figure who was still slapping at her skirts.

It was too dark to see him clearly, but when he picked her up and carried her over to the settle she realised that he was very large. He picked up the candelabra, knelt in front of her, and began to examine the damage to her gown.

'No harm done!' he said at last. 'You've lost a gown, but not your life. Have you no sense at all? Headstrong you may be, but I must doubt that you are fireproof.'

'I...I wasn't thinking...' she faltered weakly.

'I won't argue with that.' Satisfied that he had extinguished the flames, her rescuer tugged at the bell-pull and ordered brandy.

Sophie shook her head as he thrust a brimming glass towards her. 'I hate the taste,' she said.

'Drink it, ma'am! You've had a shock!' His tone brooked no argument. Certain that he would be obeyed, he turned away, filled his own glass, and sat down, studying her intently.

Sophie returned his gaze. She had never seen this man before and she felt a twinge of panic. The harsh features, thrown into strong relief by the faint glow of the candles, were forbidding. Deep lines seamed his face across the brow and beside his mouth and his dark eyes held no trace of warmth.

Sophie regained her composure slowly as she sipped at the brandy. She could not imagine what this man was doing here. The inn was closed.

'I must thank you, sir,' she said cautiously. 'I believe you saved my life.'

The stranger said nothing.

Sophie tried again. 'May I know your name?' she asked.

'I am Nicholas Hatton. The name can mean nothing to you.'

'How should it? We have not met before. I'm grateful for your help, but how came you to be here?'

She heard a short laugh. 'Why, ma'am, I am staying here. Is this not a public hostelry?'

'It is, but we are closed. I have few servants here…'

'No? Your man gave me a key…'

'Matthew should not have done so. I'm sorry, but you must leave…'

The man glanced towards the windows, which were rattling in their frames, obscured by the pelting rain.

'Come now,' he said smoothly. 'Will you turn me away on such a night?'

Sophie was alarmed by his persistence. Tall and broad, he might prove to be an ugly customer if thwarted, and Matthew would be no match for him.

Now she regretted her folly in admitting that most of her servants had left. Had this stranger come to rob her? If so, he would find little of value on the premises. There was nothing here worth taking, but she and Kit might be in danger if he didn't believe her. At best he might search the place, and at worst he might attack her.

The man seemed to read her mind.

'I don't have rape in mind,' he drawled.

Sophie blushed to the roots of her hair. 'I didn't think you had,' she lied.

'Then, Mistress Firle, you are a fool. You have no protection here. Your man looks none too strong to me.'

Stung by his words, Sophie leapt to Matthew's defence. 'He can still fire a gun,' she snapped.

'He will find no need to do so.' Nicholas Hatton leaned back, totally at ease. 'Is this a bad day, or do all your customers receive a similar welcome? You dispatched your last visitor with scant ceremony.'

Sophie glared at him. 'How dare you eavesdrop upon a private conversation? How long have you been sitting there? Why did you not reveal yourself?'

'Why, ma'am, I found it fascinating.' The hooded eyes held a mocking glint. 'Besides, I might have embarrassed you.' He grinned and she saw the gleam of perfect teeth.

Sophie could have struck him.

'My affairs are no concern of yours,' she retorted sharply.

'On the contrary, Mistress Firle, they concern me deeply…' His smile had vanished and she saw him then for what he was—a dangerous man. The hard lines of his mouth and jaw did nothing to reassure her.

'How do you know my name?' she demanded. 'And what do you want from me?' Poised for flight, she rose to her feet and seized the candelabra. If she could slip past him, she would barricade herself in Kit's room.

Hatton removed the lighted candle from her grasp. 'I must hope that you keep a salve for burns, my dear. Hot tallow on your hands can be extremely painful. You will sit down, if you please, and listen to what I have to say.'

'I have nothing to say to you. Please go. It isn't far to the nearest town…you would be more comfortable in Brighton—'

'I'll go when my business is concluded.' His tone did not brook argument.

'And what exactly *is* your business?' Sophie decided to humour him. She didn't expect to hear the truth, but she was beginning to suspect that her visitor must be connected to the smuggling fraternity. The inn lay on the route from the coast to London, but if he hoped to use it as a safe house she would have none of it.

'Why, Mistress Firle, it is with you.' His smile did not reach his eyes.

Sophie backed away, but he reached the door in a couple of strides, blocking all chance of escape.

'Don't be afraid!' he said more gently. 'I don't mean to harm you.'

'Then let me go,' she breathed.

'As soon as you've heard what I have to say…'

'Sir, you may save your breath. This inn will not be used by the ''free traders'', as they like to call themselves.'

'Now you are jumping to conclusions, ma'am. I thought merely that you might care to know exactly how your husband died…'

Sophie looked up at him. Then the world went dark.

When she recovered it was to find herself seated in a chair, with her head pressed firmly between her knees. A strong hand rested on her hair. Then a finger slid beneath her chin and dark eyes held her own.

'Better?' His voice was softer as he questioned her.

She nodded briefly, but she could not speak.

Hatton began to pace the room. 'Forgive me!' he said quietly. 'That was brutal, but I had to find some way of breaking your reserve.'

'You succeeded.' Her voice was barely above a whisper. 'Must you torture me? Richard's death was an accident. The cliffs are crumbling. In the darkness he didn't see the edge.'

'Not so! Is not the path always clearly marked with a line of painted stones? They are visible even through a mist.'

'What are you trying to say?' Sophie found that she was shaking uncontrollably.

He didn't answer her at once. Instead he offered her another glass of brandy. 'Drink this! I believe that you will need it.'

Sophie waved the glass aside. 'Go on!' she whispered.

Hatton hesitated, but there was no easy way of telling her. Best to get it over with at once.

'Richard Firle was murdered,' he said at last.

He thought that she would faint again. The huge grey eyes had closed and her pallor was alarming, but at length the shallow breathing eased. Sophie made an effort to regain her self-control.

'You can't know that,' she whispered. 'I won't believe it. My husband hadn't an enemy in the world. He fell…they found him on the rocks below…'

'You never wondered why he ventured out in such inclement weather?'

'There was a message. He was asked to help. Someone had been injured…'

'And was that person ever found?'

Her silence gave him his answer.

'It was a trap,' he continued calmly. 'The stones had been moved. They led him to his death.'

'But why?' Sophie looked up at her companion. It was becoming increasingly difficult to doubt him. If his words were true, they would answer many of the questions which had tormented her since the day of the tragedy.

Richard had known the cliffs so well. As a Revenue Officer he'd been well aware of the dangers of the Sussex coast. He'd ridden over the land for years, discovering every cove and possible landing place for the men who ran their illicit goods ashore, mostly at night, but sometimes in broad daylight.

In those days she'd feared often for his safety, though he tried to keep the worst excesses of the smugglers from her. It wasn't possible. Those stories were common knowledge. How often had she heard tales of blackmail, beatings, torture and even murder.

When two of his colleagues were discovered in a well, bound and stoned to death, she had begged him to resign, but he'd refused.

It had made it all the harder to believe the charges laid against him. Yet in a way she'd taken the news of his dismissal with a feeling of relief. At least he would be safe.

It had been hard for her, but she had chosen to share poverty with him since the day of their elopement.

Did she regret it now? Of course not. Yet even in those first few months of marriage a tiny worm of doubt had begun to eat away at her belief in him. There were too many mysteries...too many unexplained absences, accounted for by what she'd later found to be lies.

Then she had Kit, and that made up for everything.

Lost in thought, she became aware that her companion had not answered her.

'Why?' she repeated. 'Why should anyone wish to harm Richard? He left the Preventive Service long ago.'

'You are mistaken, ma'am. I can tell you that he did not.'

'But those charges...? I knew that they were lies, but somehow they were proven and he was dismissed.'

Hatton gave her a long look. 'You were unconvinced of the truth of it? I thought that we had done better.'

'What do you mean by that remark? What had it to do with you?'

'I organised it, Mistress Firle. Your husband was my man. We needed an informer. Who better than a disgraced Revenue Officer, accused of taking bribes?'

'So it was you? You were the cause of my husband's death?'

'Firle knew the risks,' Hatton told her coldly. 'He accepted them. He wasn't the first to die, as you must know. I want the men who killed him, and the others.'

'Why come to me?'

'I am convinced that you can help. I won't continue to send brave men to their deaths. Now, I too intend to lay a trap.'

'You shan't use me!' Sophie said firmly. 'My son comes first. I won't put him at risk. What do I care about a few kegs of brandy, or some packages of tobacco?'

'I hoped that you might care about murder.'

That silenced her.

'You won't be at risk, I promise. Who will suspect a woman? I can give you a couple of bruisers for protection. Use them as ostlers if you wish.'

'I won't do it!' Sophie's mouth set in a mutinous line. 'You shan't use me in any of your plans. I intend to sell the inn and move away from here.'

'Unfortunately, you can't do so. The inn does not belong to you.'

'My husband left me everything in his will.'

'It wasn't his to leave. This inn belongs to the authorities. I put him in the place myself.'

'You are lying. I don't believe you. This is a trick. You would say anything to get your way...'

Hatton shrugged. 'Speak to your lawyer if you doubt me. The inn is in my name.'

'Are you telling me that you could turn me out?'

'I could, but I should be sorry to do so. All I ask is a few months of your time. Open up your doors again. If I'm not mistaken, your previous customers will return.'

'So I am to be the bait?'

'Those are crude terms, ma'am, but, to put it bluntly, that is so. Did you know any of your customers?'

'I did not!' she retorted. 'My husband did not wish me to enter the public rooms.'

'Did he say why?'

'He told me that for the most part they were unsavoury characters. He tolerated them for their lavish spending habits.'

'Quite! There were also other reasons. Now I suggest that in future you make yourself agreeable to these men, make yourself amenable to suggestions, plead poverty if you must…'

'That won't be difficult,' she assured him grimly. 'What else am I to do?'

'Keep your eyes and ears open. Men speak freely when they are at their ease and primed with drink. Such talk will be of interest to me.'

'So I am to be your spy?'

'Dear me, what a way you have of speaking straight. Then, yes, if you will have it so…'

'How do I know that I can trust you? I've seen no proof of your identity. You could be a member of a rival gang.'

'Read this!' Hatton pulled a document from his pocket.

Sophie looked at him uncertainly. Then she began to read. The authorisation left her in no doubt of his probity.

'You could have stolen this,' she accused.

'Very true! But I did not. However, you are wise to doubt me. You have more sense than I imagined.'

'You are insulting, sir.' Sophie eyed him with acute dislike.

'Am I? I meant that as a compliment, but I have no notion of how to deal with women.'

'That, Mr Hatton, is all too obvious. You force your way in here with these preposterous suggestions, and expect me to fall in with your plans—'

'You have no choice,' he told her calmly.

'You are mistaken. I could leave this place.'

'Where would you go? Have you any money?'

Sophie did not answer him.

'I thought not. Firle was never the thriftiest of men. You could, of course, return to your father's home, but I think you will not leave your son.'

'You monster!' Sophie was ready to choke with rage. 'I see that spying is your forte. You listened on purpose to my conversation.'

'It was instructive.' He didn't trouble to deny it. 'I had to be sure of you.'

'So you would use my son to get your way? You disgust me! I owe you nothing, Mr Hatton. In fact, it would be a pleasure to trick you—'

'Others have tried it, ma'am. Let me assure you that the consequences would be unpleasant.'

'More threats? Why, you are naught but a common blackmailer—'

'We are wasting time.' Clearly Hatton was impervious to insult. 'I am waiting for your answer.'

Sophie thought quickly. There must be some way of outwitting him.

'I need more time to consider,' she said at last.

'You have an hour. When we dine tonight you will give me your decision.'

'You plan to dine here? That will not be possible. We have no food to spare.'

'So I understand, but I have no intention of going to bed upon an empty stomach. I sent out for provisions. If I'm not mistaken, Matthew's wife is already busy in the kitchen.'

'Sir, you take too much upon yourself. How dare you walk in here and give orders to my servants?'

'You prefer to starve?'

'There was no question of that,' she told him stiffly. 'I meant only that we should be unable to provide a meal which would satisfy your high standards.' She hoped that her sarcastic tone would anger him. To her fury he began to laugh.

'That's better!' he approved. 'I'm glad to see that you haven't lost your spirit. In the future it will serve you well.'

'And you?'

'I live in hope that it will serve me too. Now, ma'am, you will wish to change your gown before we dine.'

Sophie followed his eyes as he glanced down at her shirt and saw to her horror that the singed cloth was in tatters, revealing a generous expanse of shapely leg.

Hot colour flooded her cheeks. What a spectacle she must present. She jumped up in confusion, expecting some sly remark, but Hatton had turned away.

'You must excuse me now,' he said. 'I have work to do. Shall we say in my rooms at seven?'

'Your rooms?' she echoed blankly. 'I thought I had explained. You can't stay here. The inn is closed.'

'But not to me, I think.' He held up a hand to still her protests. 'Must you always argue, woman? This place is mine, and for the present you are here on sufferance.'

Helpless and seething with outrage, Sophie pushed past him and went to find her son.

Chapter Two

Anger turned to panic when she found that Kit was not in his room. Hideous images filled her mind. Had Hatton already spirited him away, holding him hostage against her good behaviour? She wouldn't put anything past that ruthless creature.

Wildly, she searched the upper floor, but she could find no trace of the child. Then, as she hurried down the stairs she heard his gleeful laugh. Thank heavens! He was in the kitchen.

She burst into the room to find him seated at the old deal table, playing happily with a ball of grubby dough.

Half-fainting with relief, she caught him to her, raining kisses on his face and neck until he tried to wriggle free.

'You're squashing me!' he complained.

'I'm sorry, my pet. You gave me a fright. How did you get down here?'

'Mistress, I brought him down. He'd been calling for some time…' Matthew's wife gave Sophie a reproachful look.

'Oh, Bess, I'm sorry. I hadn't realised that it was so late. Our unexpected visitor kept me talking.' Sophie swallowed hard. 'He intends to stay, I fear. Have we food enough for a decent dinner?'

'Enough for a week, I shouldn't wonder. The gentleman sent round to the nearest farm as soon as he arrived, and without so much as a by-your-leave...' Bess gave her mistress a curious look. 'Do you know him, ma'am?'

'He convinced me that he is perfectly respectable.' Some inner voice warned Sophie not to mention Hatton's connection with the Preventive Service.

'That's as may be, but I thought that we were closed. Matt told him to go on to Brighton, but he wouldn't hear of it.'

'That's understandable. The storm is growing worse...'

'The weather weren't too bad when he arrived.' Bess was unconvinced. She gave her mistress a worried look. 'T'ain't right to have a stranger in the place when you have no one to protect you.'

'Mama has me!' Kit struggled from his chair and went to his mother's side.

'That's right, my love!' Sophie ruffled his hair. 'Now, Bess, can you manage? Mr Hatton wishes to dine with me at seven.'

'I'll do my best, but you should have warned me—'

'How could I warn you when I didn't know that he was coming?' Sophie said wearily.

'Well, mistress, be it on your own head. A gentleman yon customer may be, but there ain't no call for you to sit with him alone.'

'Nonsense, Bess! Pray don't allow your imagination to run away with you. If you must know, Mr Hatton has a proposition for me. He suggests that I re-open the inn.'

'Why would he do that?' Bess stood with arms akimbo, bristling with antagonism towards the stranger.

'I have no idea.' Sophie was losing patience. 'That is what I intend to find out.'

She rose to her feet, and froze as Bess gave a piercing shriek.

'Whatever is the matter?' she cried in alarm.

'Mistress, your gown! It's burned to shreds!'

'I stood too close to the fire, that's all.' Sophie looked down at the tattered garment. 'Don't worry, I am quite unharmed.' She glanced at Kit and then at Bess, warning the woman not to pursue the subject.

'No more!' she hissed into Bess's ear. 'If you throw your apron over your head and have a fit of the vapours, I shall slap you hard!'

Kit had returned to his pile of dough. Now he was sticking currants into the grubby mass, attempting to create a face.

Sophie held out her hand. 'Will you come with me, love, or are you happy here with Bess?'

'I'm busy!' The small boy bent over his task with an air of intense concentration. 'This is for your supper, Mama. Bobbo is helping me.'

'Then I shall look forward to enjoying it.' Sophie dropped a kiss upon his hair. She often worried about her son, believing that he needed playmates, but Kit was an inventive child. He was never bored, finding something of interest in everything about him, and clothing his little world in the vivid colours of a capricious imagination.

His best friend was Bobbo, a mysterious creature invisible to the human eye. Bobbo had appeared when Kit was three, and in the past two years he had become a part of the family.

Bobbo was a demanding creature. Sometimes he fitted happily into the routine of the household, but on occasion his ideas could be outrageous. In the usual way, Sophie found this figment of her son's imagination vastly entertaining, but now she was unable to raise a smile.

Hatton's story filled her mind to the exclusion of all else. Could it possibly be true? In the years since her marriage she and Richard had grown apart, but his death had been a crushing blow. She mourned for the love they had once known and agonised over the accident. Had he lain injured on the rocks below the cliffs, unable to move, and knowing that the incoming tide would drown him?

The men who found him had assured her that it wasn't so. Richard had been killed outright and his body had not been carried out to sea. She'd forced herself to believe that he hadn't suffered and she had come to accept the accident, tragic though it was. Murder was something else.

A tap at the door roused her from her dark imaginings.

'I've brought hot water, mistress. Will I help you change your gown?'

'Thank you, Abby. I haven't much time…'

'Mother says I am to serve you with your dinner.' Abby glowed with self-importance. 'And I'm to tell you that Father and Ben will be close at hand.' The girl gave her a curious look.

Sophie managed a faint smile as she slipped out of her damaged gown. 'Your mother is as bad as Kit,' she observed. 'They share a wild imagination…'

'She worries about you, Mistress Firle, left on your own like this.'

'I know it, Abby, but there is no need. Our visitor is perfectly respectable.'

'Well he frightens me,' the girl announced. 'He is that big, and my, don't he know how to give orders?'

'I think he means well.' Sophie was anxious to bring the conversation to an end. 'Will you fetch me a gown?'

'Which one, ma'am?'

The question brought a smile from Sophie. 'There isn't much choice,' she replied drily. 'The grey will do, and I'll wear my cap tonight.'

'It don't match,' Abby protested.

'That is the least of my worries!' Sophie washed her hands and face and allowed herself to be buttoned into a simple round dress, long-sleeved and cut high at the neck. 'Help me pin up my hair.'

With some difficulty she pushed the abundant locks beneath a modest widow's cap and glanced at herself in the mirror. Behind her Abby pulled a face.

'You look like one of they Puritan women in Kit's picture book...' Abby was clearly unimpressed by her mistress's toilette.

'I'm not attending a reception at the Prince's Pavilion in Brighton,' Sophie replied severely. 'You may put Kit to bed for me when he has had his supper. He'll want a story, but none of your ghosts and hobgoblins, if you please. I don't want him to have nightmares.'

'As if I would!' The girl threw her an injured look. Then she hesitated in the doorway.

'Yes, what is it?' Sophie picked up her reticule.

'Mistress, is it true that you'll stay here at the inn? We've been that worried. We've nowhere else to go, you see.'

'My dear child, I'm well aware of that, and I haven't forgotten how kind your mother and father have been to me. They have stayed on without wages…'

Abby blushed with embarrassment. 'They take no account of that, ma'am, being as they have a roof above their heads, and food enough to eat.'

'But I take account of it, Abby. If I'd sold the place, your father would have had his share, but…well…I haven't decided yet.'

In truth, her decision was already made. Hatton had been right. She had no choice but to fall in with his wishes. To do otherwise meant destitution, not only for Kit and herself, but for Matthew and his family.

All she could do now would be to hold out for the best conditions she could think of.

She hurried down to the kitchen, intending to bid her son goodnight, but was stopped on the threshold by Bess's look of amusement.

'Abby said that you was got up like a nun,' the older woman observed. 'Quite right too, if I may say so. No man in his right mind would—'

'Bess, that's quite enough!' Sophie was tempted into a sharp retort. 'I'm not expecting to be raped!'

'No chance of that!' Bess chortled. 'Take care, ma'am, or you'll get grease upon your gown. I'd say naught if it were to fall upon your cap.' She eyed the offending garment with disfavour.

'You know that I must wear it,' Sophie told her coldly. 'It is perfectly suitable…'

A snort of disgust was the only reply, and Sophie was not prepared to argue. Clearly she was in the way, and she was already late for her appointment with the dreaded Mr Hatton.

He was not in his rooms, so she sat by the fire, searching her mind for some solution to her problems. She could think of nothing.

'Brooding upon your sorry fate?' a deep voice enquired.

Sophie swung round to find Hatton standing in the doorway, a bottle of wine in either hand.

'I took it upon myself to inspect your cellars,' he explained. 'They are quite a revelation, ma'am. The Prince himself would be happy to own such a stock.'

Sophie glared at him as he walked towards her. Then he stopped.

'Dear God! What have you got upon your head?' A hand reached out and twitched the cap away, allowing the mass of auburn curls to fall upon her shoulders. 'That creation is enough to frighten the French!'

'How dare you!' Sophie tried to clutch at the cap, but Hatton held it out of her reach. 'I am a widow, and widows are supposed to wear such things.'

'Widows' weeds?' he mocked. 'Forget it!' He tossed the cap into the fire. 'Black ain't your colour, ma'am, and nor is grey. You'll be of no use to me if you insist on looking like a crow.'

Sophie's eyes flashed with anger. 'Don't you mean a crone?' she cried.

'No, I think not!' He gave her a long, considering look. 'You are too thin, of course, but you will pay for dressing. Blue, I think, or possibly green…?'

'If you think to dress me up as some alehouse strumpet you may forget it,' she cried hotly.

Her anger increased as she heard a low laugh. 'Not even I could manage that. You will always look the gentlewoman, Mistress Firle. It is no bad thing. Who is more likely to elicit sympathy than a pretty widow, fallen upon hard times?' He poured the wine and offered her a glass.

'I've had no sympathy from you, sir.'

'None whatever! But then you must remember that I am impervious to women's wiles. Stubborn hot-heads, most of them, and you are no exception.'

'Then I wonder that you should care to trust your plans to me.'

'Don't worry! I shall keep an eye on you.'

'Then kindly keep your opinions to yourself. I shall take no notice of them.'

'Oh, I think you must,' he answered cheerfully. 'They are so sensible, you see.'

For a moment this outrageous statement threatened to rob Sophie of the power of speech. Then she found her voice.

'How true! What could be more reasonable than an invitation to become your spy and put my life and that of my son in danger? Why, such suggestions must be commonplace in genteel circles!'

Hatton's eyes twinkled as he looked at her. 'So the kitten has claws? Well done, Mistress Firle!'

'Don't try to patronise me!' she snapped.

'I shouldn't dream of it. I am accustomed to respect my colleagues.' Hatton was grinning at her.

A sharp retort died upon her lips as Abby entered the room, carrying a laden tray.

With formal courtesy, Hatton drew out a chair for his bristling companion. Then he seated himself at the table with the resigned expression of a man expecting an indifferent dinner.

Sophie eyed him with malicious amusement as he bit into a fluffy golden omelette stuffed with mushrooms. He said nothing as he cleared his plate.

Then Abby served the fish which had been intended for Sophie's supper. Bess had cooked it in her special way, coating it with herbs and seasoning before rolling it in a muslin cloth and steaming it gently above a pan of boiling water. When it was unwrapped the skin came away with the cloth, leaving the flesh firm and white, and ready to be bathed in a delicate butter sauce of her own devising.

Hatton raised an eyebrow. 'Do you always dine like this?' he asked.

'Very rarely, Mr Hatton. At least, not in these past few weeks. We keep chickens and a pig, of course, and we grow our own vegetables. The goose, I fear, would have been beyond our resources… I understand that we have you to thank for that.'

'I like to eat well.' He brushed the implied thanks aside. 'Let us hope that Bess has done it justice.'

Sophie gave him an acid smile. 'You need have no fear. You won't go hungry, sir.'

When the bird arrived she was pleased to see that it had been roasted to perfection. The rich dish was accompanied by a sharp apple sauce, designed to clean the palate, and a selection of winter vegetables, including Sophie's favourite mixture of carrots and turnips, mashed together with pepper, salt and butter.

Hatton was won over when he tasted it. 'I wonder why I haven't sampled this before?' he said. 'It should be served with every meal.'

Sophie smiled. 'You sound like the man who ordered apricot tart with every meal, whether he ate it or not.'

Hatton pushed his chair back from the table. 'Let us hope that Bess has mercy on us,' he announced. 'I couldn't eat another bite.'

His hopes were dashed when Abby arrived with apple pie and some local cheese. He was about to wave it away when Sophie frowned at him.

'Try a little of it,' she insisted. 'Bess will be disappointed if you don't.'

Obediently, he inspected the tray. Then he held up a square of grubby pastry decorated with a large initial.

'What is this?' he demanded.

'Oh, dear, that offering is for me. Kit made it for my supper...'

Hatton's smile softened his harsh face. 'You are fortunate in your son, ma'am.'

'I believe so, Mr Hatton, and I will defend him with my life.'

'That won't be necessary, Mistress Firle. I have promised that you will be in no danger.'

'How can you promise that?' she cried in irritation. 'Unless this is a wild-goose chase? I believe it to be so. Why should the free traders choose to use this inn? You have been misinformed, I fear.'

'Have I? I think not! Be honest with me, ma'am. Have you noticed nothing amiss since you came to live here?'

'I have told you. I did not enter the public rooms.'

'I am aware of that, but you are not blind, my dear. Did you sleep well at nights?'

Sophie stared at him. 'I kept my shutters closed,' she admitted.

'Even in summer? Were you told to do so? And what reason were you given?'

Sophie lost all patience with her questioner. 'I didn't care to ask,' she cried. 'How well do you know this area, Mr Hatton? Smuggling takes place along the coast, but there is a reason for it. These fishermen have lost their livelihood due to the French war. They can earn as much in a night as they can in a month by other means. Must their families starve?'

'And what does it lead to?' he asked coldly. 'You have your own answer to that.'

'The government could stop the trade overnight,' she insisted. 'All they need to do is reduce the duty.'

'Is it so simple? Taxes are needed to run this country—'

'To subsidise a war?' Sophie regretted the words as soon as they were out.

'You disappoint me!' he told her sternly. 'Brave men have given their lives in the fight against Napoleon. Would you give up our hard-won freedom?'

Sophie hung her head. 'Of course not? Forgive me, I spoke in haste! If I were a man I should fight too.'

'You can still fight, ma'am, but in a different way. Well, will you give me your decision? We are to be colleagues, are we not?'

'Only if you agree to my conditions.'

'Go on!' Hatton prepared to listen.

'In the first place, I must have your assurance that my son will not be put at risk.'

'Agreed!'

'I hope so, sir.' Sophie gave him a dagger-look. 'Should any harm come to him I'll kill you myself.'

She had expected some sneering taunt in reply, but Hatton said nothing.

'Also, there must be a limit to this arrangement. You mentioned six months, I believe?'

'I did.'

'And then there is the matter of payment...'

'You have some figure in mind?'

Sophie named a figure so large as to force him to withdraw his offer. She was prepared for a refusal, but to her astonishment he nodded.

'Done! You'll earn it, never fear! Anything else?'

Sophie shook her head.

'Very well, then. Shall we shake hands upon our bargain?' He reached across to her, aware of her reluctance to allow him to touch her, and amused by it.

Sophie looked down at the clasped hands. Enclosed within the lean brown fingers, her own looked very white.

At least his grasp was warm and firm. To her surprise she realised that she had expected nothing else, but she drew her hand away as if she had been stung. There was something deeply disturbing about Nicholas Hatton, and it had nothing to do with the perilous adventure upon which they had embarked.

Her companion led her over to a seat beside the fire.

'Now to practicalities, Mistress Firle. Time is of the essence in this present matter. If we delay, the trail will grow cold.'

In spite of her misgivings, Sophie felt a sudden spurt of excitement. If Richard's murderers could be brought to justice her task would be worthwhile.

'What must I do?' she asked.

He didn't reply at once, frowning as he twirled the stem of his wine-glass between his fingers.

'How much do you know about the running of this place?' he asked at last. 'What were your duties here?'

'I thought I had explained. I didn't enter the public rooms, but there were the usual tasks such as cheese- and butter-making, brewing ale and putting up preserves. I'd hoped to make a flower garden, but it was always being trampled down.'

'By whom?'

Sophie hesitated. 'I don't know,' she admitted.

'I think you do,' he said sternly. 'If I'm not much mistaken, the damage always happened at night. Be honest with me, ma'am. You must have suspected something…'

'I may have had my suspicions, but I never saw anything. Richard always insisted that the shutters were closed at night.'

'You may have been blind, but you are not deaf, my dear. Tell me what you heard.' His eyes were hard, and faced with his implacable determination, Sophie felt constrained to tell the truth.

'I think there were ponies…many ponies,' she admitted reluctantly. 'Groups of men were with them, but they spoke in whispers. I couldn't hear their conversation.'

'But you knew they were smugglers?'

'I suspected it, but it was naught to do with me. There were always such men along this coast. For some it is the only way to feed their families.'

'Sheer folly!' he announced with contempt. 'Do you know the penalties for smuggling, ma'am? Transportation is the least of it. What of their families, then?'

'They know the risks,' she faltered.

'Possibly, but those risks have increased since the war with France. The south coast is almost an armed camp, with dragoons and militia everywhere in case of an invasion. The stakes are now so high that only the most ruthless continue with the trade. They will stop at nothing to protect their chosen territory. Now they have not only the authorities to fear, but also their competitors.'

'You mean the rival gangs?' Sophie looked perplexed. 'I've heard of them and the battles at Mayfield and Bexhill, but were they not broken many years ago?'

'They were…' A look which Sophie could not fathom crossed her companion's face. 'Others have taken their places.'

It was chilling news and Sophie's resolution wavered.

'Why should they come here?' she whispered faintly. 'The men I spoke of may not be the ones you want, but if you are right it would be sheer folly to return to the scene of their crime.'

She heard an ugly laugh. 'They think themselves to be untouchable,' he assured her. 'And especially since they have disposed of the informer in their midst.'

'Richard?'

Hatton nodded.

'But why here?'

'This was considered to be a safe house, isolated as it is. They will return, Mistress Firle. Nothing is more certain. The inn is on a convenient route between the coast and London and they won't expect trouble from a woman. You may expect an approach at any time…'

Sophie gave him a wavering smile. 'Sir, it is a terrifying thought.'

'You'll be in no danger if you keep your head,' he told her briefly. 'And I've promised you protection.'

'In what form?'

'I shall be here myself,' he said. 'I propose to appear as one of your former suitors, intent on resuming our acquaintance now that you are widowed…'

Alarm bells rang in Sophie's head. 'Why not my brother or my cousin?' she asked quickly.

'That might be too easily disproved. These men will take nothing on trust. Suspicion is their watchword. That is how they stay alive.'

'I see.' For some unaccountable reason Sophie found that she disliked his plan intensely. This charade was something she had not bargained for.

She looked at Hatton and coloured. Once again he read her mind correctly.

'Don't worry!' he mocked. 'My wooing will not be importunate. I believe I shall find it possible to resist your charms.'

'And I yours!' she cried hotly. 'More than any man alive!'

'Then we are in agreement, but you must learn to control your temper, my dear. It will not serve if you continue to look at me as if I had crawled from beneath a stone.'

'You have judged my opinion of you to perfection, sir.'

'Then perhaps I might ask you for some small example of your acting ability. Now, to business. To run this place successfully you will need more servants. I'll place some men with you—'

'That may arouse suspicion,' she told him in alarm. 'Country folk are wary of strangers. They'll expect me to employ local men.'

'And so you shall,' he soothed. 'The men I send will not alarm your clientele, and nor will you, I hope.'

Sophie stared at him. 'I don't know what you mean,' she said.

'Well, ma'am, can you unbend sufficiently to mix with the lower orders with any degree of civility?'

She eyed him coldly. 'If I can be civil to you, I should have no difficulty,' she replied in icy tones.

'Ouch!' He threw back his head and roared with laughter. 'Point taken, ma'am!'

Sophie ignored that comment. 'You spoke of haste. When must I reopen?'

'This week, I think. What will you need?'

'Servants, supplies of food and liquor... everything, in fact.' She went on to add to the list with abandon, hoping to dismay him, but he merely nodded.

'Very well, two of my own men should be enough. Hire others where you can. You made an excellent point. Too many strangers will frighten off our quarry.'

'You seem very sure that the men you seek will come here.' She gave him a curious look.

'Nothing is more certain if you play your part. How good an actress are you?'

'I can't see how that should signify.'

'Then let me explain. Suppose you should overhear some word about this recent tragedy? You strike me as a woman of some spirit. Could you keep your feelings to yourself?'

'Of course!'

'I must hope so, Mistress Firle. It might mean the difference between life and death. I want no heroics from you.'

'Must you try to frighten me?'

'Yes!' he told her bluntly. 'Try to understand what we are dealing with. These men would slit your throat without a second thought. There is too much at stake for them to show you any mercy.'

'I need no convincing, Mr Hatton.'

'Then heed my words. Dead, you are not of the slightest use to me. Alive, you are worth your weight in gold.'

'I still don't understand,' she said slowly. 'Why do you imagine that I'll succeed when your own trained men have failed?'

'They didn't fail altogether, ma'am. We have come close on more than one occasion, only to lose our quarry at the last, betrayed by an informer. The pattern has always been the same.'

'But you must have some inkling as to when and where illicit goods are landed…'

'We've had our successes, but goods, as you term them, are not my main concern. French spies arrive here on a regular basis. Worse, English gold is being smuggled from this country to pay Napoleon's troops.'

'Why gold?'

'For profit. An English guinea will sell for half as much again in Paris.'

'But fisherman have not the means to buy them.'

'Exactly. There are powerful men behind this trade, and they are the ones I want.'

'I see.' Sophie was beginning to understand the motive behind this single-minded pursuit of England's enemies. 'Do you know who they are?'

'I do, but I must have proof before they can be taken. In the meantime, my men are still at risk.'

Sophie detected a note of deep concern. 'So you *do* care about their safety?'

'They are my responsibility,' he said shortly.

'And that is all?'

'What else?' His words were a challenge, warning her to expect no softening in his attitude.

She decided to ignore the rebuff. In the course of their conversation she'd found herself in sympathy with his motives for involving her, but she could not like him.

'How long do you intend to stay here?' she asked casually. 'Surely your men will be able to give me protection enough?'

'Anxious to be rid of me?' His eyes were twinkling with amusement. 'What woman would turn down the attention of a devoted swain?'

Sophie did not reply. She was torn between a strong desire for his protection, and an even stronger dislike of his arrogance. This was a man accustomed to giving orders. It was clear that he expected them to be obeyed without delay.

This might work with his minions, she thought rebelliously, but he must learn that he could not rule her life.

'Perhaps your concern is for my safety?' he mocked. 'Pray don't worry about me, ma'am. I have the best of explanations for my presence here. Your charms are such that I could not stay away...'

Sophie rose to her feet, pink spots of colour in her cheeks. 'Another cheap gibe?' she said coldly. 'That remark is in the worst of taste.'

'Oh, do sit down!' he snapped. 'Damned if you aren't the prickliest female I have ever met! Good God, woman, can you think of a better story?'

'This story is ridiculous! No one will believe it!'

'Why not? For years I have loved you from afar. Even when you refused my suit I never gave up hope, but when you eloped with Firle my friends feared for my sanity...'

'I'm not surprised, Mr Hatton. I have doubted it myself, but I see that it amuses you to make may-game of me.'

'This is no game, I can assure you. I thought I had made that clear. Now that you are widowed, will it be thought strange that I should wish to offer my heart once more?'

'Strange, indeed, since you don't appear to have one!' Sophie did not trouble to hide her contempt.

'Temper!' he reproved. 'Now, ma'am, you must be tired. You've had an exhausting day, which, you will admit, has been overfull of incident.'

'And what has that to do with you?'

'Forgive me! I am concerned about the health of my beloved, you see.' The dark eyes danced as he looked at her. 'Your father's offer of a home and your refusal will not have gone unnoticed in this household. Sir Edward has a penetrating voice. Then there was the unfortunate incident when you burned your gown, and finally you have been forced to listen to my outrageous suggestions. May I suggest that you retire?'

'You may not! I am no schoolgirl, sir, to be dismissed at will. Pray keep your opinions to yourself. If you must know, I am not tired in the least.'

It was true. For the first time in weeks, Sophie felt alive again. Now there was some purpose to her life. She could serve her country and help catch the men who had murdered Richard. Then, too, she would earn enough to secure a decent future for herself and Kit.

If she had to work with Nicholas Hatton to achieve those ends she would do so, but it would not be easy. The longer she was in his company, the more she found herself disliking him.

She watched him as he tugged at the bell-pull. When Abby arrived he asked to see her mother.

Sophie was mystified. 'What do you want with Bess?' she asked.

'I am minding my manners,' Hatton told her solemnly. 'Is it not usual to thank the cook for a good dinner?'

She looked at him in suspicion. This kindly gesture was surely out of character. This was a devious man. He must have some ulterior motive.

He didn't leave her in doubt for long. As Bess tapped at the door a large hand seized her own and raised it to his lips. She struggled to free it, but his fingers closed. Furious, she looked up at her companion, to find that he was regarding her with a tender smile.

Then, apparently, he became aware of Bess. In some confusion he dropped Sophie's hand, and stammered out some words of thanks.

'Why, sir, it was a pleasure.' Bess smiled, disarmed at once by his compliments. 'Abby tells me that the mistress has eaten well, and high time too.'

'I fear that she has been neglecting herself.' Hatton regarded Sophie with a fond expression. 'With your help, Bess, we shall restore her to the girl I knew so long ago.'

'Mistress, you should have told me,' Bess reproved. 'Here we were, all so worried about you dining with a stranger…and the gentleman ain't a stranger, after all.'

'I didn't say he was,' Sophie told her stiffly. 'I said that Mr Hatton was respectable—'

She ignored a choking sound from her companion, but as Bess whisked out of the room she rounded on her tormentor.

'Must you behave in this ridiculous way?' she asked.

'It served. If I am not mistaken, Bess is at this moment forecasting wedding bells for you... I hope I have convinced her. As I explained to you, my experience of women is somewhat lacking.'

Recalling his seductive tones, Sophie gave him a sour look. 'Don't take me for a fool!' she said. 'At a guess, I would say that your experience is vast.'

'Then you feel that Bess is convinced?'

'Bess is a foolish old woman. She believes that no woman can survive without a man to care for her.'

'And you do not?'

'No, I do not, and in the future I hope to prove it.'

'What an innkeeper you will make! Why, in a month or two you'll have the countryside agog. Men will flock to this place in droves—'

'Why so?' She saw his smile and realised that the question was a mistake.

'Think about it, Mistress Firle! A beautiful young widow in possession of a highly desirable property? What could be more tempting?'

'I shall not encourage them.'

'Oh, yes, you will.' His smile vanished as he leaned towards her. 'For a start, you will change your manner. That cool reserve is well enough in a girl, but you are a woman grown. You have had a husband and a child.'

'You suggest that I should flaunt myself? Low-cut gowns, perhaps?'

'Not necessarily, but you will need more suitable clothing. I'll drive you into Brighton in the morning.'

'I have no money for fripperies.'

'That need be no problem.' He took out a sheaf of banknotes and pushed them towards her.

Sophie was tempted to throw the money in his face, but common sense prevailed. 'I shall need some things for Christopher too,' she warned.

'Use it as you will,' he said indifferently. 'But use it. Don't think to set some part of it aside…'

Sophie coloured, wishing him to the Devil. He had the most uncanny ability to read her mind. She'd intended to start her nest-egg with some of the money.

'I shall inspect your bills,' he continued remorselessly. 'Nothing too fancy, mind. Your gowns must be such as would become a recent widow, but no black, I beg of you.'

'Perhaps you would care to choose them?' she asked sweetly.

'I'll do so if you wish, but I'm sure that I can rely upon your taste.'

'You are too kind!' To her annoyance the sarcasm failed to move him. He only laughed and shook his head.

'Temper again!' he teased. 'Take care, my dear, or Matthew and his family will not believe our story.'

'They are not to know anything of our plans? Mr Hatton, I would trust them with my life.'

He looked at her in silence. 'Let me ask you something,' he said at last. 'Let us suppose that you were in the possession of certain information. You refuse to tell. Then your son is held in front of you at knifepoint. What would you do?'

'You know what I would do. I'd tell at once.'

'But you believe that Mathew does not have the same regard for his wife and children?'

Sophie hung her head. 'I see what you mean,' she replied. 'They shall learn nothing from me.'

'Good! Now, ma'am, if I may see you to your door?'

'Certainly not!'

'Great heavens, can you still believe that I have designs upon your honour?'

'Of course not,' she retorted. 'But it will give rise to talk.'

'And was that not what we intended? Don't worry! I will leave you at your door—'

'You will leave me at Kit's door,' she told him firmly. 'I always look in upon him before I retire.'

Kit was asleep, but, as usual, he had cast aside his coverlet. Sophie replaced it. Then she bent to kiss him, resenting Hatton's presence as she did so.

'You may leave me now,' she said.

He bowed and allowed her to proceed him from the room.

'Brighton tomorrow, then?' he suggested. 'Shall we say at ten in the morning, after breakfast?'

She was about to agree when suddenly and without warning, he caught her to him.

'Don't struggle!' he hissed. 'We are being watched.' Then his mouth came down on hers.

Sophie stood rigidly within his grasp, but her senses quickened. To her dismay she found that her own body was betraying her. She was responding insensibly to the pressure of those warm lips. Long-forgotten emotions coursed through her body. Then she pulled away.

With an inarticulate exclamation she fled to the safety of her room.

Chapter Three

Abby had missed nothing of the exchange between her mistress and the stranger. She hadn't intended to spy on them as she went about her business of turning down the covers in the bedrooms and sliding warming-pans between the sheets, but the sight of their embrace transfixed her.

Now she thrust her candle into Nicholas Hatton's hand to light his way back to his rooms. Then, agog with curiosity, she hurried after Sophie.

'Is all well, mistress?' she asked as she entered the bedchamber.

'Of course!' Sophie was pale but composed. 'Why should you imagine that aught is amiss?'

Abby was disconcerted. 'Why, ma'am, I wondered if the gentleman was taking liberties, with him being a stranger an' all…'

'I have already explained to your mother that Mr Hatton is not a stranger to me,' Sophie said mendaciously. 'If you must know it, he made me an offer before I married Mr Firle. Now he is come to renew his suit.'

Colour suffused her face. Sophie was unaccustomed to lying, but she knew that it was necessary, if only to allay the girl's suspicions.

Apparently she had succeeded. Abby beamed at her.

'Why, ma'am, it's like a fairy-tale!' she exclaimed. 'Shall you take him, do you think? We'd all be that pleased for you—'

'Great heavens, Abby, give me time! I have no thoughts of marriage at this moment. My husband has not been dead above a month...'

Her sad expression discouraged further questioning, but Abby's thoughts were racing as she helped her mistress into her night attire. Dismissed at last, she hurried down to the kitchen to relay her news.

Bess hushed her eager chatter sternly. 'You'd do well to keep a still tongue in your head,' she warned. 'If I'm not mistaken, yon Mr Nicholas Hatton ain't the man to cross.'

'I thought you liked him,' Abby protested.

'He's well enough, but I make naught of his thanking me for his dinner. That's the way of the gentry. Words cost nothing, but they'll use you if they can.'

'Then you think he's come to use the mistress?'

'I don't know. She's gentry too, of course. It may be as she says and he's hoping that she'll wed him.'

Abby whirled about the kitchen, her head filled with romantic fancies. 'I hope so, Mother. If you'd seen him reach for her… He kissed her like a starving man offered a meal at last.'

'Give over with your nonsense! Starving, indeed! Why, a man like that can take his pick of a dozen likely wenches.'

'I expect so, but the mistress is so beautiful.'

'She ain't the girl she was when I first knew her. These days she's naught but skin and bone, eating nothing even when the food was there for her.'

'But she ate well this evening.'

'Yes!' her mother said grudgingly. 'I'll grant the gentleman that much. She must have been feeling better… Perhaps it's as you say and all may yet turn out well for her, poor lass! Lord knows, she could do with a turn up in her fortunes after all she's suffered.'

'Oh, Mother, you are right. To be widowed so young…'

'That, my girl, was a blessing!' Bess said firmly. 'That ain't what I meant at all. I've watched the mistress fading away before my eyes long before yon Firle was killed.'

'You never liked him, did you?'

'I did not! To my way of thinking, handsome is as handsome does. That so-called gentleman was a liar and a cheat. What did he want, I wonder? He had a beautiful wife and a healthy boy, and he paid no heed to either of them.'

'That doesn't make him a liar and a cheat.'

'No...? Well...best that you don't know the whole. I'll tell you only that he kept a close watch on your father and myself. We were advised to turn a blind eye to anything untoward around this place at night.'

Abby's eyes grew round. 'Free traders?'

Her mother hushed her quickly. 'Be quiet, you foolish creature! Carry on with your chatter and we are likely to get our throats cut!'

Abby shrieked with fright.

'Oh, get on with you! There is no danger now. For heaven's sake, go to bed—'

'I shan't sleep!' Abby wailed.

'Stuff!' her mother snorted. 'As always, it will take a gunshot to waken you come morning. Now take your candle and get to your bed. Your father won't be pleased to find you making a great goose of yourself.'

'It won't be the first time!' Matthew was standing in the doorway. 'What ails the girl, for heaven's sake?'

'Father, shall we be murdered in our beds?' Abby was still quaking.

'Lord, no! What gave you that idea? The place is locked and barred as usual.'

'And Mr Hatton is still here?'

'He is...if it is any comfort to you, and your brother sleeps here too. You have three men to guard you, you foolish creature.'

Abby was satisfied at last, but when she left them Matthew turned to his wife.

'What have you been saying to her?' he demanded.

'I warned her to keep a still tongue in her head, husband. Abby rattles on, as well you know.'

'She can do no harm. We've kept our secrets to ourselves.'

'Did you tell this Mr Hatton of our suspicions?'

'Of course not! Those cellars will stay locked. He won't find the hidden entrances however much he pokes about.'

'He has been searching?'

'I can't say. He was down there earlier this evening, choosing his wine, or so he said...' Matthew hesitated. 'Don't it seem strange to you...this notion that the mistress should open up again?'

'Perhaps. I shall never understand the gentry. Maybe the mistress has told him that it's too soon for her to wed again.'

'Perhaps!' Matthew grew thoughtful. 'He doesn't intend to waste much time. I'm to send to the village at first light tomorrow with an offer of work for those as wants it.'

'And who's to pay them? The mistress has no money.'

Matthew patted his breast pocket. 'We've had our wages, wife, and more beside. The gentleman is grateful for our care of Mistress Firle.'

'But extra men? I doubt that we shall need them. There will be no trade along these roads at this time of year.'

'Bess, it has naught to do with us. Let him waste his blunt if he should wish to do so. I doubt if it will trouble him. His carriage is plain enough, but his cattle are among the best I've seen.'

Bess sighed. 'I wish that we were out of this. Many's the time we've heard and seen too much...'

'That's foolish talk! Where would we go? We'd best stick it out and hope for the best. The mistress may yet sell this place, and she's promised us a share. A chance like that don't come along too often for the likes of us.'

'But, Matt, she must have agreed to stay, else why should she be taking on more men?'

'It may not be for long,' he soothed. 'Now stop your worrying, wife. We must be up betimes tomorrow.'

Bess sighed again. 'I'm glad the gentleman is here, for all that. Mistress Firle will sleep sounder in her bed with someone to protect her.'

She was mistaken. Sleep was far from Sophie's mind as she tossed upon her pillows. The day's events had been extraordinary. She'd been startled by the unexpected arrival of her father, and deeply saddened to find him in the same inflexible state of mind. He'd spurned her son as if the child had been a bastard.

It was little wonder that when he'd gone she'd been blind to the danger of standing too close to the fire. She shuddered. Without Hatton's intervention she might have burned to death, leaving her son an orphan. It was high time she pulled herself together.

Now, with the arrival of this mysterious stranger, it was essential that she did so. His mission might be worthy. That she could accept. But the man himself was ruthless. In any dealings with him she would need all her wits about her. He would use any means to achieve his object.

Her cheeks burned as she recalled his kiss, and she drew a hand across her lips as if to wipe away the memory of his mouth upon her own. The sensation had been disturbing, and her blush grew deeper as she remembered her own response.

What must he think of her? Would he see her as a lusty young widow, desperate to satisfy her physical needs? She hoped not, but the fact remained that she had melted in his arms.

Then she grew calmer, although it was with an effort. She had agreed to this elaborate charade, for that was all it was.

His own words gave her comfort. He'd told her in no uncertain terms that she held no charms for him. Her manner was too cold? It would remain so as far as he was concerned. It was just that…well, he had taken her by surprise. Next time she would have her own emotions well under control.

A faint smile touched her lips as she lay awake for hours, planning revenge not only upon the men who had killed Richard, but also upon the arrogant Mr Hatton.

Quite how this desirable state of affairs was to be achieved she couldn't decide. There would be danger, but to her own surprise she found that she wasn't afraid. After years of misery she felt alive again. Danger there might be, but beneath that awareness lay a strong current of excitement.

Still wondering at her own response, she fell asleep at last.

By the next day her mood had changed. She had planned to treat her unwelcome visitor with freezing dignity, but she quailed at the thought of meeting him again. The memory of his embrace still troubled her.

His brisk greeting set her mind at rest, though his casual manner piqued her. Clearly the events of the previous evening had not troubled him in the least. As he assured her, he had been merely acting.

Sophie did not care to examine too closely the reason why this should annoy her. Without a word she allowed him to hand her up into his carriage, and for the rest of the journey into Brighton she answered him in monosyllables.

'Are you always so silent in a morning?' he asked at last. 'You can't have a sore head, you didn't drink enough.'

'I see no need to chatter,' Sophie told him coldly. 'If you wish for entertainment, you must not look to me.'

'But I do!' He turned to her and grinned. 'I find you vastly entertaining, ma'am, even when you do not speak. There is something in your eyes which is a challenge, or could it be that charming curl of your lips? It must have reduced many a man to despair.'

'You are talking nonsense, Mr Hatton. I don't find it amusing—'

'No? You would have me think of something else?' His leer made her recoil.

'Keep your distance!' she cried sharply. 'We are unobserved. There is no need to pretend. You are…you are…'

'An affront to maidenly modesty?' he suggested smoothly. 'Will you tell me that no fire lies beneath that cool exterior? I won't believe you.'

At that moment Sophie could have struck him. He was taunting her, reminding her of their embrace and the way she had responded. She glared at him, disliking him more each time she was forced to endure his company.

He had claimed to be lacking in experience of women. She turned away in disgust. She had little experience herself, but enough to realise that Hatton was a skilful lover. His kiss, demanding and insistent, was something beyond her wildest imaginings. It had brought her to life again.

That unwelcome knowledge enraged her further.

'Sir, you are no gentleman!' she cried. 'If I were a man you would not insult me so.'

'If you were a man you'd be of no use to me,' he replied carelessly. 'I doubt if we'd have met.'

Sophie tried for a firm grip on her temper, and when she spoke again her voice was calm.

'Are you not forgetting our purpose, Mr Hatton? You do yourself no service. At this present time my dislike of you is so intense that I find it difficult to hide. That was not your intention, I believe?'

'Certainly not. You must forgive me, ma'am. I'm a plain man, and I fear that my manner is uncouth.'

Sophie gave him a dagger-look. He was laughing at her again and she found it maddening.

She maintained a haughty attitude until they reached the Steyne in Brighton. Then a lively interest overcame her feelings of resentment. She'd longed to visit the place, but Richard had never brought her here, although they lived so close.

Now she gazed out of the carriage window, hoping to see the parade of fashionable celebrities who frequented that famous thoroughfare. To her disappointment the place was almost empty.

Hatton saw her expression. 'The keen wind from the sea has cleared the streets,' he observed with a smile. 'Those around the Prince prefer the comforts of a hot-house atmosphere, and then, you know, it is much too early for a promenade.'

'And the Prince's cottage? Is it close by?'

'You shall see it later. Call it a cottage if you will. Inside it is a palace.'

'You have been inside?' Sophie's curiosity outweighed her determination to betray no interest in anything he might have to say.

'Upon occasion!' The curt reply discouraged further questioning as they turned into North Street.

'Now, ma'am, on your left is Hannington's. The shop is newly opened and you will find it useful for such purchases as reticules, gloves and scarves—'

'You recommend it, sir, from personal experience?' Sophie could not resist the opportunity to goad him.

Hatton refused to be drawn. 'I propose to leave you here for a time when we have completed our business with the mantua-maker. I have another appointment.'

Sophie was careful to betray no interest in this statement. Doubtless he was about to make further plans for her discomfiture, but she would not give him the pleasure of snubbing her again.

Hatton rapped sharply upon the roof of the carriage.

'Back into Kemp Town, Reuben,' he ordered.

'Oh!' Sophie could not hide her disappointment. 'I thought we were to stay in Brighton.'

'Kemp Town is a part of Brighton...the oldest part, in fact. It is but a few hundred yards away.' Hatton gave her a curious look. 'You have not been here before? I had thought that since you lived so close…?'

'There was never time enough,' she replied shortly. It was pointless to explain that when Richard was alive there was never money to spare for outings. 'As you know, we did not keep a carriage.'

'But before your marriage? Your father did not bring you for the Season? Young ladies have been known to make excellent matches here.'

'My father had other plans for me.'

'Ah, yes, the estimable William Curtis! How unfilial of you to spurn him!'

Sophie eyed him with contempt. 'Must you remind me of your eavesdropping? It is nothing to be proud of, sir.'

'No, I expect is isn't.' He was unrepentant. In fact, he was smiling as the coach drew to a halt in front of a modest terraced house.

'What is this place?' she asked as he stretched out an arm to help her down.

'The mantua-maker, of course. Did you suppose that I had brought you to a den of vice?' Hatton looked about him. 'I'll admit, however, that this is not the most salubrious of neighbourhoods.'

Sophie could only agree as she looked up at the dilapidated building with its peeling paintwork. She had never trusted Hatton. Was this suggested shopping expedition merely a ruse?

She hesitated on the doorstep, shivering as the icy wind tore at her shabby clothing.

Hatton hurried her indoors. 'I suggest that you make a warm cloak your first purchase,' he suggested not unkindly.

Sophie bridled. Was he sneering at her? She would not be patronised. Pride alone kept her head high as the maid showed them into a comfortable parlor.

Then her spirits sank as a tiny creature hurried towards them with hands outstretched. Her simple elegance put Sophie's toilette to shame.

'Welcome, my l…' The words died upon her lips as Hatton gave an imperceptible shake of his head. He was quick to offer his own greeting.

'I'm glad to see that you haven't forgotten your old friend Nicholas Hatton, madame. May I present Mistress Firle to you? She has need of a new wardrobe.'

He turned to Sophie. 'Madame Arouet will take care of you. She has much experience of fashion. Perhaps you will allow her to guide your choice…'

Startled by these uncompromising words, Madame looked from one face to the other. She was no fool, and she sensed the hostility in Sophie's manner.

'I expect that Mistress Firle will have her own ideas,' she said agreeably. 'Perhaps if I were to show her certain patterns and fabrics…?' This suggestion was accompanied by a charming smile.

Sophie's manner softened a little, sensing that she had found an ally. She nodded her agreement.

'Then if madame would care to step into the workroom?' Claudine Arouet shot a warning look at the man who called himself Nicholas Hatton. There was some mystery here, but clearly the girl had spirit. Bullying would not ensure her co-operation.

Hatton's arrogant manner had surprised her. On previous occasions she had found him kind and courteous. Now she looked at him and raised an eyebrow.

Hatton smiled then. He knew her very well, and understood the unspoken question.

'Mistress Firle has been widowed recently,' he explained. 'She has been too distressed to care for her appearance.'

Madame threw her eyes to heaven. Men would do well to hold their tongues on these subjects, she thought decidedly. Was he trying to rob the girl of all her confidence?

She smiled again at Sophie. 'That is understandable,' she agreed in her prettily accented English. 'But Mistress Firle looks charmingly, in spite of all. It will be such a pleasure to dress a lady with the slender figure of a model, when so many of my customers show evidence of spending too much time at the dining-table.'

Even Sophie smiled at that.

'She'll pay for dressing,' Hatton admitted grudgingly. 'But you'll agree that she's too young for widow's weeds?'

Madame resolved to speak to him as soon as the opportunity arose. Now she hid her feelings.

'There is always a happy compromise,' she said bluntly as she led Sophie into the other room.

Sophie's purchases did not take long. She found that she and Madame were in complete agreement as to styles and colours. Madame summoned her head seamstress and, leaving Sophie to be measured, returned to the parlor to find Hatton gazing through her window. She attacked at once.

'My dear sir, what are you about?' she asked. 'This is no way to bend a lady to your will.'

Hatton took her hand and kissed it. 'Am I in your bad books, my dear? A bull in a china shop, perhaps?'

'Most certainly! Would you take one of your famous thoroughbreds, and try to break it with cruelty?'

'Was I cruel!' Hatton looked disconcerted. 'I didn't mean to be. It's just that…well…the lady hates me. I see no remedy for that.'

'You might try using some of your charm.'

'That would not serve,' he told her shortly.

'Well, at least refrain from these unfortunate comments. If the lady is recently widowed, as you say, she cannot be feeling herself again just yet.'

'I stand corrected, Madame. I'll try to mend my ways. Am I forgiven?'

'Always, you shocking creature! You will give my regards to your father?' A look of infinite sadness passed fleetingly across her face.

Hatton took both her hands in his. 'I promise,' he said quietly.

Madame was quite herself again when Sophie came to join them, and she responded quickly to the girl's unfeigned thanks. She was too well bred to betray unseemly curiosity about her customer, though she could only wonder at the connection between this young woman and Nicholas Hatton. The lady's shabby clothing did not trouble her. Since the troubles in France, some of her dearest friends had been reduced to abject penury…among them, some of the highest in the land.

But Mistress Firle was an Englishwoman, and obviously gently bred. Perhaps the lady had fallen upon hard times, but how had Hatton become involved?

Was this some affair of the heart? She thought not. She was fond of Hatton and she owed his family much, but she had never ceased to wonder why he was still unmarried. He seemed impervious to female charms, and in all their dealings she had never seen him with a woman. Possibly there had been some unfortunate incident in his past.

She brushed the thought aside. It was none of her concern. She returned to the business in hand.

'The garments will be ready in a day or so,' she promised. 'If you will give me your direction, madam, they shall be sent to you…'

Blushing, Sophie gave her the name of the inn.

'And the account is to go to Mr Hatton?' Madame realised that her question was indiscreet, but she was anxious to see the reaction of her customers.

'Certainly not!' Colour flooded Sophie's face as she opened her reticule and took out the roll of notes. 'Will you let me know the total, please?' Her cheeks were burning. Did Madame Arouet imagine that she was Hatton's light o' love?

Anger made her careless. 'I do not know this gentleman well,' she said coolly. 'I met him only yesterday.' She stopped in some confusion. Hatton had warned her to watch her tongue. Had she said too much?

Madame was quick to set her customer at ease. Her hearing was acute, but she assumed a sudden deafness.

Hatton was swift to cover Sophie's gaffe. 'The ladies of my family suggested that I recommend you to Mistress Firle,' he announced. 'I must hope that she is pleased with her purchases…'

Sophie was ashamed of the sudden spurt of anger which had led to her indiscretion.

'Madame has been most helpful.' Sophie smiled then and Madame Arouet was startled into silence.

That smile lit up the room as the girl's face was transformed.

She revised her thoughts at once as to the strange connection between Hatton and her latest customer. The young man would be well advised to watch his step. Shabbily dressed though she was at present, this slender girl had a certain quality about her which was totally disarming. When dressed as Madame intended her to be, not only Hatton would be in danger of losing his heart.

Then she chuckled to herself. Match-making? She could be as guilty of it as many another lady of advancing years. Hatton was so eligible. Years ago she'd hoped of a match for her daughter, Eugenie, but her quarry had insisted on treating the girl as if she were a younger sister.

Hatton picked up his gloves and cane. 'We must go,' he said. 'We have much to do today.' Then a thought struck him and he turned to Sophie. 'You remembered to buy a cloak, I hope?'

Sophie nodded, annoyed once more by his arrogant manner. 'It was my first purchase,' she told him shortly.

'And an excellent choice, if I may say so.' Madame picked up the finely woven garment and settled it about Sophie's shoulders. 'Mr Hatton, I'm sure you will agree that the colour is becoming?'

Her eyes held his, daring him to disagree with her.

Hatton laughed, but he could not resist the chance to tease. 'Turn round,' he ordered.

Mute with resentment, Sophie did as she was bidden.

Then, to her astonishment, he bowed and kissed her hand. 'A delightful choice,' he agreed. 'That glowing shade of blue is quite your colour, Mistress Firle.'

Nonplussed by the compliment, Sophie could only stare at him. Then she remembered her manners. 'Thank you!' she said in some confusion.

Madame accompanied her customers to the door, shivering as a blast of icy wind swept in from the street.

''Tis a bitter day,' she complained. 'But then you English are a hardy race. For myself, I long for the south of France. Perhaps, one day…?'

Hatton threw a comforting arm about her shoulders. 'Claudine, your day will come,' he promised.

Settled once more in the carriage, with a rug about her knees, Sophie gave him a curious look.

'You know Madame well?' she asked.

'She is an old friend of my father…my family,' he amended hastily. 'What did you think of her?'

'I liked her very much,' Sophie told him frankly. 'She was so kind. I was at a loss to choose from all those wonderful fabrics, but she understood exactly what I needed.'

Hatton chuckled. 'Is anything left of your nest-egg?' he enquired.

'Of course. I told you. I need some things for Kit.' She hesitated. 'Mr Hatton, I know you said that I should spend the money, but I don't feel comfortable doing so.'

'And why is that?'

'Matthew and his family have not been paid for weeks,' she blurted out. 'Their wages must come first...'

'That matter is settled, Mistress Firle. I took care of it last night.'

'Oh, I see!' Sophie faltered out her thanks, wondering as she did so if this masterful stranger intended to take over her entire life. She returned to a less controversial subject.

'How came Madame Arouet to Brighton?' she asked. 'To me she seemed a most unlikely mantua-maker, although, of course, she has great expertise.'

'Need you ask? Like many another, she is an aristocrat driven from her home in France by the revolution.'

'And her husband?'

'Arouet was beaten to death before her eyes. She and her daughter were lodged in a French prison for some months.'

Sophie gasped. 'How brave she is! One would never imagine that such a tragedy had happened to her.'

'She is a courageous woman,' he agreed. 'There are many such, forced to use what skills they have simply to survive.'

Sophie fell silent.

'Something troubles you?' he asked.

'Not exactly, but I was thinking. It is very strange. When tragedy strikes…I mean, when Richard was killed it was a fearful shock. I was so overcome with what it would mean for me and Kit that I thought of no one else. I should have remembered that I was not the only woman in the world to suffer such a loss.'

She stole a look at her companion and was surprised to see an expression of compassion on his face.

'You are growing up, my dear,' he told her gently. 'Believe me, I was sorry to hear of your husband's death.'

'Yes,' she said thoughtfully. 'I do believe you. That's why I'll help you catch his killers.'

He handed her down as the coach drew up before Hannington's in North Street.

'You have an hour to make your purchases,' he announced. 'Don't keep me waiting, Mistress Firle.'

'I wouldn't dream of it,' she told him stiffly. She turned away and hurried into the store. Now that she was sure that Matthew's wages had been paid, she could use that comforting roll of bills to buy flannel for Kit's shirts and woollen cloth to make him a coat. Sophie had learned to grow clever with her needle. Without those skills she and her son would have been reduced to rags in this last year or so.

It was a sobering thought. Her fingers closed about the roll of 'soft' as Richard had called it. She hadn't seen so much money since that dreadful day when she'd opened Richard's desk in search of paper for Kit's painting.

She'd gazed at the bills in disbelief. Richard was always pleading poverty, but there was enough here to keep them in comfort for a year. When she'd questioned him he'd flown into a rage, accusing her of spying on him and a lack of trust.

Well, it was true. From that day on, she'd never trusted him completely. They had become estranged, though it had grieved her deeply.

She glanced at the clock across the street. She had an hour. Swiftly she moved from one department to another, ignoring the tempting fripperies on display. Then, hurrying past the gaily coloured ribbons, she bethought herself of Bess and Abby. Stuff for gowns would be more welcome, she decided. She added two lengths to her purchases of wool and flannel, and gained the entrance to the street before the appointed hour.

Hatton raised an eyebrow in surprise. 'Good God!' he exclaimed. 'A punctual woman? I can scarce believe it!'

Sophie ignored the gibe.

'Are you hungry?' he asked in a jovial tone.

'No, Mr Hatton. I don't eat luncheon.'

'Well, I do!' he replied. 'And you'd be better for it. With more flesh on your bones you wouldn't feel the cold so much.'

'Thank you for your concern!'

'Think nothing of it,' he answered in airy tones.

'I don't think anything of it, sir, knowing as I do that your concern is merely for your own ends.'

She heard a maddening chuckle. 'Still furious? Blest if you ain't the prickliest creature I ever met in my life.'

'But did you not say yourself that your experience is not vast?'

'Touché!' Hatton laughed aloud. 'I led with my chin on that one, did I not?'

'Fencing *and* boxing, my dear sir? What a marvel you are, to be sure!'

'Compliments, ma'am? I did not expect them, I'll confess… How do you come to know so much about these manly sports?'

'You forget…I have a son,' she told him coldly.

'I don't forget. He is a fortunate lad, though I must hope that you don't frown at him as you do at me. That slight furrow on your brow may become permanent, you know. It will do nothing for your looks.' A long finger reached out to trace the almost imperceptible line.

Sophie thrust his hand away and stared out of the window.

Then, as the carriage stopped at the Castle Hotel, she attempted to assert her independence.

'Sir, I explained to you that I was not hungry, but pray don't let that stop you from dining. I will take a turn about the Promenade for an hour or so.'

Hatton looked at her in disbelief. 'Are you mad?' he exclaimed. 'Look at that sea. A single wave could knock you off your feet and suck you under.'

Sophie followed his pointing finger. The leaden waters of the English Channel did indeed look threatening. Whipped up by the wind, great sheets of water crashed inland, submerging the Promenade.

'Very well! I will wait here in the carriage for you. You must know that I cannot dine alone with you in public.'

'Of course you can't!' His lips twitched. 'That is why I took the liberty of bespeaking a private parlour!' He clamped an arm about her waist and half-lifted her from her seat.

To struggle would have been both useless and undignified. Sophie suffered herself to be led indoors.

She wasn't surprised to find that the food which was set before her was excellent, and in spite of her protestations she found that she was very hungry.

Hatton helped her liberally to the oyster patties and the roast beef, making no comment as she began to eat with evident enjoyment.

He confined his conversation to the question of staffing at the inn.

'I suggest that you interview my men at the same time as any others who may apply for work. I'll give you their names beforehand. That way, they will not arouse suspicion.'

'*I* am to interview these men?'

'Of course! After all, you are to be their employer.'

'But what am I to ask them?'

'All the usual questions,' he said carelessly. 'You will ask for previous experience, reasons for leaving their last position, honesty, sobriety and so on...' His eyes were twinkling. 'I'm sure you'll think of many more.'

'They may not tell me the truth,' she objected.

'Of course they won't, but you must use your judgement. See them in the room where we first met. It's dark enough for me to sit quietly in the corner—'

'Spying on me again?' she said bitterly.

'Purely out of interest.' His voice was smooth. 'Now, ma'am, there is something else.' He took a small package from his pocket and gave it to her.

'What is this?' she cried.

'Why not open it and see?'

Sophie tore aside the wrapping to reveal a small square shagreen box. She opened the lid and gasped. Inside lay the most beautiful brooch she'd ever seen. The large and glittering jewel at its centre was exactly the same colour as her cloak.

Sophie was no expert, but she knew at once that this was no trumpery piece of paste. The sapphire alone must be worth a fortune.

She coloured. 'I can't take this!' she said stiffly.

'You must!'

'Well, I won't! You go beyond the terms of our agreement. When you said that you'd pretend to be my suitor I did not expect you to give the impression that...that... Well, Madame Arouet believes already that I am your—'

'My light o' love? That is certainly my intention, Mistress Firle.'

Sophie pushed the box across the table. 'Keep it!' she said. 'You cannot force me to wear it!'

Hatton's patience snapped at last. 'You will wear it, madam, and you will wear it here, where it is in plain sight!' He jabbed a finger at her bosom. 'Now let us have no more of your nonsense. I am tired of it! Your ill temper is the outside of enough. Any more of it and I will turn you out, with your son and your baggage, before this day is out.' His voice was silky with menace.

Sophie knew that she had gone too far, but she would not apologise. She sat in silence for the whole of the return journey to the inn.

With cool courtesy, Hatton handed her down from the carriage.

'I shan't dine here this evening,' he informed her. Without another glance in her direction he stalked away.

Chapter Four

Sophie was shaken by the day's events, and Hatton's threats had terrified her. What a fool she was! She could not afford the risk of being turned out of her home, however much she disliked him. Above all, there was Kit to think about. What demon had persuaded her into behaving so badly?

She must keep a firm grip on her temper. Just let her gain her ends, and then she might enjoy the pleasure of telling the arrogant creature exactly what she thought of him. She doubted if it would make much difference. This man cared nothing for opinions other than his own. But I'll do it, she vowed to herself. If nothing else, it would give her so much satisfaction.

Refusing Bess's offer of a light supper, she went to find her son.

'Shall I read you a story, Kit?' She drew the boy on to her lap.

'Yes, please, Mama! I'd like the one about the pirates.'

Sophie began the oft-repeated tale. She deplored the violence and skirted around the worst excesses of those tigers of the seas.

Kit stopped her halfway through the tale. 'You've forgotten the blood on the deck,' he accused.

'Oh, dear, so I have!' Sophie smiled to herself. Her son could not yet read, but he remembered every word of the tales she told him.

She finished the story and tucked him into bed. 'Now I have a surprise for you,' she said.

The eager little face looked up at her. 'Is it something very nice, Mama?'

'I hope you'll think so. It's a fishing rod.'

Kit's look of rapture was reward enough for her. She'd stolen out of Hannington's and into the shop next door to make her purchase. An extravagance, perhaps? But then, Kit had so little.

Now he lay down with the rod beside him, his fingers curled about it. Within minutes he was fast asleep.

Sophie looked down at the impossibly long lashes curling against his cheeks. Kit was such a little boy. Asleep, he seemed so vulnerable. She bent and kissed him, vowing as she did so that she would protect him at whatever cost to herself.

What had she suffered, after all? Merely a day spent in the company of an unpleasant creature who seemed to take a positive delight in goading her. And she had risen to the bait, she thought in disgust. She, who had always prided herself upon her calm and her even temper. Hatton, alas, seemed to bring out the worst in her.

In future she must not allow herself to be teased into fighting with him. A dignified silence appeared to be the answer to his gibes. He would soon grow tired of the game if she did not respond.

Then she heard the sound of carriage wheels. Hurrying to the window she was in time to see her tormentor driving away, handling the ribbons himself. He'll never take the corner at that speed, she thought with some satisfaction.

She was mistaken. Driving to an inch, Hatton negotiated the bend in the lane in style.

Robbed of the pleasure of watching him overturn the coach, Sophie wandered down to the kitchen.

There she found a cosy scene. Matthew and his family were seated round the table, deep in conversation with Hatton's coachman.

The man was on his feet at once, and Sophie acknowledged his salute with the briefest inclination of her head. Doubtless he, too, regarded her as his master's latest bird of paradise.

She eyed him sharply, but in his demeanour she could find nothing but respect. Reuben was an unprepossessing fellow, in spite of that. Short and squat, his arms seemed to her to be unnaturally long. Without a hair on his gleaming pate, his head merged into a bull neck above a barrel chest.

Clearly Hatton did not require elegance in his servants.

'Mistress, won't you let me send you up some supper?' Bess coaxed. 'I could make you an omelette.'

'I have dined well today,' Sophie told her with a smile. 'I couldn't eat another bite. I believe I shall retire early tonight.'

'Abby has lit your fire already. Mr Hatton thought you might need it.'

Sophie bit back a sharp retort. The redoubtable Mr Hatton took far too much upon himself, but it would not do to let her servants see her annoyance. She bade them goodnight, and went up to her room.

It was pleasant, after all, to enjoy the unaccustomed luxury of such warmth. In the past she had wakened often to find ice encrusting the inside of her windows, and it could not be denied that the night was bitter.

Settling into her fireside chair, she picked up her book and tried to read without success. Her eyes were closing. At last she sent for Abby, slipped out of her gown, and sought the comfort of her bed.

Sophie slept late next day. It was full daylight when she awoke to the sound of Kit's voice in the stable-yard. Her fire had been replenished as she slept, so the room was warm.

She slipped on a robe over her night attire and hurried to the window. Peering out, she could see that Kit, muffled to the ears in scarves and a woollen hat, was absorbed in drawing a large circle on the frosty ground with a long stick. He seemed to be chanting some strange song.

Intrigued, she watched as he divided the circle into segments. Then he stood in the centre with closed eyes, and pointed the stick in each of four directions.

She smiled. The child must be absorbed in some mysterious game of his own. Then, as she turned away, she heard a bellow of rage.

'Stop it!' her son shouted. 'You are spoiling the magic!'

A glance was enough to show her that an older boy, almost into his teens, was scuffing the circle with his boots, jeering as he did so.

'Spoiling the magic?' he mimicked. 'Well, I don't mind spoiling your game.'

'You will! You will!' Almost as red as a turkey-cock, her son doubled up his fists.

Sophie gathered her robe about her. Kit would be no match for the older boy. Then she heard a leisurely voice.

'You're magic, aren't you?' Hatton enquired. 'Why not turn him into a frog?'

Kit stood very still. 'Yes,' he said thoughtfully. 'I might just do that.' He pointed his stick at the older boy who gave a cry of fright and ran away.

'You must be Kit,' the deep voice continued. 'Allow me to introduce myself. My name is Hatton.'

'Thank you, Hatton. Do you know my mother?'

'Indeed I do. I'm on my way to see her now. You might care to accompany me.'

Sophie hurried herself into the old grey gown. Then she ran downstairs to find her son and his mentor engaged in a serious discussion as to the relative merits of worms or maggots when engaged in the art of fishing.

'My dear Kit,' she reproved. 'Will you never learn that it simply is not wise to fight boys older than yourself?'

'I didn't fight him,' Kit said simply. 'I said I'd turn him into a frog. Hatton thought of it.'

'*Mr* Hatton, if you please,' Sophie said severely.

'He said his name was Hatton,' Kit replied in injured tones.

'It will do well enough, since it is my name. Kit, your mother and I have some matters to discuss. Shall you mind very much if I ask you to help Reuben with my horses? They need to be groomed and fed.'

'Will he let me drive them?'

'He'll show you how to handle the ribbons. Later, I may take you out myself.'

Kit made a headlong dash for the door.

'One moment, Kit. I need your promise first.'

'What's that?'

'Will you promise not to turn my horses into frogs?'

Kit came back to rest a grubby hand upon Hatton's immaculate buckskins.

Sophie winced, but her companion did not appear to recognise the threat to his appearance.

'I wouldn't do that,' her son said earnestly. 'I don't use magic on my friends.'

Hatton rose to his full height and bowed. Then he held out his hand. 'Thank you,' he said with dignity. 'Good friends are hard to come by.'

Kit took his hand and shook it warmly. 'May I go now?' he asked.

Hatton nodded. When he turned back to Sophie he found that she was smiling, but she shook her head in reproof.

'You shouldn't encourage him in such nonsense, Sir. Kit has too vivid an imagination.'

'Don't try to stifle it, ma'am. It is a gift not given to many.'

She gave him a curious look. 'Have you children of your own?' she asked.

'I am not married, Mistress Firle, and to my knowledge I haven't fathered any bastards.'

Sophie's cheeks grew pink with embarrassment. 'I didn't mean to pry,' she said with dignity. 'It is just that you seem to have a way with children.'

'I don't talk down to them, if that is what you mean. They are human beings, like the rest of us, and often possessed of far more sense than their elders.'

Sophie was aware of the implied criticism, but she let it go, mindful of her good resolutions.

'He has no notion of danger,' she replied in a worried tone. 'Without your intervention he would have tried to fight that young lout.'

Hatton laughed. 'Your little game-cock isn't short of spirit. In time he'll learn that there are other ways to skin a cat.'

'I suppose so, but I cannot like the notion of his helping to groom your horses. They are thoroughbreds, are they not, and doubtless highly strung?'

'He'll come to no harm in Reuben's hands.' Hatton was growing impatient. 'You must not mollycoddle him, Mistress Firle. Let him try his wings a little.'

'He's only five years old!' Sophie cried indignantly. 'Besides, he's all I have!'

'Then get out of his way, ma'am. The lad has promise, but he must learn. You can't protect him from every bump and blow.' Brusquely he dismissed the subject. 'Are you ready to interview your new servants?' He laid a sheet of paper in front of her.

'What is this, Mr Hatton?'

'Just a reminder of the questions you should ask. You will take Besford and Fraddon, of course. They are my men. Besford will make a suitable ostler, and Fraddon is an experienced cellarman.'

Sophie hoped devoutly that the two men would be less frightening in appearance than the terrifying Reuben. Her heart misgave her at the thought of her precious Kit in that strange creature's company, but Hatton recalled her quickly to the task in hand.

'There are four others from the local villages,' he told her. 'I must hope that you won't allow yourself to be influenced by appearances.'

'I can't accuse *you* of that, Mr Hatton. I've seldom seen a more villainous-looking servant than your coachman.'

'Reuben? I'm sorry that he doesn't meet with your approval. I didn't choose him for his handsome face.' Hatton tossed aside his cloak. Then he rang the bell. 'Your mistress will see the men now,' he informed Matthew.

With that he walked over to the darkest corner of the room, turned the wing-chair away from the door, and became invisible to the casual observer.

Sophie saw his own men first. Each of them was powerfully built and roughly dressed, but somewhat to her surprise they were not ill spoken.

Knowing that the interviews were merely a formality, Sophie did not keep them long, explaining their duties as best she could. Having engaged them on the spot, she left them in Matthew's hands, with instructions to unload the cartload of supplies which had arrived that morning.

Then her next candidate sidled into the room. Sophie took him in dislike at once. For one thing, he bore a striking resemblance to the boy who had tormented Kit that morning.

Apparently respectful, there was a knowing look about him as he took in every detail of the room. Sophie suspected at once that he had an eye to the main chance. She would never rest easy with this creature about the premises. Thieving, she guessed, was already on his mind.

The next man was a surprise. 'Why, Ben!' she exclaimed. 'What are you doing here?'

'Bess sent word that you needed help, ma'am. I hope you'll consider me. My sister can vouch for me…'

'I'm sure of it,' she told him warmly. She'd met Bess's brother on several occasions and always found him willing to turn his hand to any task about the inn, even though she could not pay him.

Pleased that she was now able to do so, she offered him a generous wage and was rewarded with a look of gratitude. Then he hesitated.

'I hope you won't think me forward, Mistress Firle, but I've brought my son along o' me. He can't get work nowhere…'

'But why is that?'

'I'm sorry to say, ma'am, but he's an innocent.'

'What do you mean?'

'If you see him, you'll know what I mean. He's never been quite right in the head, but he's a strong lad, and he's willing.'

'Will you call him then? I'd like to speak to him.'

As Ben turned to the door Sophie heard a slight cough from the direction of the window. She decided to ignore it.

Hatton had told her to use her own judgement and she would do so.

'This 'ere is Jem.' Ben preceded his companion into the room. 'He don't say much, ma'am, but he can understand you.'

Sophie looked up and gasped. Ben's son was enormous. He had to bend his head to negotiate the doorway and his giant bulk seemed to fill the room. Now he stood in front of her, smiling shyly.

'Would you like to work here, Jem?' she asked. 'Your father could show you what to do.'

The lad's smile grew wider, and he nodded. His bright blue eyes were fixed upon her with a pleading look.

Sophie studied the guileless face, and was captivated. Jem might not be bright, but she knew at once that she could trust him.

'Very well!' she said. 'Ben, will you tell Matthew that I have engaged you both?'

'You won't be sorry, ma'am.' Ben's look showed her what her decision had meant to him, but she stilled his fervent thanks. 'Make yourselves known to the other men,' she told him. 'They are strangers hereabouts.'

'Aye! Fishermen in from the coast, so they tells me.' Ben shook his head. 'There's no work there, they says, since the war with France.'

'Will you send the last man in?' she asked. 'I doubt if I shall have work for him as well...' Hatton had told her to engage four men, and she had already done so. Now she was at a loss as to what to say to the last of the applicants.

'He's gone, ma'am. He went off with the one you turned away.'

Sophie felt relieved, guessing that he was likely to be another undesirable.

As the door closed on Ben and his son, Hatton rose from his chair.

'You did well!' he told her. 'Better than I expected.'

'Good heavens, don't tell me that you approved of my choice? When you coughed I thought that you were warning me against accepting Jem.'

'It had the opposite effect, I believe.' Hatton was laughing openly.

'What! Oh, you wretched creature! You meant me to take him all the time.'

'Why not? I had already spoken to all the applicants, you see. I saw them earlier this morning, when you were still asleep.'

Sophie stared at him. 'You were here? Oh, I thought...I mean, I saw your carriage leave the inn last night, and I had imagined that you had not slept here.' Hot colour flooded her face as she realised the implications of her words.

'Never judge by appearances, Mistress Firle. For the present I can control my vile male appetite for female company, if that is what is worrying you.'

'What you do does not concern me in the least,' Sophie said scornfully. 'In any case, my disapproval would not alter your behaviour.'

'No, it wouldn't!' he agreed with a cheerful smile. 'I'm sure you feel the same about your own behaviour.'

As this happened to be true, Sophie saw no point in denying it.

'I'm glad to see that you are wearing your brooch,' Hatton continued smoothly. 'It looks well on you.'

'I found it useful,' Sophie admitted with some reluctance. 'The man I turned away never took his eyes from it. If I'd engaged him, I am persuaded that it would have disappeared.'

'An ugly customer!' Hatton agreed. 'His friend was of the same ilk.'

'What would you have done if I'd engaged them?'

'I thought it unlikely, but the question doesn't arise. Are you pleased with your new staff?'

'With two of them, at least. I'll reserve my judgement about your men, but I can trust Ben and his son.'

'True, and the lad, in particular, will be an asset.'

'Why do you say that? He is said to be touched in the head, you know.'

'We are not looking for scholars, Mistress Firle. Jem's size alone is enough to discourage trouble-makers, but there is no harm in him. He'll serve you well, I believe.'

Sophie looked her surprise. 'I shall never understand you, sir. I had not expected this from you.'

'Sympathy for a troubled mind? Well, ma'am, you do not know me well. Let us hope that your opinion of me will improve on further acquaintance.' He opened the door and sniffed the air in appreciation. 'Time for our nuncheon, I believe. May I persuade you to join me?'

Mollified by his good opinion of both Ben and his son, Sophie preceded him into the dining-room.

She was feeling confused. It was true. She would never understand this man. She'd been astonished by the way her son had accepted him without demur. Children, she knew, had an amazing way of sensing sincerity in adults.

Of course, Hatton had made it his business to be agreeable to Kit, entering into the spirit of his game and treating him with respect. She hadn't expected it.

Nor had she supposed that he would see beyond the childlike demeanour of Ben's son. Had she been asked beforehand she would have sworn that Hatton would have forbidden her to engage the lad. Now, apparently, he approved.

As he seated her at the table, she realised that she was looking forward to her meal. He looked on with approval as she allowed Abby to help her to a dish of mushrooms bubbling gently in a coating of cheese sauce.

'The outing to Brighton did you good,' he observed. 'Today you have more colour in your cheeks. With plenty of good food we'll soon turn you into a buxom wench.'

Sophie laid down her fork. 'I may not care to become a buxom wench,' she told him stiffly.

'You couldn't!' he teased. 'That racehorse build will never carry spare flesh. Eat up, my dear! You need not fear to rival the fat lady at the fair.'

Sophie ignored these pleasantries. She found that she was hungry, and Hatton's teasing would not stop her from enjoying her meal. She attacked a generous slice of ham braised in Madeira wine, and dared him to comment further.

He didn't do so. 'Shall you be ready to open the inn by the end of the week?' he asked.

'I think so, now that we have enough staff and plenty of stores,' Sophie told him thoughtfully. 'What will happen then?'

'Why, let us hope that you will attract some trade, ma'am.'

'At this time of year? Sir, you are an optimist. Who would venture on these roads in winter?'

'More folk than you may suppose,' came the smooth reply. 'This place is isolated. Nevertheless, it is on the main route into Brighton. Possibly you may be visited by some of the young bloods in the town. Not all of them have the means to keep up with the Prince and his entourage. They seek other diversions. A pretty widow may be just the bait to attract them.'

Sophie frowned, but she was not displeased by the compliment. 'Yet these are not the men you seek, surely?' she objected.

'No, they are not, but a busy inn provides better cover for our quarry than one which is almost empty. I think you may expect some unusual visitors within the next few weeks.'

Sophie shuddered, but Hatton did not appear to notice. He pushed back his chair and bowed to her.

'Will you forgive me if I leave you, Mistress Firle? I have urgent matters to attend.'

Leaving her to her thoughts he walked away, and within minutes she heard the sound of his carriage wheels upon the drive.

Oddly, Sophie felt at a loss without him. In just a day or two she had grown accustomed to countering his taunts, and she had enjoyed the challenge to her wits.

Of course, he was not the type of man she admired. Sophie knew her own weaknesses. She'd always been attracted by a handsome face and figure. In her late husband's case she had persuaded herself that his appearance cloaked a character of sterling worth. She couldn't have been more wrong, as she now knew to her cost.

Hatton, at least, would never be described as handsome. High cheekbones and a strong jaw gave him a predatory look. If she'd been asked for an adjective to describe him she would have chosen 'merciless'. A dangerous man, by any standards. With that dark hair and eyes, and his swarthy complexion, he might have been taken for a pirate.

Sophie smiled to herself. She was allowing her imagination to run away with her. Kit was not the only one at fault in that respect. Hatton was a gentleman, she told herself. That fact was apparent in his manner, his carriage, and his air of authority. On occasion his formal courtesy had confirmed these views.

It had not made her soften towards him. He had shown the most ruthless disregard for the situation in which she found herself through no fault of her own. For the moment, it suited her to agree to all his plans, but that agreement would not last for ever.

She made her way down to the kitchen, and was astonished to find her son seated upon the fearsome Reuben's lap, sharing his meal of bread and cheese and pickles. The new fishing rod lay in the place of honour on the table, and Kit was absorbed in discussing the relative merits of worms or maggots as bait.

The man rose to his feet as Sophie entered the room, his huge hands setting Kit aside with surprising gentleness. His manner was respectful, but without the least trace of subservience.

'I hope that Kit is not making a nuisance of himself?' she ventured. 'If he interferes with your work, you must send him back to me.'

'The young gentleman has been a help to me,' Reuben told her. 'He has a feel for horses…he ain't afraid of them.'

Sophie quailed. Hatton's team looked skittish to her inexperienced eye. Kit could be kicked, or bitten, or crushed against the wall of a stall.

Reuben smiled at her, and his ugly face was transformed.

'Don't you worry, ma'am,' he assured her. 'Master Kit pays heed to what I tells him. He'll come to no harm along o' me.'

Kit threw a chubby arm round Reuben's neck. 'We haven't finished our work, Mama. Reuben says that we must clean the tack. That means the saddles and the bridles of the horses, you know.'

'Very well, then, as long as you do what Reuben says, but you must come indoors before it gets dark.' Sophie smiled at the ill-assorted pair and left them.

Once again she had been guilty of judging by appearances. Reuben might be ill favoured, but in those few minutes he had warmed to his evident kindness to her son.

*   *   *

She mentioned it to Hatton when he returned late in the afternoon.

'You are learning fast, Mistress Firle,' he told her drily. 'It's always as well to watch what people do, rather than what they say or how they look.'

Sophie said nothing. There was much truth in his remarks, and she could not argue.

'Now I have a surprise for you,' he told her.

'A pleasant one, I hope?'

'I trust that you will think so.' He rang the bell to summon Matthew. 'You may send the girl in now,' he said.

Sophie stared at him in astonishment, but she was even more surprised by the appearance of a woman not much younger than herself. The newcomer was an enchanting creature, flaxen ringlets framing a little heart-shaped face. A pair of large blue eyes looked at her briefly. Then they were hidden by impossibly long lashes as the girl bobbed a curtsy and kept them fixed on the carpet.

Sophie stiffened in anger. If Hatton thought to install his mistress at the inn she would have none of it.

'What is this?' she said sharply. 'I do not know this person.'

She looked at Hatton and caught a flash of anger in his eyes. 'Of course you don't!' he said in a curt tone. 'Nancy is not a native of these parts, but she is a skilled serving wench.'

'Serving whom?' she snapped out without thinking.

Hatton turned to the girl. 'Will you wait outside for just a moment?' he asked. 'I'd like a private word with Mistress Firle.'

As the door closed behind her he rounded on Sophie.

'Does your folly know no bounds?' he demanded in a furious tone. 'Can you run this place unaided? Who is to serve your customers?'

'Abby has always done so.' Outwardly defiant, Sophie was quaking inwardly.

'I see. In addition to serving food and ale she will also clean the place, make the beds and see to the wants of yourself and your son?'

'She is a capable girl.' Sophie was still defiant.

'She will need to be a marvel. Twenty-four hours each day will scarce be enough for her to carry out her duties. Don't tell me that her mother will help her. Bess will have more than enough to do to feed the men and any travellers who stop here.'

'I shan't be idle myself,' Sophie cried. Her anger now threatened to match his own. 'Abby and I will work together.'

'Indeed? With your vast experience of a servant's duties you are certain to be a wonderful help to her...'

The biting sarcasm made Sophie flinch. She did not answer him.

'It will be difficult to carry out the task I asked of you if you spend your time in scrubbing floors and emptying slops.' Hatton's logic was relentless, and she could think of nothing to say to him.

She gave him a look of hatred, but his reply was a contemptuous laugh.

'More dagger-looks? They'll cut no ice with me. What is your objection to Nancy? She is a willing worker, I assure you.'

Willing to do what? Sophie was tempted to fling the question at him, but she thought better of it.

'I prefer to choose my own female servants,' she replied in icy tones. 'I'd have chosen a girl from the local village—'

'You would have found it difficult, ma'am. I have made enquiries. We are close enough to Brighton for the local girls to find well-paid employment and easier conditions there.'

'Then why has this…this Nancy chosen to come here? To martyr herself, perhaps?'

It was a gibe unworthy of her, and she expected to be punished for it, but Hatton had been studying her stubborn expression. A slight smile lifted the corners of his mouth.

'Are you being quite honest, Mistress Firle? I think not. You object to the girl because she is well favoured. Tell me, would some ancient crone attract more custom to this inn?'

'She'll cause trouble. Respectable, you say? With that face and figure I take leave to doubt it.'

'Jealous, my dear?'

Sophie jumped to her feet. Anger had driven all thoughts of caution from her mind. She lifted a hand to slap his face, but he caught her wrist in an iron grip.

'Don't try it!' he said grimly. 'Sit down, you little fool! Dear God, you must have had wenches working for you in the past. Were they all ill favoured?'

'No! They were not! That is why…why…' Her voice broke and she could not go on. Appalled, she realised that she was close to tears. It would be the ultimate humiliation to break down in front of this detestable man. She turned her face away.

'Look at me!' he said more gently. 'I can only guess at what has happened in the past. Am I to believe that your husband was unfaithful to you?'

A large hand covered her own and to her horror she saw that a tear had fallen upon his skin. She tried to brush it away, but a second fell and then another.

'It wasn't Richard's fault,' she whispered. 'He was so handsome. They threw themselves at his head…'

'He could have refused them, my dear.' Hatton thrust his handkerchief into her hand. 'And now, I suppose, you have no faith in any man?' He was tempted to slide a comforting arm about her slim shoulders, but he thought better of it. It would only confirm her poor opinion of his sex.

'Not all men are the same,' he assured her. 'But now I understand. You believed that Nancy was my mistress, did you not?'

Sophie nodded. She was still incapable of speech.

'I should be angry with you, Mistress Firle. She is not, but had she been a connection of mine I should not have insulted you by bringing her here. I know that your opinion of me is not high, but that you must believe, at least.'

'I'm sorry!' she said in muffled tones. She could no longer doubt his word. 'I'll speak to her if you will call her in.'

'One moment, then!' He took the handkerchief from her and dried her eyes. 'We mustn't allow her to think that I've been beating you, or she may flee back to Brighton.'

Sophie managed a watery smile.

'That's better!' Hatton lifted her face to his and looked into her eyes. 'I wish that you could learn to trust me,' he said in an altered tone. 'We could deal well together, you and I.'

Chapter Five

That night it wasn't only Hatton's words which robbed Sophie of her rest. After lying awake for hours, she'd fallen into an uneasy sleep only to be awakened by a fearful clap of thunder, so loud that it seemed to shake the very foundations of the inn.

Then a livid flash of lightning lit her room, to be followed within seconds by another thunderclap. She realised that the storm must be immediately overhead.

Jumping out of bed, she threw on her robe and hurried into Kit's room, fearing that the child would be terrified. Her worries were needless. Kit was fast asleep. As usual, he'd cast off his coverlet and lay with his arms above his head, oblivious to the raging elements which tore so fiercely at the countryside.

Sophie listened to his steady breathing as she covered him again. She dropped a kiss upon his cheek. Then she checked the oil-lamp which burned far out of his reach on top of a high chest. As an extra precaution she'd installed a metal cage about it, holding it firmly in place in case a sudden draught should blow it over.

The lamp had been a source of some contention between herself and Richard. Her late husband had accused her of mollycoddling their son, insisting that Kit must learn to sleep in the dark.

'You'll turn him into a coward,' he'd sneered.

'I could never do that! Kit has plenty of courage, but he also has a vivid imagination…'

'Monsters under his bed? I never heard such nonsense! Perhaps you'd prefer that he burns to death? If that lamp goes over…'

'I'll make sure that it doesn't!' Sophie had replied with spirit. She would not give way on this matter, but it was then that she'd asked Matthew to construct the metal guard.

'Is he all right?'

She heard a low voice in the doorway and turned to find Hatton watching her. Clad in a patterned dressing-gown of silk brocade, he looked larger than ever.

'He hasn't wakened, thank goodness!' Sophie jumped as yet another violent clap of thunder crashed overhead. Then she managed a wavering smile. 'Oh, dear! I am not usually so foolish. In the ordinary way I do not mind a storm, but this is exceptional, is it not?'

'It is, and it will last for some time yet, I fear. Sleep will be out of the question. Do you care to join me in a glass of wine?'

As another flash of lightning lit the room, Sophie saw that he was smiling. Then, as her eyes followed the direction of his own, she gasped. Not expecting to find anyone about at that hour of the night, she hadn't troubled to fasten her robe securely. Now she saw in dismay that it was open to the waist, revealing a thin nightgown which left little to the imagination.

Blushing, she buttoned up her robe. 'Thank you, but I intend to stay with Kit,' she said with what dignity she could summon. 'He may yet wake.'

'Then I'll make up the fire in here,' he told her easily. 'May I suggest that you fetch your slippers, Mistress Firle, otherwise your feet will freeze.'

Shocked, Sophie looked down at her bare feet. In her haste she hadn't thought to wear her slippers.

'I won't be above a moment,' she exclaimed. 'Will you stay with him?'

'Certainly!' Preoccupied with coaxing the dying embers of the fire into life, he did not look at her.

Sophie ran back along the passageway, gained her room, and thrust her feet into her slippers. As an afterthought she picked up a heavy woollen shawl. Then, as she was leaving the room she caught a glimpse of herself in the mirror. Dear heavens, she looked a positive fright! Déshabillé was not the word for it. She looked flushed and rumpled, and her hair was loose, lying in a tumbled mass about her shoulders. She snatched up a ribbon and tied it back.

When she reached Kit's room again the fire was burning brightly. Hatton was installed in a battered nursery chair, perfectly at ease as he stretched long legs towards the warmth.

'Thank you!' Sophie said briskly. 'The storm is moving away, I think. You may yet be able to sleep.'

'I doubt it! Just listen to the rain!'

Sophie looked up in alarm as a torrential downpour hammered against the roof.

'Don't worry!' he soothed. 'This place is in good repair. I insisted on it.' He rose and fetched another chair for her, setting it on the other side of the fireplace.

'Fires in bedrooms are one of life's pleasures, are they not?' he observed. 'As a child I used to lie and watch the flames and fancy that I could see faces in the embers. It was even better when the weather was inclement and it snowed.'

Sophie tried to hide her surprise. Somehow she had not thought of this sophisticated creature indulging in childish fancies.

Hatton read her expression correctly and his lips twitched. 'Is it a shock to find that I am human, ma'am?'

'You have succeeded in hiding that fact up to now, Mr Hatton.' Sophie smiled back at him. He was trying to be agreeable, and life would be much more comfortable if she met him halfway. 'I must confess that it is an unexpected pleasure to be able to have fires in all the rooms again. I hate the cold. It seems to freeze my brain.'

'Then we must keep you warm, ma'am. There is nothing of you, after all.' He leaned forward and pulled the ribbon from her hair, allowing it to fall about her shoulders. 'That's better!' he approved. 'Don't you value your crowning glory, my dear? Why must you try to hide it with a hideous cap, or scrape it back from your face behind a ribbon?'

'Oh, please!' Sophie's hands flew up to the errant curls. 'Mr Hatton, you must leave this room. We are both of us in—'

'In a state of undress? So we are! But is it not comfortable to be sitting here in the warmth, listening to the storm outside?'

It was both comfortable and reassuring, but Sophie did not care to admit it, even to herself.

'Bess or Abby could waken up at any time,' she pointed out. 'They might come to look at Kit.'

Hatton sighed. Then he rose to his feet with some reluctance. 'And we must not forget the proprieties,' he teased. 'Very well, ma'am, I will leave you. You will call on me if anything untoward should occur?'

'Such as what?' Sophie was perplexed. Then she realised that whilst apparently attending to their conversation, Hatton had been listening closely to the storm. Or was it to the storm?

He saw her look of alarm. 'Just a precaution,' he assured her. 'You'll have no unwelcome visitors tonight, if I'm not much mistaken. This weather will deter the hardiest of men. They won't be able to move their goods. This rain will have turned the clay to a morass. The lanes will be impassable.'

'Then let us hope that it continues,' Sophie said with feeling. 'I don't feel very brave tonight.'

He gave her a long look. 'You'll do well enough,' he said. Then he bowed and left her.

For some time Sophie sat lost in thought. What had persuaded Hatton to look in on her son? Was it simple kindness, or had he been alerted by the sound as she opened Kit's door? Then a more sinister reason crossed her mind. Perhaps he'd been expecting someone else to enter the inn at night.

She thrust the thought aside. Had he not assured her that on this, of all nights, no one would venture out into the storm? As she listened to the pattering of the rain it no longer seemed so threatening. She must think of it as protection for her little household, even as a few drops came down the chimney and hissed on the glowing embers of the fire. Lulled by its warmth, she fell asleep.

She awakened to find herself in her own bed. As small fingers attempted to prise her eyelids apart, she heard a whispered voice.

'Are you awake, Mama?'

'I am now!' Sophie looked up sleepily at her son.

'There, now! Didn't I say that you should let your mother sleep?' Abby tried to pull the boy away from Sophie's bedside.

Kit wriggled out of her grasp. 'I did as you told me,' he said indignantly. 'I counted up to nine when the clock was striking. I *can* count, you know.'

'Heavens, is that the time? Abby, you should have wakened me—'

'I guessed you couldn't have had much sleep, what with the storm and all. I was frightened out of my wits. I hid beneath the bedclothes...'

'It *was* very wild,' Sophie admitted. She was not really attending to Abby's words. Her eye had fallen upon her robe, draped neatly over the back of a chair, with her folded shawl beneath it and her slippers arranged precisely at the side.

She could not have put them there herself. Her slippers lay always beside her bed, with her robe placed within easy reach across her counterpane. Then, if Kit wakened in the night and called to her, they were readily to hand.

'Will I fetch your breakfast, ma'am?' Abby had to repeat the question twice before her mistress answered her.

'Oh, yes...yes, thank you! Though I suppose I should get up at once...'

'No hurry, ma'am. There ain't much you can do, and blest if it ain't still raining. It's hard to tell night from day. Father is busy lighting all the lamps and finding extra candles.' With that she hurried away.

Sophie plumped up her pillows and settled Kit in the crook of her arm. He loved to snuggle close to her first thing in the morning.

'What will you do today?' she asked. 'I thought we'd go for a walk, but the weather is too wet. Perhaps we could have a reading lesson?'

'Could we do that later?' The eager little face looked up at her. 'Reuben has promised to show me how to cast with my fishing rod.'

'Oh, my darling, he doesn't propose to go down to the river? The water was running high even before this storm and the banks were crumbling. It would be far too dangerous—'

'Oh, no, Reuben says that it would be a waste of time. We are going to practise in the barn. He's going to draw a line on the ground, and I'm to try and reach it.'

'Mr Hatton may have need of Reuben,' Sophie reminded him. 'You mustn't make a nuisance of yourself.'

'Hatton doesn't mind. I spoke to him this morning. He won't be going out today. Did you know that Reuben can bend a poker in his bare hands?'

'No, I didn't. He must be very strong.'

'Reuben says that it's because of all the good food he ate when he was as old as me. We had ham and eggs and kidneys for breakfast this morning…though I didn't like the kidneys much, but I did eat them up.'

It was becoming all too clear that Reuben was the oracle. His word was law as far as Kit was concerned. Sophie resigned herself to the fact that what Reuben said was likely to be her son's main topic of conversation in the coming weeks.

Sophie looked up as Abby entered the room, bearing a laden tray. In the usual way she would nibble at a roll as she sipped her chocolate. Today the covered dishes held a hearty breakfast. She was about to send it back when she saw Kit's solemn look. Apparently Reuben's dictum was to apply to her as well.

She did her best with the ham and eggs, and found to her surprise that she enjoyed it.

'I must go now,' her son remarked. 'Reuben says that it is rude to be late when one has made an appointment.'

Sophie chuckled to herself. Reuben was clearly a man of strong opinions, but to date she could not fault his observations of her son. Kit had been a poor eater. If Reuben could persuade him into enjoying his meals, she could only be grateful to the ugly little coachman.

She slipped out of bed, feeling for her slippers. Then she remembered. They were on the far side of the room.

Sophie frowned. She had no recollection of returning to her bedchamber on the previous night, but she must have got there somehow. A dreadful suspicion crossed her mind. Had Hatton returned when she was unaware of him? Who else had the strength to carry her sleeping form? Neither Bess, nor Abby, nor Nancy were capable of such a feat, and Matthew, she felt, would have considered it an impertinence to take her in his arms. Hatton would have had no such scruples.

She went downstairs to find him deep in conversation with Fraddon, the new cellarman.

Sophie's tone was brusque as she interrupted them.

'Mr Hatton, I'd like a private word with you,' she announced.

'Certainly, Mistress Firle. Shall we go into the snug?'

Once again, he'd taken the initiative, but Sophie would not be deterred. Her face was set as she looked at him.

'Did you return to Kit's room in the early hours?' she asked in icy tones.

'I did!' Hatton's eyes never left her face. 'You have some problem with that?'

'Merely that I found myself in my own room this morning. I have no recollection of returning there.'

'No, you would not!' he said agreeably. 'You were fast asleep.'

Sophie flushed to the roots of her hair. 'You admit, then, that you took me there yourself?'

'Why should I deny it? It seemed the sensible thing to do. You would have awakened cold and stiff, I can assure you.'

'That is none of your concern, though I accept that you meant well.'

Hatton bowed.

'Even so, I don't seem to be able to make you understand. My reputation means as much to me as it does to any other woman. Suppose you had been seen carrying me to my chamber? Only one conclusion would be drawn—'

'I think it unlikely. At a glance you were an unlikely subject for seduction. Not only were you unconscious of your surroundings, but your mouth was open and you were snoring.'

Sophie gave a shriek of dismay. 'You are lying! I don't snore, you hateful creature!'

Hatton grinned at her. 'How do you know?' Then he relented. 'I was teasing,' he admitted. 'No, ma'am, you do not snore. In truth, you looked quite charming as you lay there in my arms.'

'Spare me your compliments, sir. I am not joking when I tell you that you go too far. Is it your intention to destroy me? If you don't mend your behaviour, my servants will lose all respect for me.'

'They won't do that,' Hatton told her lightly. 'They think highly of you, Mistress Firle, as you must know.'

She looked at him. 'Then will you tell me that you did not...I mean...well, my robe and my slippers were not in their usual place?'

Hatton sighed. 'I did remove them, ma'am. I thought it unlikely that you were accustomed to sleeping in your shoes. Then I drew your coverlet over you. Believe me, I took no liberties with your person.'

Sophie wanted to believe him, but she had no recollection whatever as to what might have happened in her room.

He read her mind correctly, and his expression hardened.

'I am not in the habit of forcing my attentions upon helpless females, whatever else you may think of me. Had I made love to you, my dear, you would certainly have known about it. In view of your condition it seemed pointless. You are no virgin, Mistress Firle. Surely you must know that the participation of both partners is needed to obtain the fullest pleasure.'

Sophie was scarlet with embarrassment. She had not expected such forthright speaking from any man. Now she realised that Hatton was furious. His honour had been impugned. No gentleman would take advantage of a sleeping woman.

'Please stop!' she cried. She wanted to cover her ears, but she knew that it would bring fresh sarcasm upon her head. 'I've heard enough! I do believe you.'

Hatton was not finished. 'I suppose I should be flattered by your estimation of my prowess with the ladies. I'm sorry to disappoint you, but dalliance, I find, requires a disproportionate amount of energy. I have neither the time nor the inclination for it at the present time. There are more important matters to attend. May I suggest that you try to remember them?'

Sophie could have struck him. 'I do remember it,' she said in icy tones. 'Perhaps you have forgotten that I have been widowed and my son has lost his father?'

Hatton did not reply and her fury grew.

'What a creature you are!' she cried. 'I'm not surprised that you are still unwed. You are the most insulting, arrogant, selfish man I've ever known.'

Hatton bowed again. 'Your assessment of my character is not original, madam. My mother echoes your sentiments at frequent intervals.'

'I'm not surprised.' Sophie turned away.

'Where are you going?' he demanded.

'Do I need your permission to return to my room?'

'Feathers still ruffled?' Hatton was unperturbed. 'I think we must call a truce, my dear. I shall need your help this morning.'

'Whatever for?'

'I propose to try a certain experiment.' He strolled across the room and pulled at the bell-rope. When Matthew appeared he was asked for the keys to the cellar.

Sophie was only half-attending to the conversation. She'd planned to cut out flannel shirts for Kit as the weather was still too poor for her to take her daily walk.

She had no idea what Hatton had in mind, but if he wished to inspect the cellars he could do it without her. He must know the place quite well. After all, he owned it.

Then she heard an odd note in Matthew's voice. It was unlike him to prevaricate.

Sophie looked at his face and was surprised to see that he was very pale.

'If you should wish for a particular wine, sir, I'll fetch it for you at once,' he said uneasily.

'Just the key, Matthew, if you please.'

Still Matthew hesitated. The gentleman had paid his overdue wages, and for that he must be grateful, but what could he want in the cellars? Mr Hatton, to his knowledge, had no connection with the running of the inn. It was Mistress Firle to whom he was responsible. He threw her a pleading look.

'What is it, Matthew? Are you not well?' Sophie looked at him more closely and was surprised to see a strange expression in his eyes. She could think of no reason for it, but the man was obviously terrified.

'Have you found rats down there?' she asked. 'We'll send down the terriers to clear them out if that is what is worrying you.'

'No, ma'am, it isn't that. Perhaps if the gentleman will tell me what he wants, I can get it for him.'

'Matthew, I asked you for the keys. Your mistress wishes to check the stock of wines and spirits. As you know, she intends to re-open the inn within a day or two.'

Matthew's sigh of relief was almost audible. 'If that's all, sir, I can give my mistress the cellar book. It's all in order. She won't find a single bottle missing…'

Hatton looked across at Sophie and she understood him at once. He intended to inspect the cellars in spite of Matthew's clear reluctance to hand over the keys, and his injured expression.

'You must not think that I don't trust you, Matthew,' she soothed. 'But Mr Hatton is concerned about the conditions under which we keep the wines. We've had such heavy rains, and there may be a danger of flooding. Now, bring me the keys and we'll go down together.'

Matthew dared not argue further, but he didn't return himself. It was Fraddon, the new cellarman, who brought the keys.

Hatton motioned to Sophie to accompany him. In his hand he held a lantern of curious appearance which he shone ahead of him as he descended the steep flight of steps down to the cellars. Then he nodded to his man to light the oil lamps set at frequent intervals in the walls.

As the clear light flooded the cellars, Sophie looked about her. She could see nothing to account for Matthew's uneasiness. The barrels were neatly stacked along three of the walls, whilst the fourth and longest held a series of wine racks which reached from floor to ceiling.

'All seems to be in order here,' she observed. 'There was no need for you to badger Matthew.'

'No?' Sophie heard an ugly laugh. 'Then let me show you!'

Hatton walked swiftly to the middle section of the racks, pulled out two of the bottles and slid his hand into the aperture.

Sophie gasped as a part of the high rack swung towards her revealing not the brickwork which she had expected to see, but a massive wooden door.

'The key?' Hatton looked at Fraddon.

The man removed another bottle, felt behind the rack and handed an iron key to his master.

Then Sophie heard an anguished cry as Matthew thrust her aside. With his back to the door he spun round to face Hatton.

'Don't open it!' With arms spread-eagled, he tried to cover the lock. 'You'll get us killed!'

Hatton put him aside without the slightest difficulty.

'Stand back!' he ordered sternly. 'You have much to answer for, I think.'

Matthew's face was working. 'What could I do?' he whispered. 'Master, you don't know—'

'Perhaps I don't, but I intend to find out!' Hatton inserted the key into the lock, and the door swung back on well-oiled hinges. Then he shone the lantern ahead of him.

Sophie was close upon his heels and she gasped in astonishment as they entered yet another cellar of which she'd had no previous knowledge. It was very large, and the goods which it contained were strange to her. Much of the floor space was piled high with oilskin bags, filled to capacity. The kegs which filled the rest of the store were much smaller than a beer barrel.

Long ropes with iron hooks attached hung from the walls, as did an implement which bore a close resemblance to Kit's fishing rod, apart from the odd-looking pincers at the tip.

Then she shuddered. Stacked in one corner lay a heap of cutlasses. Shining in the lamplight they looked well-greased and ready for their murderous task. There were firearms too, and a great pile of heavy wooden staves.

Sophie swallowed hard. 'I don't understand,' she faltered. 'Is this some kind of store?'

'You might say that!' Hatton told her grimly. He turned to the trembling Matthew. 'Where do the tunnels lead?'

Matthew's resistance was broken. 'As far as the first copse on the hill,' he muttered. 'That's the entrance.'

Sophie was horrified. 'Oh, Matthew, do you mean to say that anyone could have entered whilst we slept?'

'No, ma'am. All the doors are bolted from this side. It ain't possible to get in through the tunnels.'

'Then that must mean…?' Sophie was thinking fast. Someone from inside the inn must have opened up the entrance to allow the smugglers access to their store. 'Who could have—?'

Hatton cut her short. 'This is not the place for a discussion,' he said brusquely. He turned on his heel and led the way out of the cellars.

The others were subdued as he settled himself behind a table in the parlour, and Sophie was unaccountably annoyed. Hatton was not a magistrate, and he must not behave as such.

Her fears were confirmed when he spoke to the unfortunate Matthew.

'You have much to answer for, have you not?' he enquired coldly. 'Why did you not see fit to inform your mistress when you realised what was happening here?'

'That were down to me, sir!'

Sophie turned to find Bess standing in the doorway with arms akimbo. She looked fully capable of taking on the redoubtable Mr Hatton and a dozen like him.

'I see. Won't you sit down, Bess?' Hatton rose and indicated a chair.

'No, I won't, sir, if it's all the same to you.' Bess was not to be mollified by such courtesy. 'My Matthew had naught to do with any of this. It was me that found out what was going on.'

'How did you do that?'

'It was quite a while ago. Matt had a putrid throat. He was coughing, so I came down very late to fetch him a hot drink. I saw 'em then.'

'But, Bess, who did you see?' Sophie persisted. 'Was it someone who used to work for us?'

'No, ma'am, it weren't...' Some of Bess's belligerence had vanished. 'I'd rather not say...'

'Quite right, Bess!' Hatton was quick to intervene. 'You followed them, then, right into the cellars? That was a dangerous thing to do.'

'I know it, Master. A worse band o' cut-throats I never did see. I told Matt that we must never speak o' they cellars, but he would find out for hisself.'

Bess paused and then she turned to Sophie. 'If you think that we done wrong, Mistress Firle, you won't want us to stay. We can be out of here by morning.' Her lips were trembling, but she stood her ground.

'Oh, Bess, I wouldn't think of letting you go!' Sophie threw her arms about her servant. 'You were not to blame. You found out these things by chance, but I do wish that you would tell us the name of the person whom you saw that night.'

'I can't!' By now Bess was weeping openly.

Hatton signalled to Matthew to take his wife away.

'I hope you are satisfied,' Sophie gritted out as the door closed behind them. 'You have succeeded in upsetting two kindly people who have become involved through no fault of their own. In future you will leave my servants alone.'

She had expected a sharp retort, but as Hatton looked at her she saw a curious expression in his eyes. Could it be sadness? Surely not? To hide her perplexity she picked up the oddly-shaped lantern.

'How did you know of the hidden cellar?' she continued. 'Was it because of this strange object? I imagine it is something to do with the smuggling fraternity, for I have not seen its like before. It looks more like a watering-can than a lamp and for all the light it sheds it might as well be so.'

Hatton took it from her. 'It serves its purpose well,' he told her. 'This is a spout lantern, used for signalling out to sea. The long spout prevents the light from being seen on land. The opening at the end is uncovered briefly to send messages in code.'

'Where did you find it? Did it lead you to look for the second cellar?'

'Fraddon found it hidden behind some barrels, but I've always known of the second cellar. Don't forget that I own this place.'

'I'm unlikely to forget it, since you lose no opportunity to remind me,' Sophie replied bitterly. 'If you knew of the secret place, why did you feel the need to torment Matthew? Did it give you pleasure to frighten him?'

'It gave me not the slightest pleasure,' came the cool reply. 'But I had to know if Matthew was involved with the smuggling gangs. He was hiding something. That was obvious. He was already badly scared. I had to know why.'

'Well, now you *do* know!' Sophie said with some asperity. 'I hope you're satisfied.'

'Your loyalty does you credit, ma'am. It does not encourage me to trust you. In defence of your friends, you would help them bury a body, I believe.'

'Yes, I would!' she told him boldly. 'But this is nonsense. There is no question of burying a body—'

'As a mere figure of speech!' Hatton said in some amusement. He pulled at the bell-rope to summon Matthew once again.

'Tell me what you wish to know and I will question Matthew.' Sophie was determined to save her servant from further brutal interrogation.

'With your permission, I will speak to him alone. I think that you should leave us, Mistress Firle—'

'Certainly not! I shouldn't think of it.'

'Very well, if that is your decision. I hope you won't regret it.'

Matthew entered the room before she could reply. She looked at him in alarm. Matthew seemed to have aged before her eyes.

Hatton spoke without preamble. 'I want the truth from you,' he said. 'When was this last cargo delivered to the cellar? Don't try to gammon me by saying you knew nothing of it. I won't believe you.'

Matthew crumpled. 'I ain't a free trader,' he whispered. 'It was naught to do wi' me.'

'Of course it wasn't,' Sophie intervened. 'We don't suspect you, Matthew, but you must tell Mr Hatton everything you know.'

'Well, ma'am, once I knew of the cellar I kept an eye on it. Sometimes it was empty, and sometimes full. I 'ad to be careful, you understand, but the place was quiet in day time.'

'You haven't answered my question,' Hatton said coldly. 'That last cargo…when was it delivered?'

Matthew looked at Sophie and encouraged by her nod he was persuaded to reply.

'It was just afore the Master died, begging your pardon, ma'am, for reminding you of your trouble. That cellar had been empty for weeks aforehand, as if it had been cleared a-purpose for something special.'

'Special indeed!' Hatton muttered almost to himself. He turned again to Matthew. 'Since then you have not been approached?'

Matthew looked baffled. 'Approached, sir? You mean—?'

'I mean has anyone requested to inspect the cellars, perhaps on the pretext of buying up your stocks of wines and spirits?'

Matthew frowned as he tried to recollect. 'We've had one gentleman,' he admitted. 'Don't you remember, Mistress Firle? You refused to see him…'

'Yes, I recall. I had no interest in his offer. Matthew, is this all you know? As I understand it, the door of the cellar can only be opened from inside the inn. You must have seen who used the key?'

For some reason this question troubled Matthew more than any that had gone before. He kept his eyes fixed on the carpet and his mouth was set in a tight line, but his hands were shaking.

'Won't you tell me, please?' Sophie pleaded.

Matthew shook his head.

'I'll tell you, ma'am!' Again, Bess was standing in the doorway. 'Sorry I am to say it, but it were the Master.'

Sophie glanced at Hatton and knew what she had to do.

'Oh, no!' she cried. 'That can't be true!'

'As true as I'm standing here, Mistress Firle. Yon gentleman weren't all you thought him, though I know it's wrong to speak ill of the dead.'

Sophie turned away as Hatton dismissed her servants, on the pretext that she had suffered serious shock.

'Well?' he asked.

'Of course Richard let the smugglers in,' Sophie insisted. 'Was he not supposed to be a member of their gang?'

'He was!' Hatton did not look at her. 'Have you any idea of the value of that cargo in the cellar?'

'I couldn't begin to guess, since I don't know what it is. Those bundles wrapped in oilskin? What were they?'

'That was tobacco, ma'am, protected from immersion in the sea. Did you not see the grappling hooks? Our friends are in the habit of ''sowing a crop'' as they term it. They sink the cargo beneath a marked spot when threatened by the preventive officers. Then they collect it later. They do the same with the ankers.'

'Ankers? I do not know that term.'

'You saw them in the cellar. They are the small tubs of wines and spirits.'

'There were so many of them,' Sophie mused. 'The cargo must have been huge…worth many thousands of pounds?'

'A fair assessment, madam.'

Sophie had been thinking fast. 'I understand you now,' she said. 'The goods in the cellar are the bait, are they not? You believe that the smugglers won't give up the opportunity to continue with their operation?'

'Something like that,' Hatton agreed. 'Too much money is at stake here. They won't let it go.'

Sophie stared at him. 'What will happen now?' she asked.

'I think you may expect an approach. I can't tell you from which direction, or how it will be phrased. All I ask is that you be on your guard. Whatever is suggested to you, you will show reluctance to agree.'

'That won't be difficult!' she told him grimly.

'I don't expect it will, but remember, you will be surprised and shocked to learn that goods have been stored here in a cellar of which you had no previous knowledge. You will protest that it can't possibly be so. When it is proved to you, you will be terrified, fearing that the authorities will learn of the contraband. As you know, the penalties for smuggling are savage.'

Sophie swallowed hard. 'Transportation?' she breathed.

'That, or death! Your terror will seem natural enough.'

'You are convinced that they will come here?'

'Nothing is more certain. Someone made a serious mistake in killing your husband before the goods could be moved. If I'm not mistaken, there are certain gentlemen in London impatient for their profits on that cargo. Their initial outlay would have been enormous.'

Sophie was very pale. 'Would it not be simpler for them to kill me too?'

Hatton's smile transfigured his face. 'And lose a possible ally? No, my dear! They will know you to be in need of money. If they can get you on their side with soft words and promises, so much the better for them. The trade will resume as if nothing had happened.'

His hands rested lightly on her shoulders as he turned her to face him. 'Above all, you must be on your guard. They must not suspect a trap. Can you do it?'

'I can…if you…'

'Yes, Mistress Firle. I shall be here.'

Chapter Six

In spite of Hatton's reassurance, Sophie felt deeply troubled as she went back to her room. She'd had no alternative but to agree to his scheme, but the thought of the coming ordeal filled her with dread.

Could she play her part? He'd made it all too clear that the slightest slip would mean disaster. She could recall every word of their conversation and now it seemed to her that he was asking far too much of her.

She'd been shocked by the discovery of the second cellar and its content, and Matthew's terror had added to her own.

How could she succeed in acting as Hatton's spy when his own men, highly trained and experienced, had lost their lives in the attempt?

She caught a glimpse of her face in the mirror, expecting to see panic written there. True, she was pale and the great grey eyes seemed larger than ever, yet her inner turmoil did not show. She took a turn about the room in an effort to calm herself. She must remember Hatton's purpose and her own.

He'd been clever, she thought ruefully. Not only had he promised that Richard's killers would be brought to justice, but he had offered her the chance to help her country. Could she do less than the men who were dying in their thousands on the continent of Europe in an effort to defeat Napoleon? It would be craven to even think of it.

With an effort she thrust her misgivings from her mind. The thing to do was to occupy herself, taking one day at a time.

She looked at the bolt of flannel cloth which she'd bought at Hannington's, and the pieces of Kit's shirt, carefully unpicked to act as a pattern. Then she laid out the flannel on the carpet, trying her pattern first one way and then another so as to make the best use of her purchase. Heaven knew when she would have the means to buy such cloth again.

Satisfied at last, she began to pin the pieces down. If she cut wide of the seams and extended the length of the garment at the sleeves and tail, her son would be well clad for the rest of the winter.

Her mouth was full of pins when she heard a tap at the door. In response to a mumbled command to enter, Nancy came towards her, bearing a number of boxes.

'The carrier brought your purchases from Brighton, ma'am,' she said.

Sophie was puzzled. Then she remembered. 'The gowns? I had forgot! Will you help me unpack them?'

Nancy lifted out the garments one by one, laying them on the bed, and Sophie quailed. She could not recall having ordered so many. She recognised the green with the black stripe, and the blue with its matching pelisse, but the bronze?

'How beautiful!' Nancy said softly. 'It is almost the colour of your hair, Mistress Firle—the same shade as autumn leaves. Must I put them away?'

'Please do!' Sophie's eyes had fallen upon an expensive dark-green redingote and a number of spencers. Long-sleeved and waist-length with revers and a collar, they were designed to provide extra warmth, but she had not ordered them.

Nor did she recognise a braided pelisse in french merino cloth. There were a number of scarves in printed, knitted silk and yet another gown in dark blue kerseymere, buttoned high at the throat. Sophie picked up a tippet edged with fur.

'What is this?' she demanded.

Nancy looked her surprise. 'You didn't order it, ma'am? Perhaps there has been a mistake.' She smiled at Sophie. 'I believe it is known as a Bosom Friend because it protects the throat and chest…must I leave it aside to be returned?'

'I think so.' Sophie picked out the garments which had been her choice. 'These may be put away. Please leave the others on the bed.'

She was seething. Her order had been more than doubled. Hatton must have had a private word with Madame Arouet. Well, she would not allow him to dictate her choice of clothing. Nor would she allow him to pay for it.

'Where is Mr Hatton?' she asked.

'He left here at first light, Mistress Firle.'

'I see!' Sophie tried to contain her fury. 'When he returns, will you tell him that I wish to see him?'

'Yes, ma'am!' Nancy glanced at the pattern laid out on the floor. 'Would you like me to help you with that? I'm handy with my needle...'

'Why, yes, of course, if you'd like to do so.' Sophie was surprised, as much by the fact that Nancy's rich Sussex burr seemed to have vanished, as by her offer of help.

Nancy knelt down and began to pin the pattern with skilful fingers.

Then she saw the ring on Nancy's hand.

'A wedding ring?' she exclaimed. 'Nancy, you did not wear that when you came to see me first of all.' Then realisation dawned. 'Oh, I see! When we re-open it will serve to keep away the most importunate of our customers?'

She could not blame the girl. Nancy was quite lovely. She would be the target of every man who fancied himself as a devil with the ladies.

'The ring is my own,' Nancy told her quietly. 'I am a widow, ma'am.'

Sophie's heart went out to her. 'Oh, my dear, I am so sorry. You are young to suffer such grief...'

'I had been married six months.' Lost in memory, Nancy seemed to have forgotten the presence of her listener. 'They tortured him, you know. Then they threw him down a well, and stoned him to death.'

Sophie's blood ran cold. Wide-eyed with horror, she stared at her companion.

'But why? And who would do such a dreadful thing?' She had already guessed at the answer, and it terrified her.

'The same man who killed your husband, Mistress Firle.' Nancy's voice betrayed no trace of emotion and that deadly calm chilled Sophie to the heart.

'Who...who are you?' she whispered.

'I was Nancy Welbeck, the daughter of one of the Collectors on the Kentish coast. Then I met John Tyler. He was one of my father's Riding Officers. We married less than a twelve-month ago...'

Impulsively, Sophie reached out and took the girl's hand in her own.

'Then this is why you are here. You seek justice, just as I do?'

'Justice?' Nancy looked at her then and something moved in the depths of her eyes. They were swiftly veiled, but Sophie was undeceived. For this fragile-looking girl justice would not be enough. In her implacable hatred she sought nothing less than revenge.

'Justice?' she repeated. 'They owe me more than that. They took two lives when they killed John. I lost my unborn child when the news was brought to me.'

Sophie slipped an arm about the slender shoulders.

'Won't you try to remember the happy times?' she urged. 'Your husband would have wished that for you. The memory of those months, short as they were, will stay with you always.'

Nancy did not reply. She sat as if turned to stone. Her sorrow was too deep for any words of comfort to reach her. Vengeance was her overriding passion, and Sophie sensed its corroding influence.

'Did you mean it when you said that you would help me with this pattern?' she asked as she returned to the task of pinning the cloth. 'Can you think of a better way to arrange the pieces? I must not cut the flannel to waste.'

In silence Nancy knelt beside her, swift fingers laying out the pieces of Kit's shirt to best advantage.

Sophie was appalled by the story she'd just heard, but she hid her feelings well. Nancy needed help to recover from the tragedy which had overtaken her. It would be best to keep her busy.

Perhaps it was not tactful to engage the girl in cutting out garments for her own child, but Nancy seemed to be absorbed in her task. The sight of any child must sadden her, but Kit was an affectionate little soul. His unerring instinct led him always to offer love where it was needed. Nancy might yet find comfort in his company.

With the cutting-out completed, Sophie smiled at her companion. 'How skilled you are,' she said in admiration. 'You have done this before, I think.'

'I enjoy it, ma'am. I had some hopes of setting up a business…that is…before I married. I was often asked for copies of my gowns.'

'You designed them?'

Nancy managed a faint smile. 'They had a particular advantage, Mistress Firle, which I did not advertise to everyone. I chose always the best cloth, but the garments were put together with running stitches. That meant that they were easily taken apart, and the material re-used.'

'What an economy! I must remember it. And, Nancy, there is only one other thing. Pray do not call me ma'am, or Mistress Firle. My given name is Sophie.'

'Thank you!' the girl said gravely. 'It is kind in you to suggest it. Perhaps when we are alone? Otherwise it will give rise to comment in the kitchen.'

'Oh, I had not thought of that.' Sophie's face fell. 'I have so much to learn about the spying game.'

'You must be cautious at all times,' Nancy warned. 'It will become a habit.'

With those parting words she returned to her duties below stairs.

Sophie was anxious to make full use of the remaining hours of daylight, so she spent the rest of the afternoon stitching together the pieces of Kit's shirt. When he popped his head round the door she suggested that he try it on.

Kit pulled a face. 'Must I, Mama?'

'It won't take a moment. Then, if you like, I'll tell you a story...'

This promise kept Kit still for long enough for her to make sure that the garment fitted him. Then she laid it aside.

The parlour was already filled with shadows, but the fire provided enough light without the need to send for candles as Kit climbed on to her lap.

'Have you had a busy day?' she asked tenderly.

Kit gave a sigh of deep content. 'Yes,' he told her. 'We've been tying flies.'

'Tying flies?' Sophie was perplexed. 'How do you catch them, darling?'

Her son's laughter echoed about the room. 'Not those kind of flies, Mama. We were making fishing flies. Reuben says that they are better than worms for catching trout.'

'I see. Is it difficult to make them?'

'*Very* difficult. Reuben says that what is needed is dex…dex…'

'Dexterity?' Sophie supplied helpfully.

'Something like that. They are so pretty. I'll bring one to show you when we've finished them.' Kit snuggled closer. 'You smell good,' he announced.

Sophie hugged him close. 'Which story would you like?' she asked.

Kit's reply was prompt. 'The one about the pirates, please.'

Sophie smiled to herself. It was what she had expected. Kit never tired of her tales of adventure upon the high seas, the running up of the skull-and-crossbones when a prize was sighted, and the hoards of treasure to be found upon the Caribbean islands.

Blackbeard was his favourite. The exploits of the infamous Captain Teach fascinated him, and he tried to excuse the worse excesses of his hero.

'Did he *always* make his prisoners walk the plank?' he asked anxiously.

'Not always, I expect, especially if they begged for mercy. Besides, you know, most probably they could swim.'

'But what about the sharks, Mama?' Kit gave a delicious shudder. 'I'd have been so frightened.'

Sophie laughed. 'I doubt if you'll ever meet a shark, my love…'

'But I might find buried treasure,' Kit insisted. 'You promised that we should go down to the coast.'

'And so we shall when the weather improves. Sometimes the storms uncover treasure upon the beaches, though it isn't always gold and jewels.'

'Tell me about the jewels...' Kit fingered Sophie's brooch. 'Did they look like this? It's beautiful!'

'Blackbeard had chests full of such things, but he buried them far away, in the Indies.'

Kit would not give up his cherished hopes. 'You said he was an Englishman,' he insisted. 'He may have brought some back with him.'

'Perhaps he did.' She kept her thoughts to herself. No amount of treasure would have been much comfort to the famous tiger of the seas as he stood upon Execution Dock with a rope around his neck. He had taken his secrets with him to his Maker.

'If I dig deep enough I'll find it.' Kit was growing drowsy. The warmth of the fire and the comfort of his mother's arms finally overcame his efforts to keep his eyes open and he fell sound asleep.

Sophie looked down at him. She ought to rouse herself and put him to bed, but the moment was too precious. This vulnerable little creature was her entire world. She would protect him with her life.

Carefully she moved her arm to settle him more comfortably. Then she leaned back and closed her eyes. After a succession of troubled nights a lack of sleep was beginning to tell on her. She did not stir as Hatton entered the room. Then, suddenly, she was wide awake, aware that she was being watched.

'No, don't get up!' His hand rested lightly on her shoulder. 'You must be much in need of rest.'

There was a note in his voice which she had not heard before and she looked up quickly. As the flickering firelight played upon the harsh planes of his face she thought she detected an expression which astonished her. In another man she would have described it as tenderness. It vanished quickly, confirming her belief that she must have been mistaken. Once more his look was unfathomable.

'Nancy informs me that you wish to see me,' he continued. 'How can I serve you, Mistress Firle?'

The mention of Nancy brought Sophie's concerns to the forefront of her mind.

'Mr Hatton, I feel that you are making a mistake,' she said earnestly.

'Another one? What do you have in mind?'

'How well do you know Nancy?'

'Well enough! Don't tell me that you are still convinced that she will be unsuitable? Too young? Too beautiful? Such sentiments are unworthy of you.'

'Those are not my main concerns. Why did you not tell me who she was? I learned today that her husband has been murdered. Is she yet another woman whom you seek to use for your own ends?'

Even in the dim light Sophie could see that his face had hardened. 'It may surprise you to know that I did not seek her out. Nancy came to me.'

Sophie was silent for a time. 'No, it doesn't surprise me,' she said at last.

'Well, then, what is worrying you? You must believe that she will play her part in apprehending her husband's murderers.'

'My dear sir, you told me once that you have no great understanding of a woman's heart. I must tell you now that you are playing with fire.'

She heard a snort of disgust. 'Dramatics, Mistress Firle? I can well do without them.'

'You would do well to listen to me. Nancy is beyond your control. She is obsessed by hatred.'

'You think that a bad thing?'

'I can understand it, but I think it dangerous. She could put us all in jeopardy. If she finds the men who killed her husband and robbed her of her unborn child, I shouldn't like to be responsible for her actions. No words of yours will sway her.'

Hatton regarded her in silence. 'You may be right,' he admitted reluctantly. 'I'll watch her closely.'

Privately, Sophie thought that it would take more than that. Nancy was adept at concealing her true feelings. It had taken another woman to discover them.

'So you won't send her away?' she asked.

'I think not. If you are right, she might take matters into her own hands and ruin our entire operation. Better to keep her here. Don't you agree? Of course, if you and she are at daggers' drawn...?'

'We are not!' Sophie told him sharply. 'I like her very much. I'm sorry only that she is so obsessed. Hatred is the most corrosive of emotions. It harms the person who feels it far more than the object of their loathing.'

'You are right.' Hatton sank into the armchair opposite. 'I have often felt the same. In one way we play into the hands of our enemies by hating them. It can cripple a person for life, robbing them of normal pleasures.'

Sophie was surprised to find that he was in agreement with her. His philosophy was unexpected. She had imagined that this ruthless creature was no stranger to the worst excesses of hatred.

Now she looked down at the sleeping child upon her lap. 'I must put Kit to bed,' she said. 'Will you excuse me, sir?'

'Let me!' With astonishing gentleness he took Kit from her, bending so close that his lips almost brushed her cheek.

Sophie turned her head away. For some unaccountable reason she was disturbed by his nearness as an unfamiliar scent of tobacco, clean linen, soap and the outdoors assailed her nostrils. It was not unpleasant, and it stirred long-forgotten feelings in her breast.

What must it be like to feel those massive arms about her once more? The memory of his bruising kiss returned to trouble her. Her response had been immediate. He had sensed it immediately, as he had reminded her. It was humiliating to find that she had so little control over her natural instincts.

Now she held out her arms for Kit, but Hatton nodded to her to precede him from the room. If she tried to argue she would waken the child, so she led the way to Kit's chamber.

Hatton laid him on the bed, and proceeded to unfasten his shoes.

'What a family you are!' he joked, 'I seem always to be removing shoes from sleeping figures…'

The colour rose to Sophie's cheeks. 'There is not the least need for you to do so, sir. I am perfectly capable of undressing my son.'

She was seething with indignation. It was ungallant of him to remind her of the previous night when he'd carried her to her own bed and removed her clothing.

Now he seemed to have read her mind. 'Forget it!' he advised. 'Now, if you'll lift the lad I'll slip him out of his coat and breeches.'

He was surprisingly deft and Kit showed no signs of awakening even as Hatton eased him into his nightshirt.

'There, ma'am!' he said with satisfaction. 'You'll hear no more of him before morning. He has become Reuben's shadow, and the pair of them are busy from morn till night.'

Sophie hesitated. 'Your man is very good to him,' she admitted.

'Why not? The boy is quick to learn and interested in everything about him. Besides, Reuben has no objection to being regarded as some kind of demi-god.'

Sophie saw the gleam of perfect teeth, and she laughed in spite of herself. 'I'm afraid he takes up far too much of Reuben's time, Mr Hatton. I wonder that you allow it.'

'It is no great problem at the moment,' he replied with a dismissive gesture. 'Now, ma'am, since your son is safely bestowed in his bed, I hope that you'll agree to dine with me?'

Alarm filled Sophie's head. Had she not decided to keep Hatton at a distance? She searched her mind to think of a plausible excuse to refuse him. She could not plead a previous engagement. The very idea was ludicrous. She had no friends in the locality. Nor had she any transport.

Hatton noticed her indecision. 'Come, you won't tell me that you prefer to dine alone? That is bad for the digestion, ma'am. Companionship is essential for full enjoyment—of a meal, I mean of course!'

He was teasing her again, and to her annoyance Sophie found that she was blushing furiously.

'Quite charming!' he announced with a twinkle. 'And rare indeed in a wife and a mother... Naturally, if you feel that you can't trust yourself to my company I shall understand.'

Hatton was enjoying himself and Sophie determined to give him a sharp set-down. Anything to wipe that infuriating smile from his lips.

'Were we not agreed that your understanding of women is limited, sir? I shall be happy to dine with you.'

She heard a shout of laughter.

'What a fib! Unconvincing, my dear, when that look would turn a man to stone. Shall we say at seven, then?'

Sophie could not bring herself to speak. She swept past him with her head held high.

She reached her room to find that Abby had put away all the garments which she had intended to return, leaving out only the bronze gown.

'I won't wear that!' she said. Her tone was sharper than she had intended and Abby looked surprised.

'Why, ma'am, is something wrong with it? I thought it quite the prettiest of all.'

Sophie saw the girl's downcast look and was ashamed of her ill-temper. 'You are right,' she admitted. 'The difficulty is that I did not order it. The garments left on the bed were to be returned. There must have been some mistake.'

Abby's face cleared. 'I'd keep them if it were me,' she told her mistress with a mischievous look. 'Oh, ma'am, you won't send back the fur-lined tippet? It's fit for a queen!'

'And I am not a queen, Abby.' Sophie was strongly tempted to change into her drab black gown, but she could imagine Hatton's reaction. He would realise at once that it was a childish attempt to annoy him. She would not give him that satisfaction.

'You may bring me the blue which is buttoned to the neck,' she said.

Abby brightened. 'It will go well with your brooch, Mistress Firle. My, that's a fine piece of jewellery! Mother says that it's high time a gentleman took care of you.'

This remark did nothing for Sophie's state of mind. She was almost tempted into another sharp retort, but she bit her tongue. She walked over to the wash-stand and poured some water into the basin.

'Is it still hot?' Abby asked anxiously. 'Mr Hatton told me to bring it up for six o'clock...'

'Did he, indeed?' Sophie's feelings threatened to overcome her. She washed and dressed quickly. She had had more than enough of Hatton's arrogance. This evening she would make it clear that she would brook no further interference.

He needed her to help him carry out his plans. He had made that clear enough. She was beginning to suspect that his threats to turn her out were simply an attempt to ensure her co-operation. Now she sensed that he would never do so.

She couldn't quite decide why she felt so certain of that fact, but tonight she would test out her belief. The challenge excited her and she made her way to his private parlour relishing the battle of wills ahead.

He was standing by the fireplace, but he turned as she entered the room, immaculate as always in a well-cut coat of the finest broadcloth, snowy linen and tight pantaloons with gleaming Hessian boots pulled over them. He had an excellent leg for the prevailing fashions, she noted grudgingly.

Sophie walked towards him with a smile which would have graced a crocodile, and his eyes narrowed.

'You are in looks tonight, Mistress Firle. Is this one of Madame Arouet's gowns?'

'It is.' Sophie's smile did not waver.

Hatton bowed. 'It is most becoming. The woman is a genius. Don't you agree?'

'I do, but sadly, her accounting system leaves much to be desired. I had not ordered more than one half of the goods which I received.'

'Really? Perhaps it is no great matter, ma'am. Can you make use of them?'

'Possibly…if I could afford them. Mr Hatton, please don't try to gammon me. This is your doing, is it not?'

'I may have suggested a few additions…'

'You had no right to do so. I won't accept them, sir!'

'Very well then, send them back!' he said indifferently. 'It does not matter to me.'

Sophie was nonplussed. She had expected a fierce argument.

'On the other hand, you could pay me for them when this sorry business is ended,' he continued smoothly. 'You may find them useful at some later date.'

'Possibly!'

He had cut the ground from under Sophie's feet and she knew it. She ground her teeth in frustration. It was impossible to get the better of him.

Now he looked up with pleased anticipation as Abby entered the room bearing a tray. He seated Sophie at the table with his usual formality, and favoured Abby with a smile.

'I'm starving!' he announced. 'What does your mother offer us this evening?'

'Dressed lobster, sir. It was brought up from the coast today. Mistress Firle will enjoy it—it's one of her favourites.'

'Your mother spoils us, Abby, with gourmet foods. How can she top that?'

'You are to have broiled fowl with mushrooms, Mr Hatton, and then a Celerata cream.'

'No apple pie?'

Abby looked confused. 'We finished it off,' she said timidly. 'The men were that hungry, but Mother will make another for you if you wish it.'

'No, you shall not worry her. Let us enjoy the Celerata cream, possibly with some cheese to follow. With that I shall hope to survive till morning.'

As Abby scurried from the room, Sophie gave him a look of reproach.

'You must not tease her, Mr Hatton. Now she will go back to the kitchen and tell Bess that you are not satisfied with your meal.'

'I doubt that, ma'am. Bess knows that I appreciate her cooking. I have been at some pains to get her on my side, you know.'

'I wonder that you bothered.'

'I had my reasons. Bess's opinion goes for much among the servants. I'm relying on her to back up my cover story. I wish her to consider me a suitable candidate for your hand...'

'You ask too much of her, Mr Hatton. With your lack of concern for the properties, it may have escaped your notice that a recent widow would be in mourning for at least a year. Most certainly no lady in that situation would think of offering encouragement to another man...however charming.' She gave him a smile which would have frozen daffodils.

Hatton grinned at her. 'Compliments, ma'am? That is a pleasant change. At the risk of causing you some distress, I should inform you that Bess had no time for your late husband. She will not find it strange that you would seek for happiness so soon.'

Sophie glared at him. 'Have you been gossiping behind my back, and with the servants too?'

'No, I have not! My information comes from Reuben. Bess does not speak out in front of Kit, of course, but when the child is absent she makes no secret of her opinions. She feels that you were cheated by a man unworthy of you.'

'Richard's behaviour was none of her concern,' Sophie replied stiffly.

'You are mistaken, Mistress Firle. Your servants are fond of you. They did not care to see you duped. You were kept in ignorance of much that was happening here.'

'Then why did they not tell me?'

'Would you have believed them? Loyalty alone would have prevented it, and you say yourself that you will not listen to gossip.'

Sophie was silent.

'Or was it loyalty?' he continued inexorably. 'I find it astonishing that you did not question your husband's frequent absences, or the reasons for his tolerance of a clientele too dangerous for you to meet them.'

'He did not say that they were dangerous,' she replied. 'Just that they were rough and noisy.'

'You have not answered my question, ma'am. Perhaps you did not care to know the answer…?'

'Oh!' she cried. 'You shall not blacken his name. He was your own man, after all. I had thought you must be proud of him. He died in a worthy cause.'

'Your loyalty to a man you did not love is admirable, my dear, but it is misplaced. It is high time you knew the truth. Firle was a double agent.'

Sophie stared at him. 'I don't know what you mean,' she whispered.

'Then let me explain. He fed us a certain amount of information, most of it useless. However, the information he supplied to his friends was of great value to them. They were warned well in advance of possible seizures, or a long-planned ambush at their landing beaches.'

Sophie felt that her throat had closed. It was almost impossible to breathe. She shut her eyes as the full implications of his words came home to her.

'You can't mean it!' she whispered at last. 'Do you tell me that he was working with the smugglers?'

'Beyond a doubt, ma'am. For a time we could not understand why our most secret plans appeared to be known to them. It became clear that we had an informer in our midst. The trail led to your husband.'

'I can't believe it! You must be mistaken. Why, that would mean that he was privy to the deaths of some of your own men...his friends...'

Hatton said nothing.

'I can't accept that you are right,' Sophie said more firmly. 'What possible reason could he have for agreeing to such a betrayal?'

A grim smile crossed her companion's face. 'Money, Mistress Firle! His share of the trade would have been substantial, but he must have realised that fortunes were being made by the men who backed the smugglers. I suspect that he tried to blackmail them, and in doing so he signed his own death warrant. They would not have hesitated to remove the danger.'

'But Richard had no money. We had no carriage and we lived so sparingly…' Then Sophie remembered the huge sum she had found in Richard's desk, and her face clouded.

'Yes?' Hatton prompted.

'Why would he need so much?' she pleaded. 'I did not ask for it.'

Her pitiful expression wrenched at Hatton's heart. The girl had courage, but she had borne enough. He would not explain that a womaniser such as Richard Firle would need bottomless pockets to keep his birds of paradise in luxury.

'Perhaps we shall never know,' he told her gently. 'It may be that he hoped to save enough to take you and Kit away from here.'

Tears gleamed upon her lashes, but she shook her head.

'You don't believe that, and nor do I. You said that I did not love him. That is true, but I thought

I loved him once, and I thought he loved me. I soon learned the truth of it. My father was right. Richard was a fortune-hunter. When my father cast me off he had no further use for me.' She bent her head, but Hatton cupped her chin in his huge hand and forced her to look up at him.

'Don't fail me now!' he urged. 'You have your son to think about, remember?' He strode over to the bell-pull and summoned Abby. Then he took Sophie's hands and drew her to her feet.

'Can I persuade you to sit upon my lap, my dear? I feel that Abby needs convincing of my ardour.'

Sophie was too shocked by his revelations to put up much resistance. It was oddly comforting to feel his massive arms about her, but it was also embarrassing.

'There is no need, I'm sure...' she said half-heartedly.

Hatton settled her more comfortably. 'This is no hardship, ma'am. Of that I can assure you.'

Chapter Seven

As Sophie lay inert within his arms, Hatton showed no disposition to release her, even when Abby had left the room.

She was very pale, and he looked down at her in some concern, aware that she was trembling uncontrollably. He picked her up and moved closer to the fire.

'Are you all right?' he asked. 'My apologies, ma'am. Perhaps I should not have told you of your husband's perfidy.'

'I prefer to know the truth,' she whispered through chattering teeth. 'It's just that I seem to be so very cold.'

'That is shock, my dear.' He reached out a long arm to the tray on the table beside him and poured her a glass of brandy. 'Drink this! I know you hate the taste, but it will warm you.'

Obediently, she sipped at the fiery spirit. As it coursed through her body she began to regain some semblance of composure. For a time she had seemed to lose all power of thought, but now her mind was racing. Her son was her first concern.

'Kit must not know of this. Please, I beg that you will never tell him.'

Hatton's lips tightened. 'Nothing was further from my mind,' he said abruptly. 'No child should carry such a burden.'

Sophie nodded. Then she remembered Nancy. If the girl should ever learn that it was Richard who had betrayed his colleagues...

She shuddered as she recalled the hatred in the girl's eyes. Revenge was an obsession with Nancy, and who knew where her vengeance might fall? Kit would be an easy victim.

Hatton held her closer, chafing her hands in an effort to warm them. 'What is it?' he asked quietly.

'I was thinking of Nancy. Does she know of any of this?'

'Of course not. Why do you ask?'

'She might harm Kit if she should ever learn that his father was the cause of her husband's murder. I fear that she is unbalanced.'

'How could she hear of it? No one in this household knows, apart from you and myself.'

Suddenly, Sophie became aware that she was resting comfortably against Hatton's massive chest. She coloured deeply as she attempted to struggle to her feet. He made no attempt to stop her.

'Better now?' he enquired.

'Thank you. I do feel warmer...' She managed a wavering smile as she took the opposite chair. 'It must be the brandy, I imagine. Is it your answer to all ills?'

'Only to some of them.' The hooded eyes regarded her intently. 'You have my admiration, ma'am—'

'Oh—why is that?'

'You are honest, Mistress Firle, especially with yourself. You do not seek to play the part of the grieving widow.'

'I can't,' she told him simply. 'I won't pretend to grief because I have lost my love. Richard was no longer that. Yet I do grieve in another way, for a life cut short by evil men. My son has lost his father, and Richard, whatever his failings, was our sole support. For that, at least, I must be thankful.'

'You are generous, ma'am.' Hatton's admiration grew. This gently nurtured girl had paid dearly for her one mistake in marrying Richard Firle. He could only guess at her agonies of mind when she realized that fact. The years must have worn away at her hopes, her dreams, her confidence and her faith in her fellow human-beings, but none of it had crushed her.

'You don't regret your marriage, then?' He was surprised at his own need to hear her reply, though he knew the answer before she spoke.

Sophie gave him a radiant smile. 'Of course not! I have Kit...'

Hatton turned away. Her courage shamed him. He was beginning to regret ever having considered drawing her into his plans. She had done nothing to deserve it. There must have been some other way to gain his ends without the need to involve this girl and her young son in such danger.

He was under no illusions. Sophie's life and that of the boy could be snuffed out like candles in the wind if anything went wrong. Only days ago he had thought the price worth paying. Now he knew that it was not. The realisation hit him hard. Hatton was no fool. He knew that he was growing dangerously fond of both Sophie and her son.

The knowledge shook him badly. It could put all his plans at risk. His expression was carefully controlled when he turned back to her.

'Will you open the inn tomorrow, Mistress Firle?' he asked. 'You have everything you need?'

'I believe so. We are well stocked, though I can't imagine that in the depths of winter we shall have much trade.'

'Then we must try to encourage it. Lamps in all the windows to offer a welcome to the traveller, and roaring fires. Bess may possibly wish to do some cooking…. There is nothing like the smell of fresh-baked bread, or the prospect of a juicy roast…'

Sophie shook her head at him. 'Mr Hatton, you are an optimist. Sometimes in the past we have gone for weeks without a single customer. I cannot think that it will change.'

Sophie was wrong. By noon on the following day she was surprised to hear the sound of carriage wheels. Glancing through the window, she saw six young men striding towards her door.

Hurrying down the stairs, she moved to greet them, warmed by the admiration in their eyes. Clearly her bronze gown was a great success.

'Gentlemen, what may we do for you?'

'Why, ma'am, we are in need of sustenance. The drive from Brighton has given us an appetite. What can you offer us?'

The man who spoke was in his early twenties. Tall and dark, he reminded her of someone, though she could not think why.

Sophie recited the menu quickly and was vastly amused when her customers ordered everything from soup through turbot to chicken, ham and mutton. She doubted if they would be able to eat one half of it, but she hadn't reckoned on a young man's hearty appetite. The food vanished like snow in summer. Then her customers set about Bess's apple pie with evident enjoyment.

Sophie was intrigued. 'How did you hear about the inn?' she asked as she served them with a sixth bottle of wine. 'We have only just reopened.'

They all beamed at her. 'Word gets about, ma'am.' The speaker's eyes had strayed to Nancy, who was engaged in clearing the tables. 'I suspect that we shall become your most faithful customers. Brighton can be dull, you know.'

Sophie laughed at him. 'Surely not? There are so many diversions…'

'But none that include the company of the most beautiful women in this part of Sussex.' The speaker gave her a gallant bow.

'Nonsense, sir! I suspect that your stomachs are your main concern. Have you enjoyed your meal?'

A chorus of approval convinced her, and Sophie beamed at them. 'We had not expected company today,' she told them. 'Next time you must let us know your wishes.'

'Ma'am, they have been more than fulfilled.' The young man bowed again. 'The Prince himself could not have dined with more pleasure.'

Sophie laughed. 'I doubt if his Royal Highness will venture along these country lanes in winter. You may not know that Sussex roads are said to be the worst in England.'

'And why is that, ma'am?'

'The county lies on clay. You were fortunate that we had frost last night, so that the ground is firm.'

'How true, Mistress Firle!' Hatton had entered the room. 'Yet this weather cannot hold. The wind is bringing rain from the west.'

The six young men looked up at him and he favoured them with a pleasant smile. 'Just a warning, gentlemen,' he told them smoothly. 'The clay is a serious hazard. In summer it bakes to the consistency of rock, but rain turns it into a morass. In the past it has taken as many as twenty oxen to drag a wagon free.'

The young men looked at each other. They seemed reluctant to leave the comfort of the inn. One of them walked over to the window.

'No rain as yet,' he announced. 'Sir, won't you join us in a game of cards before we leave?'

Hatton nodded. 'As you wish. You stay in Brighton, so I hear. What brought you out into the country?'

Their leader grinned at him. 'My dear sir, it was a need to practise our driving skills. Ned there almost overturned the mail coach last time he took the ribbons. It cost him a small fortune to soothe the driver's feelings.'

His friend objected strongly to this slur upon his abilities. 'His lead horse was almost blind,' he insisted.

'And so were you when you took that corner, Ned,' the man beside him teased.

Ned maintained a dignified silence as he shuffled the cards. Then there was a pause as each man studied his hand.

Sophie left them to their game. She had enjoyed the company of these unexpected customers, feeling quite at ease with them. They had reminded her of the sons of family friends known to her since childhood. How long ago it all seemed now, the parties, the picnics, the village fêtes and the balls when young men such as these had presented themselves at her father's house, all vying for her attention.

She'd lost her heart to none of them, much to her father's satisfaction. His choice for her was William Curtis, the neighbouring landowner, whom Sophie had always held in keen dislike. For a time she had had an ally in her mother who pleaded Sophie's youth, but that excuse had worn thin as the months passed and she reached her seventeenth birthday.

Then she had met Richard. It was just a random trick of fate that he'd been sent to ask her father, a local magistrate, for a date when certain captured smugglers might be tried.

And my head was full of nonsense at that time, Sophie thought sadly. She'd been reading about the Vikings, half-thrilled and half-repelled by their exploits, but always intrigued. The splendid creature who rode up to her father's door might more fittingly have stepped ashore from a Norwegian galley.

She could remember every detail of that first encounter. She'd been standing at the foot of the steps about to mount her horse. The groom was already bending with locked hands to help her into the saddle. Then he'd been thrust aside, and Sophie turned to look into the bluest eyes she'd ever seen.

And I behaved like an idiot, Sophie thought bitterly. Richard must have found her the easiest of conquests. She had positively gaped at the impossibly handsome vision before her, marvelling at the sculptured perfection of his face, the wonderful curves of a mobile mouth, and the way the sunlight gleamed upon his blond head. She had discounted Viking ancestry immediately. This man looked more like a Greek god.

A wry smile lifted the corners of her mouth. Susceptibility to good looks had always been a weakness in her character, but from that day she had never looked at another man.

She'd braved her father's wrath, the indignity of being locked in her room and even threats of a diet of bread and water and serious beatings, until Richard had come for her that fateful night.

She'd gone with him without a backward glance, untroubled by the fact that she scarcely knew him. Their meetings had been few and, of necessity, fleeting. Love at first sight was true romance, as he had assured her, and she hadn't doubted the truth of it.

They had married on the day of her escape and, lost in dreams of happiness, Sophie could see no clouds upon the horizon.

Had not Richard assured her that once they were wed her father would relent? If she showed herself penitent and begged the forgiveness of both her parents, she would be restored to the bosom of her family.

It had not happened. Richard had reckoned without her father's implacable opposition to the match. It had been a body blow to him. Sophie had been the child of his heart, but she had spurned his wishes and his love. Even the thought of her was like a dagger-thrust. His only solace was to forget that she existed.

Richard had refused to believe at first that he had married a pauper, rather than an heiress, but as the truth came home to him, his manner towards Sophie changed. She'd been terrified by his coldness. How was she to live if he decided to abandon her? She loved him still, rejoicing when she found that she was pregnant. That, surely, would bring him back to her.

It didn't. Only when disgrace and dismissal from the Revenue Service threatened to crush him had he turned to her. She had stood by him, refusing to believe the accusations levelled against him, but troubled even as she defended him.

Richard seemed to lead a life apart from her, marked by mysterious meetings and frequent absences. When she'd tried to question him he'd frown, surly and abusive. On that last day of his life she had looked at him clear-eyed, wondering, not for the first time, how this man, handsome beyond belief and with the physique of an athlete, could have failed to live up to all she had expected of him.

Sophie shook her head, as if to rid it of troublesome thoughts. She could not change the past. Now she must think about the future. She looked up as Hatton entered the room.

'Your game is over?' she asked in surprise.

'Yes, your guests are leaving. I told them again that they must not underestimate the poor state of the roads. I reminded them that the oxen, the swine, the women and all the other animals in Sussex are noted for the length of their legs. It is said to be from the difficulty of pulling their feet from the mud… It is thought to strengthen the muscles and lengthen the bones.'

Sophie laughed in spite of herself. 'I had best come and bid them farewell,' she said. 'I enjoyed their company, and they enjoyed their meal. We shall have made a splendid profit.'

'Congratulations!'

Sophie detected a sardonic undertone and she stared at him.

'Mr Hatton, you can't suspect these young men. I should have thought them harmless.'

'But then, you are easily deceived, are you not, Mistress Firle?' Hatton saw her angry look and relented. 'No, you are right. These puppies are not the men we seek.'

Sophie saw to her surprise that he was booted and spurred. Over his arm he carried a cloak with many capes.

'Do you go with them to Brighton?' she asked.

'No, my dear. My duties take me elsewhere. I shan't be away above a day or two.'

Sophie was horrified. 'No!' she cried. 'You can't! You promised us your protection. You shall not leave us now.'

'Your concern for me is touching…' Hatton's tone was sarcastic. 'Do you believe that I shall be lost upon the roads?'

'I don't care about you,' she cried wildly. 'I am thinking of my servants and my son.'

Hatton took her hand and drew her down to sit beside him. 'I wish that you could learn to trust me, ma'am. Believe me, you are not in danger for these next few days. With all this rain upon the western wind the roads will be a quagmire within hours. Wagons cannot move in such conditions, and the consignment in your cellar is too large to be carried by packhorses. In any case, some approach is certain to be made to you beforehand.'

Sophie was unconvinced, and her pallor alarmed him.

Hatton took her hands in his once more. 'You have done so well,' he told her gently. Absentmindedly, he was stroking the back of her hand with his thumb and she found the sensation disturbing. She drew her hand away as if she had been stung.

'When…when will you return?' she cried. She was torn between her dislike of him and an urgent wish for his protection.

'As soon as possible!' Unexpectedly he raised her fingers to his lips and kissed them. 'You are not without protection, Mistress Firle. You have both my men and your own. Jem is someone to be reckoned with, I feel…' He was smiling down at her.

Pride stiffened Sophie's resolve. 'Very well, then, go if you must,' she snapped.

'Sophie, please!'

'I don't recall giving you leave to use my given name, Mr Hatton. I see your promises now for what they are…completely worthless!' She turned on her heel and left him.

It was but the work of a moment to bid farewell to her guests. Then she stalked away without another glance at Hatton.

She heard the carriage leaving, to be followed by a single horseman, and she felt bereft. Beneath a ridiculous temptation to burst into tears she was furious. Hatton had drawn her into his plans, ignoring all her objections. Now, when it suited him, he was quite willing to leave her alone to face whatever dangers might be in store, and she was terrified.

It was all very well for him to claim that the servants would protect her. They might be willing to do so, but they knew no better than she did herself from which direction that threat might come.

Now she could only hope that he'd been right about the weather. For the next three days she blessed the leaden skies and the constant rain. Not a single customer had crossed her threshold. The greyness was depressing, but she could cope with that. What she feared most was the sudden arrival of strangers.

She tried to banish Hatton from her mind, telling herself that he wasn't worth a thought, but she found it difficult. She had grown accustomed to his teasing and that lazy smile and the comforting sight of his enormous figure about the place.

On several occasions during those few days she was tempted to pack her bags and leave with Kit, but where could she go? She had no money, and with a small child at her heels she would find it difficult to gain employment.

Try as she might, she could see no way out of her predicament, other than to stay where she was. Oh, if only Hatton would return! As the days passed she missed him more and more.

Of course, it was simply that he had promised to protect her. On this occasion, at least, she could not berate herself for being swayed by a handsome face. Hatton was no Adonis. His features were too strong for that. In repose his expression could be daunting. Not a person to whom one would readily apply for mercy, she thought rebelliously.

Well, she, at least, was not afraid of him, and when he returned she would give him a piece of her mind. Sophie spent much of her time thinking of sharp set-downs and crushing retorts which would reduce him to abject apology for his ill behaviour. That is, if he ever came back again. The sudden notion that he might not do so filled her with despair. Then common sense returned. Hatton had laid his plans with care. He would not abandon them now, however little he cared for her own welfare, or that of her child. It would be duty alone which drew him back to the inn, and she should admire him for his dedication.

But she didn't...at least, not altogether. Duty was important, naturally, and she would be the first to admit it, but other things were important too, such as consideration and affection.

Alarmed at the direction which her thoughts were taking, Sophie picked up her book. The small volume of poems had been left behind by a casual visitor some months ago. The beauty of the language, the various rhythms and the rich imagery of the work had proved to be a solace in the past, and now she knew many of the poems by heart, reciting them to herself as she went about her daily routine.

Her eye fell upon some lines penned by William Blake, an author new to her:

Tyger, Tyger, burning bright
In the forests of the night.
What immortal hand or eye
Could frame their fearful symmetry?

In the past the raw power of the poem had delighted her, but now it brought Nicholas Hatton forcibly to mind. Man and animal seemed as one in their predatory quest.

Sophie thrust the book aside. She must be losing her sense of proportion. Most probably the poem was not about an animal at all, but a symbol of some deeper meaning.

As for Hatton? He was just a man, possibly more ruthless than most, but a man for all that, and not a wild animal.

Yet the image stayed with her and she could not shake it off. That night she dreamed that she was running through a jungle, with some beast in hot pursuit.

She wakened with a cry, to find that her room was flooded with moonlight. The skies had cleared, and the rain had stopped at last.

Sophie lay there trembling. Now Hatton *must* return. He would know, even better than she, that once the roads were passable his quarry would return to the inn to collect the contents of her cellars.

The London men behind the trade would be growing impatient. They'd wait no longer for their profits on the vast cargo.

Further sleep was impossible. She waited until the first grey fingers of dawn had lightened the eastern sky and then she summoned Abby to fetch her water and help her dress.

'You are up betimes, Mistress Firle.' Abby was still half-asleep, and clearly unappreciative of Sophie's sudden desire to be up before the birds.

'I thought I'd go for a walk,' Sophie told her. 'I'm tired of being forced to stay indoors.'

'Can I come too?' A small face peeped around her door.

'Of course you may,' Sophie corrected. 'But first you must eat a good hot breakfast and let Abby dress you in your warmest clothes.'

'You'll catch your death,' Abby predicted in gloomy tones. 'There's been a frost, and the ground's like iron.'

This statement did nothing for Sophie's peace of mind, but she thrust aside her fears. Perhaps they would have no customers today.

When the sun was up she took Kit by the hand and set off down the lane. It was good to be out of doors on such a perfect winter's morning. A white rime clung to the verges of the road, untouched as yet by the weak rays of the sun as it glanced off trees and hedgerows bejewelled by the frost.

Sophie pointed to a solitary robin which regarded them with interest. Now she handed a bag of crumbs to Kit. The bird seemed almost tame. He hopped towards them, pecking eagerly at the bread.

'I bet I could train him to sit upon my hand. That is, if we could catch him, Mama.'

'No, we can't do that. He's a wild creature. It would be cruel to put him in a cage. Why not look for him when you are out of doors? He may stay close if you feed him every day.'

'That's a good idea!' Kit looked up at the sky. 'Will it snow, do you suppose? Reuben is making me a sledge.'

'I think it is too cold for snow. See how the ice has formed upon this pond. No, my dear, don't put your weight on it. It is too thin, as yet.'

'If it gets *really* thick, Hatton has promised to teach me how to skate,' Kit said with pride. 'He's very good, you know, he can do twirls and jumps, and he can skate backwards…' Clearly, this last astonishing achievement outweighed all the others in Kit's mind.

'Good gracious, how do you know all this?'

'He told me,' Kit said simply. 'He showed me, too. Just watch!' Kit ran along the icy lane and jumped in the air with his arms spread wide.

Sophie's lips twitched at the thought of the redoubtable Mr Hatton displaying his skating skills on dry land for the benefit of her son. She would have given much to have seen it.

'Of course, it's easier on the ground,' Kit told her gravely. 'The ice is slippery and first I have to learn to balance.'

'I expect it's rather like learning to walk,' she agreed.

'Well, I did that, didn't I?' Kit chuckled at his own joke and ran ahead of her.

She didn't keep him out of doors for long. The east wind was too cold, and she might have been naked for all the protection her warm clothing offered.

She hurried indoors to the comfort of a roaring fire, praying that the change in the weather had come too suddenly for the smugglers to have made their plans.

She had few customers that day. A carrier selling fish from the coast stopped by to ask for trade. Bess bought generously, knowing that the fish would keep well in the icy temperature of her food cellar. The man stayed only long enough to drink a tankard of mulled ale. Then he pushed on, clearly anxious to be rid of his load before nightfall.

Sophie ran to the window as a single horseman rode up to her door, but it was only a stranger, asking the way to Brighton. He was followed by the occupants of a carriage. A lady and two gentlemen came in to warm themselves and take refreshment, debating as they did so whether or not to continue with their journey.

'We might stay here, Matilda,' one of the men suggested. 'The food is excellent, and it will be much cheaper than the town.'

'Penny-pinching again, husband?' the lady sniffed. 'I *must* be at Brighton. My doctor insists upon it.'

'My dear, you can't intend to go on with his nonsensical suggestion of winter bathing? In this weather? Why, it is like to kill you.'

The lady would not be swayed. 'Much you would care,' she snapped. 'Dr Deaton has a splendid reputation and he knows my condition well.'

'Be it on your own head!' Her husband threw up his hands. He was not prepared to argue further. Then the other gentleman intervened.

'It may be as well to go on,' he suggested. 'If it should snow we might be trapped here for a sennight.'

'A week in this place?' the woman cried in anger. 'I won't have it! We must leave at once.'

Sophie saw them off without regret. She was in full agreement with the sentiments of the lady's husband. Anyone foolish enough to immerse themselves in the icy waters of the English Channel in the dead of winter was asking for trouble, whatever their doctor's orders.

Then she smiled. The woman might try the treatment once, but she doubted if the experiment would be repeated. There were other diversions in Brighton which would be much more to her taste and would provide a more agreeable cure for her ailments, real or imaginary.

So far things were going well, but one hour later a coach driver came in with news that his coach had overturned a mile away. The horses were down and the vehicle had toppled into a deep ditch with the passengers trapped inside.

The driver was badly shaken, half-blinded as he was by blood pouring from an ugly cut across his brow.

Sophie dispatched Hatton's coach, with Reuben at the reins. She sent the rest of her male servants with him, laden with ropes and chains. Then she turned her attention to the injured driver.

The wound was not as deep as she had at first suspected, but she bathed it carefully before winding a bandage about the pad she'd used to staunch the blood.

Preoccupied with her task she hadn't noticed that she was no longer alone. Mindful of Hatton's sovereign remedy for shock, she reached for a bottle of brandy. Then she gasped. Behind her the room had filled with a group of silent men.

Sophie smiled at them uncertainly. They were too quiet and unlike any customers she had seen before. All of them wore loose clothing, but beneath it she could see that they were heavily armed.

'I'll be with you in a moment,' she promised. 'This man has been injured in an accident. I'll ring for someone to take care of him.' Despairingly she reached out towards the bell-pull, knowing full well that only Nancy or Abby would be likely to appear. She herself had sent her menfolk away.

'No need for that. Yon chap has fainted.' One of the men twitched the bell-rope away from her. 'Bad luck to have an accident like that!' He gave his companions a knowing wink.

Sniggers were followed by loud guffaws. Then one of the men walked past her, taking bottles of spirits from the shelves and handing them to his companions.

'Just saving you the trouble of having to serve us, ma'am!' he leered.

Sophie was thinking fast. She had no weapon with her. In any case, a single pistol would be useless against this mob. She must rely on her own wits. Pray heaven that Nancy did not come to find her. The men were downing gin and brandy as if it were water. At this rate they would be intoxicated within the next half-hour. She knew what that could mean. Both she and Nancy would be at risk, and Abby too.

'You are welcome to help yourselves,' she said pleasantly. Nothing in her voice betrayed her terror. 'Would you like some food?' It was all she could think of. Food might help to keep them sober.

'It wouldn't come amiss!' The man who had handed out the bottles reached out to finger her brooch. 'That's a nice piece, mistress. Did you get it from your fancy-man?'

Sophie's anger made her incautious. 'No!' she snapped. 'I am a widow.'

'Now there's a shame!' A dirty hand caressed her cheek. 'A good woman going to waste, I call it!' The hand strayed to the bodice of her gown, tugging it so that the buttons flew in all directions.

Sophie slapped his hand away, to the accompaniment of a shout of laughter from his friends.

Her anger seemed to inflame him further. He slipped an arm about her waist, drawing her close. His fingers were entwined in her hair, forcing back her head as he bent to kiss her.

Sophie lost all her fear of him. Now she fought him like a cat, biting and scratching at his eyes, but she was no match for his superior strength. He forced her back until she was laying across a table. Then his hands tore at her skirts.

Suddenly, Sophie heard a grunt and a dull thud. She struggled upright to find her attacker lying at her feet as if he had been pole-axed.

'My apologies, ma'am,' a cultured voice remarked. 'This was an unfortunate incident. The shock must have been severe. Won't you sit down whilst I fetch you a restorative?'

Still dazed, Sophie looked at the speaker. She saw a man not much above middle height and no longer young. Silver-haired, and thin to the point of emaciation, he had the face of an ascetic or some tortured mediaeval saint.

Now the blue eyes smiled encouragement at her. 'You are quite safe,' he said. 'Those animals are gone.'

Sophie looked beyond him to find that the room was indeed empty, apart from her companion. 'I have to thank you,' she said weakly. 'Foolishly, I left myself without protection. My men are attending some accident further up the road.'

Then she remembered the smiles and winks when the accident was mentioned. 'I think they caused it,' she said heavily. 'But why, I can't imagine.'

'Possibly they hoped to commit a robbery?' he suggested.

'Then why come here?'

'The arrival of your men must have frightened them away. This inn must have seemed the next best target.'

It all sounded very plausible, but Sophie was unconvinced. She sensed that her unwelcome visitors were members of the smuggling fraternity, but no approach had been made to her about the disposal of the goods still hidden in her cellar.

Her rescuer handed her a glass of brandy, and Sophie pulled a wry face. If gentlemen continued to ply her with drinks in this way, she might get a taste for the spirit which she disliked so much. Still, she could not refuse such a kindly act, and she took a sip to please him.

'Well done!' He bent to retrieve the brooch which was lying at her feet. 'This is yours, I believe?' He was careful to avert his eyes and looking down, Sophie could understand why.

Stripped of its buttons, the front of her gown was gaping wide, revealing an expanse of snowy chemise. She jumped to her feet, holding the edges of the cloth together.

'Excuse me!' she murmured in confusion as she fled the room.

Chapter Eight

Unwilling to explain the damage to her gown, Sophie didn't summon Abby to help her change. It was but the work of a moment to slip out of the ruined garment.

She had selected another one and was fastening the buttons at her wrists when she heard a sudden scream. It came from the stable-yard and her first thought was for Kit.

She dashed to the window and caught her breath in horror. Her gentlemanly rescuer was thrashing the man who had attacked her with appalling ferocity.

A bloody weal ran across the victim's face. It had narrowly missed his eyes, and he'd put up his hands to protect them. It didn't save him. Even as she watched a second savage blow drove him to his knees.

Sophie didn't hesitate. She fled down the stairs and out into the yard, catching at the upraised arm as the whip threatened to come down again.

'No!' she cried. 'Please stop! You shall not do this, sir!'

With his arm still raised, the man swung round and Sophie flinched away in terror as she waited for the blow to fall on her defenceless head.

It did not, but her terror did not lessen as she looked up into the gaunt face. The blue eyes were empty of expression. She might have been looking through a pane of glass into the void beyond. This was the true face of evil, and she knew in her heart that this was one of the men whom Hatton sought.

Without another glance at the bleeding wretch upon the ground, he took Sophie's arm and led her indoors.

'I am sorry that you had to witness that, ma'am. A beating is all that these animals understand...' He was all solicitude as he helped her to a chair.

'There was no need for it,' she whispered faintly. 'I was unharmed.'

'The creature needed a sharp lesson,' he told her. His eyes had never left her face. 'May I make a suggestion?' He didn't wait for her reply. 'Don't leave yourself without protection. You must have men about the place.'

'I have,' she said weakly. 'But there has been an accident. They are gone to help.'

'All of them?'

She nodded. Then she realised the folly of that admission. 'They will soon return,' she said quickly.

The gentleman studied his perfectly manicured hands. Then he looked up and smiled. 'I must be on my way, ma'am. I stopped only to bait my horse, but I am glad to have been of service to you.'

Sophie tried to detain him. If she was right and this was Hatton's quarry, she should try to question him.

'I am so grateful to you, sir. Won't you take some refreshment before you leave? It is a bitter day.'

He bowed. 'Too kind! I have my failings, Mistress Firle, but a fondness for alcohol is not one of them.'

'Then a dish of tea, perhaps?'

'I thank you, but I must refuse. I have some way to go today.'

Sophie followed him along the passageway which led out to the stables, still intent on persuading him to change his mind. She was very much afraid of the strange visitor, but she had promised to help Hatton and she would keep her word.

Then an arm slid about her waist and a large hand covered her mouth to stifle a shriek, as she was drawn into the shadow of a dark recess.

'No,' a deep voice whispered. 'Let him go! He will be back, you may be sure.'

'You?' Sophie swung round to find herself face to face with Hatton. 'When did you return?'

'Some few hours ago,' he told her carelessly. 'You seemed to be handling matters well, so I did not show myself.'

Sophie was speechless with indignation, and in the darkness she saw the gleam of white teeth as he grinned at her.

'Why, you—' she began.

'Hush, and listen...'

The stranger was evidently speaking to his so-called groom. 'I blame you, Welbeck,' he said in glacial tones. 'Had it not been for that drunken fool, we might have been loaded and away by now. How came you to let the men indoors?'

'They were all but frozen, master,' came the abject apology. 'There ain't much traffic on this road. We had to wait for hours for a coach to come along, but we overturned it with a rope across the road, just as you said.'

'And you expect congratulations? Why, you lout, for all the good it did we need not have troubled. I needed time to make my case for the removal of our goods, and that you did not give me.'

'Yon's nobbut a girl,' the man said scornfully. 'You could have knocked her on the head.'

Sophie heard a chilling laugh and then a yelp as the whip was used again. 'Watch your mouth, Welbeck,' his employer advised. 'You are speaking of a lady...and a lady whose help we shall need in future operations. Now fetch my horse.'

'Must Walt go with us, master? He's bleeding bad and almost blind.'

'I should have killed him,' came the brief reply. 'Knife him or bring him with you. Either way he can't be left here. I don't trust a drunkard.'

Sophie turned and buried her face in Hatton's coat. She was appalled by the raw ferocity in the speaker's tone.

'He seemed so kind at first,' she whispered. 'I didn't suspect him in the least…'

Hatton found himself stroking her hair. 'Don't worry,' he said. 'I'm here. You are quite safe.'

Sophie bristled as memory flooded back. 'You weren't here when I needed you,' she accused. 'And what did you mean when you said that I was handling matters well? I was attacked and might well have been raped—'

'I think not,' he said lightly. He did not mention how close he'd come to rushing to her rescue, and ruining his own plans.

'You seem very sure of that,' she told him bitterly. 'Am I so ill favoured that no man would touch me?'

He hugged her to him then and she could feel the laughter bubbling in his chest.

'Typically feminine!' he teased. 'No, my dear, you are not ill favoured and you know it well enough. Allow me to tell you that it is a privilege for any man to hold you.'

Sophie struggled out of his grasp. 'I hate you!' she cried. 'I wish that I might never see you again…'

Hatton followed her into the parlor. 'That's sad,' he observed with a twinkle. 'I was hoping that my reappearance might be welcome. Must I go away again?'

'No!' she exclaimed in alarm. 'I mean, it is your duty to stay until the danger is over.'

'Quite right, ma'am! Well, then, let us get down to business. What have you discovered?'

'Nothing!' she told him flatly. 'I am useless as a spy. They tricked me all too easily. I let all the menfolk go to help out with this so-called accident—'

'Not quite all of them. My own men were undeceived. They were hiding in the barn in case of trouble.'

'And what do you call trouble, Mr Hatton? It seems to me that your idea of danger is curious to say the least.'

'Had you proved recalcitrant, you might have been abducted—that is, until you came to your senses and agreed to their demands.'

'And that would have been acceptable to you?'

'No, it would not!' Hatton had reached the limits of his endurance. Now he walked towards her and lifted her face to his. Then he kissed her long and tenderly.

'Does that answer your question?' he asked in a low voice.

Sophie broke away from him in a panic, drawing her hand across her mouth as if to wipe away the touch of his lips.

'Despicable!' she cried. 'How dare you insult me so? If I were a man I'd call you out!'

Hatton regarded her for a long moment. 'If you were a man I should not have kissed you,' he said reasonably. 'Have you forgotten our plan?'

'Who were you convincing of your ardour this time?' she snapped. 'No one is observing us.'

'I thought I heard approaching footsteps, ma'am.' His eyes were dancing. 'Anyone might have entered the room.'

'Liar!' Her anger was directed as much against herself as at him. With his mouth on hers she had wanted to throw her arms about his neck and hold him close as long-forgotten passions fired her blood. Such weakness was humiliating.

'Take care!' she cried. 'After today's experiences it would not take much to persuade me to take my son and leave this place, whatever the consequences.'

'Would you be so foolish?' he enquired mildly. 'I think not. Some of your experiences have been unpleasant, but not all of them, I trust. You seem to be none the worse for them.'

A glance at her face showed him her heightened colour, but at least she'd lost that look of terror which the stranger had inspired in her, and Hatton was satisfied.

'Now, let us a call a truce,' he cried. 'Can you tell me nothing more?'

'No! I had no time to move among the men on the chance of discovering their destination.'

'It is no matter,' he mused. 'The first approach has been made. When our friend returns he will have some plausible reason as to why his goods are stored in the cellar here. Don't be too eager to believe him...'

'You mean I should ask him for some proof of ownership?'

Hatton laughed. 'He will have nothing in writing, Mistress Firle, but he's no fool. As we heard, he would rather have you with him than against him. I would expect him to counter your objections with some hints as to how a penniless widow might provide herself with a comfortable living.'

'But what shall I say?' she cried in desperation.

'Let us play it by ear. The important thing is that you allow him to persuade you to let him move the cargo.'

'And then?'

'Then I shall follow him to his destination.'

'Suppose he should recognise you, sir? Clearly, you have been connected with the authorities for some time.'

'Worried about me, ma'am? I am flattered.' Hatton saw the glowering look upon her face and laughed. 'The gentleman does not know me by sight. It is only in this past year or so that I have taken on these duties.'

'And before then?'

'I was with Wellington in Spain, Mistress Firle. My brothers are still there.'

Sophie was surprised. It was the first time Hatton had spoken of his family. 'That must be a worry for you,' she told him with quick sympathy. 'The campaign is said to have been hard-fought...'

'It isn't over yet,' he told her grimly. 'I had no wish to leave, but it was felt that I could be of more use here.'

'But why you?'

'There are family reasons. My grandfather was instrumental in breaking up the Hawkhurst Gang. You will have heard of them?'

Sophie shuddered. 'Were they not murderers to a man?' she asked in faint tones. 'But that was fifty years ago.'

'Little has changed. My father carried on the work, but he has paid for it. When his house was fired he suffered serious injury.'

Sophie tried to swallow, but her mouth was dry. She stretched out a hand to her companion. 'Forgive me!' she whispered. 'I didn't understand. You have the best of reasons to pursue these men, apart from a wish to serve your country.'

Hatton took her hand in his and kissed it, but whatever he had been about to say was interrupted when Kit rushed into the room.

'Hatton, Hatton, you are back! The pond is frozen hard. Will you teach me to skate? You promised...'

Laughing, Hatton took the child upon his knee. 'I don't skate in the dark...but tomorrow... Shall we say at ten o'clock?'

'If it rains the ice will melt.' Kit looked crestfallen.

'We'll face that dreadful calamity when it happens. Meantime, you might like to try your skates. Do you see that parcel in the corner? Open it and see what you can find.'

As Kit flew across the room and tore at the wrapping of his parcel, Sophie shook her head.

'You spoil him, sir. You are too indulgent.' Her smile left him in no doubt that she was pleased.

He shrugged her thanks aside. The expression on the child's face was reward enough.

Kit came towards them, carrying a pair of sturdy leather boots with long blades screwed into the soles. He might have been carrying the Holy Grail.

Sophie knelt beside him to help him lace them up. She was unsurprised to find that they were a perfect fit. Now she knew the reason for the sudden disappearance of a pair of Kit's old boots.

Hatton held out his hands to help the child to his feet.

'Comfortable?' he asked.

Kit nodded. 'I'm a bit wobbly, sir.'

'You will be so at first, until you find your balance, and the boots may be a little stiff. Try them for a while, but don't wear them for too long today, or you may get a blister.'

Both he and Sophie hid their amusement as Kit tottered away, doubtless to show Reuben his new treasures.

'I hope he doesn't fall and hurt himself,' she said anxiously.

'He'll have worse falls upon the ice. Are you sure that you wish to trust him to my tender care?'

'Kit has set his heart on it. Besides, Mr Hatton, I have no fear that you will let him come to any harm.'

For the first time in their acquaintance Hatton looked embarrassed, but he made a quick recovery.

'You mollycoddle him!' he told her roughly, expecting a furious retort. It did not come.

Sophie rose to her feet. She did not trouble to hide her amusement. 'And you are worse,' she told him. 'Kit has only to express a wish to you, and it is granted. Dear me, what a father you would make!'

The implications of this remark were not lost on either of them, and Sophie hurried away before she could compound her error further.

* * *

For the next few hours she was fully occupied in caring for the unfortunate occupants of the overturned coach. One of the gentlemen had suffered a broken arm, whilst the other was nursing various cuts and bruises. Only the woman had escaped with little more than a severe shaking. The experience had done nothing to improve her temper. Demands that their coachman be dismissed without a character were interspersed with bouts of strong hysterics.

Sophie lost all patience. She ordered a hot toddy and added a couple of extra measures of strong rum. With any luck the woman would fall into a drunken stupor and could then be carried to her bed.

'Why, Mistress Firle, you shock me!' Hatton was at her elbow, grinning broadly. 'I thought you despised hard liquor.'

'I am come to the conclusion that it has its uses,' she replied with feeling as she thrust the tankard into the woman's hand. 'Drink this, ma'am! It is a powerful restorative.'

She heard a choking sound beside her. 'Powerful indeed!' Hatton whispered. 'That potion is enough to fell a horse!'

Sophie did not deign to answer him. She moved away to enquire about the condition of the others. The man with the broken arm was not complaining, but his face was twisted in agony.

'The surgeon will soon be here,' she comforted. 'Then you will be more comfortable.'

'Ma'am, will you see to my friend?' he asked. 'I fear that he is bleeding badly.'

Sophie called for hot water and bandages. Then she set about treating his companion's wounds. She was still working on them when the surgeon arrived. He set her aside at once.

'No great harm done,' he announced. 'You have stopped the bleeding, ma'am. Now let us see to this gentleman here.'

Sophie fled. She could cope with bleeding, but she could not face the thought of standing by whilst the broken arm was set.

'Squeamish?' a deep voice enquired.

Sophie turned to find Hatton looking down at her.

'I suppose so,' she admitted with some reluctance. 'It will hurt quite dreadfully.'

Hatton threw his arm about her shoulders. 'You have done enough,' he announced. 'Those travellers need rest. Leave them to their slumbers and come and dine with me.'

'No!' she told him firmly. 'There is too much to do, I have not yet enquired about the groom—'

'Thrown clear, and quite unharmed,' he assured her.

'Well, the damaged coach will need repair. I must send for the wheelwright—'

'Already done! Anything else?' She saw the challenge in his eyes and thought she knew the reason for it. 'Perhaps you do not care to be alone with me. Could that be the motive for your unwillingness to give me the pleasure of your company.'

'Of course not!' Sophie stiffened. As usual he seemed to have this curious ability to read her mind, but she would not admit to the truth. 'I am not aware that you found pleasure in my company,' she told him coldly.

'No? Then I must be slipping, ma'am. I thought I had made it clear.'

Sophie backed away from him, suspecting that he intended to kiss her again, but he laughed and held out his hand to her.

'May we not be friends for this one evening at least? Let us forget our problems for these next few hours and dine like civilised people. You shall tell me of your life before you married Firle and I will entertain you with the gossip from Brighton.'

Sophie looked at him uncertainly, drawn to him like a moth to a flame. He was a disturbing being, dangerous to her peace of mind. In his company she felt fully alive, piqued on some occasions and furious on others, but always excited for some reason she could not fathom.

And then there was his kindness to Kit. That she could not forget. It would be churlish to refuse this simple request to dine with him.

At last she held out her hand. 'Very well,' she demurred. 'But on one condition, sir...'

'And what is that, Mistress Firle?'

'My servants need no further convincing that you...I mean...they all believe by now that you are come to...to offer me your hand.'

'Do they, ma'am? I must take leave to doubt it. Matthew and his wife both know full well that I have another purpose here. That is unfortunate, but once we entered the cellars it was inevitable. Let us hope that they did not share that knowledge with the others.'

'Matthew is no fool,' she told him quickly. 'He would not tell Abby. Nor will Bess speak of it to her brother and his son...'

'Good! I trust that you are right. It means, of course, that I must continue to pursue you.' Hatton's eyes were dancing.

'From a distance, sir. I must have your word on that.'

'Agreed!' He gave her a solemn bow. 'I must not kiss you, nor may I hold you in my arms, unless, of course, Abby should chance to enter the room.'

'Even then,' she told him solemnly. 'It is unseemly.'

'Suppose you trip or faint?' he teased. 'Am I to let you fall to the ground?'

'I shall not faint, Mr Hatton. And if you continue to annoy me, you may be the person who falls to the ground.'

'Threats, my dear?' Hatton shuddered in mock terror. 'You are a modern Boudicca...'

'Then you would do well to remember that the Queen of the Iceni was said to have scythes upon her chariot wheels. They cut away the legs from her opponents.'

'Touché.' He grinned. 'A truce then, ma'am?'

'A truce!' Sophie gave him her hand. 'Now, sir, I must change my gown. Bess does not care to have her cooking spoiled by laggardly diners.'

Hatton let her go, well satisfied with her complaisance. He'd determined not to allow her to dine alone, knowing that, if she were left to her own thoughts, Sophie would continue to reflect upon the dangers of her situation.

Was that why he had kissed her? If so, it had served its purpose in diverting her attention from the ugly scene she'd witnessed. She could no longer be in any doubt as to the ruthless nature of the men he sought.

Then he cursed softly under his breath. He was deluding himself. He'd kissed her because his passion for her could no longer be denied, and it was madness to fall into this easiest of traps. What was happening to him? Every instinct warned him to stay away from her...to keep her at a distance...but it needed only the sight of her to set his blood afire. Such folly was unlike him.

In the past he'd felt contempt for those who'd been so easily led astray by a pair of fine eyes or a charming smile, combined with a winning disposition. Now he was caught in the same toils. Perhaps it was not too late to extricate himself.

He grimaced in some amusement. Sophie's disposition most certainly could not be described as winning. She'd fought him every step of the way since the moment of their meeting. She was no milk-and-water miss, fierce as a tigress in defence of her young so he could do no other than admire her.

And that had led to...what? There had been no need to make a parade of his devotion. An arm flung carelessly across the back of a lady's chair was enough to cause a scandal in his circles. He'd kissed her to annoy her, as he now admitted to himself. Well, he had been hoist with his own petard. Her response had startled him.

At first he'd thought that he must have been mistaken, but when he had repeated the experiment he could no longer be in any doubt. This was a woman worthy of capture. At another time, and in another place, he would not have hesitated, but now his hands were tied.

* * *

Nothing of this showed in his manner as he rose to greet her later in the evening. Gravely, he led her to a chair and offered her a glass of Madeira.

Sophie shook her head. She had no intention of lowering her guard. Long reflection had persuaded her that, in agreeing to dine alone with Hatton, she was playing with fire. Long months as belle of the county before her marriage had given her a certain insight into gentlemen's intentions. Now she knew that Hatton wanted her, in spite of his protestations that he was playing a part.

Strangely, the knowledge pleased her. It gave her a degree of power over him, but she could not guess at its extent. That she would only learn by trial and error.

As they sat down to dine the tension in the room was palpable. Hatton addressed himself to a dish of turbot in sauce with every appearance of enjoyment, but Sophie seemed to have lost her appetite.

'Do try this macaroni *à la napolitaine*,' he coaxed. 'The Prince's chef could not better it.'

Sophie took a bite or two to please him.

He bent a critical gaze upon her. 'Let me ask you something, ma'am. Have you ever seen a race-horse?'

'Why, yes, of course.'

'Then you will have noticed their fine condition, with gleaming coats, and every muscle in perfect harmony?'

Sophie stared at him. She could not imagine where the conversation was leading.

'That is so,' she agreed.

'And are we any different, Mistress Firle? Racehorses are fed with care, and that is the reason for their success. Human beings are no different.'

'Quite possibly. I cannot think why this should concern you.'

'It should concern you…' he said with meaning. 'You don't eat enough. It will tell on you in time, believe me. We humans have survived across the centuries because of our willingness to eat a varied diet.'

'You would have me make my way through seven courses?'

'No, ma'am, there is a happy medium. Now try these collops…' He helped her to a couple of chops, neatly trimmed of fat. 'You will find them light enough to leave room for the next course.'

Sophie was tempted to remonstrate. Instead she changed the subject. 'You promised to tell me all the Brighton gossip,' she reminded him.

'You sound like your son, ma'am.' Hatton chuckled.

'I must suppose I do, but I have always longed to hear of the doings of the great and good—'

'Or even the doings of the great and not so good?'

'Even that.' Sophie could not hide her curiosity. 'My father spoke often of the Prince and what a pleasure it was to see him strolling about the town, so popular and so much at ease with the common folk.'

'That, I fear, is somewhat changed since your father's day, though Prince George is still more popular in Brighton than he is in London.'

'Have you met him?' she asked eagerly. 'One hears so many rumours that it is difficult to judge of his character with any truth.'

'He is a curious mixture, much more so than other men. Obstinate, vain, highly strung and over-emotional, he is quick to take offence, sometimes where none is intended. He never forgives a slight to his person...'

'Then it is easy to dislike him?'

'It is almost impossible, Mistress Firle. You have not studied the other side of the coin. I think I never met a man with so much charm, when he chooses to exert it. He can be witty and entertaining, with an affability which disarms his enemies. I have seen them change their opinion of him in the course of a few moments.'

'You sound as if you admire him.'

'I do. He is greatly gifted. Did you know that he speaks four languages as fluently as English? He is fond of music, as are all the Hanoverians, and we have not had such a patron of the arts since the first King Charles.'

'But?' Sophie had sensed a certain reservation in his tone.

'But he is his own worst enemy. The people have no quarrel with his fondness for the ladies, to put the matter delicately. What they won't forgive is his treatment of his wife…his second wife, I mean.'

'Oh!' Sophie's cheeks were pink. 'You cannot mean that this story of a marriage to Mrs Fitzherbert can be true?'

'I'm afraid it is beyond doubt.'

'But that would make him a bigamist. I did not hear of a divorce before he married Caroline of Brunswick.'

'There was none. He never admitted to that first marriage.'

'But the child…the heiress to the throne? Surely that would make the Princess Charlotte illegitimate?'

'It is not spoken of. Now let us end this treasonable talk. You have told me nothing of yourself.'

'I think I should not like the Prince,' Sophie said with great finality. 'That is a pity. I always longed to see him. As a child, you know, I always imagined Brighton to be a golden city, floating in the air, with Prince George at its heart, beloved by everyone.'

'Don't give up your dreams so easily,' he teased. 'The Prince would most certainly be beloved by you. He has one great quality which would cause you to forgive all else.'

'And what is that?' Sophie looked doubtful.

'He loves children, and he is adored by them. There seems to be a mutual and instant understanding. With the young, one sees him at his best. One cannot fail to think him a kindly and good-hearted man.'

'You are generous, Mr Hatton.'

'No, I speak merely as I find. Did your father know the Prince?'

'He didn't aspire to such heights,' Sophie told him in amusement. 'Even so, he had plans for me, that is, before Sir William Curtis was widowed and he saw the opportunity to join his lands to ours.'

'You were never tempted by the offer?'

'I was not!' Sophie's reply was curt and did not invite further questioning on the subject. Then she softened. 'Even so, I should like to have come to Brighton for the season. I'd heard of the balls, the concerts, the parties and the picnics, as well as the racing on the Downs.'

'But you married Firle instead?'

'Yes!'

Her wistful expression tugged at Hatton's heart-strings. That ill-advised match had robbed her of a large part of her girlhood. Far from leading the life to which she had been bred she'd found herself in this isolated spot, bereft of friends and family and tied to a man unworthy of her, with only her son for consolation.

Sophie saw his expression. She could not bear to be pitied.

'You must not think that I regretted my decision,' she told him stiffly.

'I did not think it for a moment. Kit, after all, is not to be regretted...'

Her smile transfigured her face and Hatton's heart turned over. The temptation to take her in his arms was overwhelming, and it took all his self-control to resist it. He tried to give the conversation a lighter turn.

'I think we must be thankful that you did not arrive in Brighton some six years ago,' he said. 'You would have broken many a heart among the 10th Dragoons.'

'The Prince's regiment?' Sophie dimpled. 'Mr Hatton, are you trying to flatter me?'

'Not in the least. Those susceptible young men would have been swooning at your feet.'

'Do spare my blushes, sir. You are talking nonsense.'

Hatton tried to pour her another glass of wine, delighted to see her restored to some remembrance of her girlhood, but she covered the glass with her hand.

'No!' she said. 'You shall not persuade me into further foolish chatter.' She glanced at the clock and rose with a sharp exclamation. 'Great heavens, how the time has flown! I had no idea that it was so late. You must excuse me, sir.'

He didn't attempt to detain her. Silently he held out his hand, and when she took it he raised her fingers to his lips.

'Our truce still holds?' he asked.

'It does, sir, and I must thank you for a pleasant evening.' For once, Sophie felt much in charity with him. Entertained by his conversation, she had forgotten all her fears for those few hours.

She fell asleep almost at once that night.

By the following morning she was much refreshed. The winter sun was pouring through her windows, but the frost still held the countryside in its iron grip. She could see the starry patterns against the glass.

Kit's voice sent her hurrying to look into the stable-yard. Hatton was already with him; as she watched, he lifted the child on to his great stallion, leading the beast with one hand as he supported her son with the other.

It wasn't only the Prince who had a great rapport with children, she thought wryly. Not for the first time she wondered why Hatton had not set up his own nursery. He must be in his thirties, but perhaps those years in Spain had given him no opportunity to choose a suitable bride.

Sophie sipped at her chocolate and nibbled at a roll. Then she went downstairs to enquire about the welfare of her unexpected guests. They were still bruised, but much recovered, and the gentlemen, at least, offered their thanks for all her kindness. Their female companion was anxious to be away, chivvying her husband to expedite the repairs to their coach whilst complaining of a sore head.

'Such an experience!' she moaned. 'I fear I have suffered serious injury. My head is like to burst.'

Privately, Sophie thought it far more likely that the woman was suffering from the effects of the several rum-laced toddies which she had consumed the day before, but she made sympathetic noises.

Then she looked up as a cheerful party of young bloods erupted into the room. She recognised them at once as previous customers. These were the men who had arrived on the day of her re-opening.

Now she eyed their costume in amusement. Broad-brimmed hats and long drab coats were, she guessed, intended to mark them out as grooms, rather than the aristocrats they were. Hatton had told her that it was a popular conceit, but Sophie found it something of a mystery.

Even more mysterious was the fact that they were all carrying skates. Now they clustered about her, vying for her attention, but their leader stilled the clamour with an imperious gesture.

'We are come to beg your indulgence, Mistress Firle,' he told her with a winning smile. 'Will you allow us to skate upon your lake? It is the only stretch of unblemished ice for miles around. We've tried elsewhere, but Ned here has already come to grief through reeds frozen into surface ice.'

Sophie glanced at the unfortunate Ned. He certainly seemed to be accident-prone, and was, at that moment, nursing a bleeding nose. It had not dampened his enthusiasm for the sport.

'My lake, as you are pleased to call it, is naught but a large pond swollen by the recent rains, sir, but you are welcome to skate upon it if you wish to do so.'

'Shall you care to join us, ma'am?' the young man continued as a chorus of thanks rose about her. 'We carry spare blades in case of breakages. It would be but the work of a moment to fix them to your boots.'

Sophie was flattered by his offer, but she felt obliged to decline. 'I have never skated in my life,' she protested. 'I should be certain to break a limb.'

'Not with someone to support you on either side.' The speaker was surprisingly persistent. 'Do say you'll come. It is quite the most delightful sensation in the world.'

Sophie hesitated and was lost. A spirit of rebellion seized her. She was tired of thinking about her present worries. Why shouldn't she have some fun? Hatton might have offered to teach her, but he hadn't done so. She would show him that others were not so laggardly. Her eyes sparkled with excitement as she hurried away to fetch her boots.

Chapter Nine

They heard the others long before they reached the pond. Kit, as always, was talking twenty to the dozen as Hatton helped him into his skates. Then he fell silent, frowning in concentration as they took to the ice with Hatton skating backwards and holding both his hands.

Sophie watched as Kit made his first attempts, trying to walk rather than to glide. Then he got the hang of it and began to shout with glee.

'Watch me, Mama!' he cried. 'I'm skating!'

'There now, Mistress Firle…you see how easy it is?' The young man, who had introduced himself simply as Wentworth, held out his hands to help her to her feet. 'Just trust yourself to Jack and me. We shan't allow you to fall.'

As Sophie stood upon the narrow blades she was tempted to refuse the offer, but all eyes were upon her, and she could not act the coward in front of Kit.

Wentworth was as good as his word, so with Jack holding on to her other arm she ventured out upon the slippery surface. It soon became clear that the two young men were experts, and after the first few anxious moments Sophie began to enjoy herself as she skimmed along between them.

A keen wind brought the colour to her cheeks, but it had no power to chill her as her companions increased their speed.

'Whoa! You will make the lady dizzy!' Hatton skidded to a halt beside them, with Kit holding tightly to his hand.

'Nonsense!' Sophie told him. 'I haven't had so much fun in years. I won't stop now, just when I feel more confident.'

'I wasn't suggesting that you stop, Mistress Firle...merely that we change partners.'

Sophie's companions seemed about to protest, but a glance at Hatton's face persuaded them otherwise. It was, therefore, with good grace that they glided away with Kit between them, and, much to his delight, increasing their speed as they did so.

'You are too high-handed, sir.' Sophie wasn't pleased. 'What right have you to dictate my actions, or the company I choose?'

'None whatever, my dear. I thought merely that you might like to try your new-found skills with a single partner?' He slid an arm around her waist and, taking her other hand in his, moved across the ice with an ease that communicated itself to her.

'Relax!' he advised. 'You hold yourself too stiffly. Put yourself in my hands. I shall not let you come to harm.'

At the end of a half-hour she had acquired a certain degree of proficiency, helped by his words of advice. Then he led her off the ice. 'That is enough for today. If this weather holds we shall have you skating on your own.' Raising his voice, he called to Kit, but for once the child was unwilling to obey his instructions to remove his skates.

Hatton's frown was enough to bring the child to his side, though he looked despondent.

'I wanted to practise,' he complained. 'Ned says that the best skaters always practise.'

'So they do, but not for so long that their legs grow stiff and their feet begin to bleed. Now sit down, Kit, and let us see what these young men can do.' He made a place beside him on the fallen log where they had left their things.

With the ice to themselves the young men treated them to a dazzling display of jumps and spins. Kit applauded them, but he was strangely silent.

'What is it, Kit? I hope you are not sulking...' Sophie reproved.

'No, Mama, but Hatton said that *he* could jump.'

Sophie chuckled as she looked at her companion. 'How fortunate that you have not removed your skates, Mr Hatton! I trust you will not disappoint us!'

She was rewarded with an answering grin as Hatton got to his feet. 'Anything for a quiet life,' he teased. Then he moved out to join the others.

To Sophie's surprise they cleared the ice for him, but in a moment she understood the reason for it. Moving at great speed, Hatton executed a startling number of difficult jumps and spins which left her breathless with admiration. The sheer beauty of the movements found her clapping wildly, and Kit was open-mouthed.

Then the others joined him. They did not have his skills, but Wentworth's movements struck a chord in Sophie's mind. As the young man turned in profile, her suspicions were confirmed.

'Why have you found it necessary to deceive me?' she demanded as she walked back to the inn with Hatton by her side.

'Ma'am?'

'Mr Wentworth is a relative of yours, I think. I cannot be mistaken. The resemblance is too strong.'

'He is my cousin.'

'Indeed? And his companions? Are they your cousins too?'

'Only two of them. The others are just friends.'

'I see. We are indebted to you for their presence here, I imagine. I wonder that you did not think to tell me of the relationship.'

'It didn't seem important at the time. Does it matter to you?'

'Of course it does not matter, Mr Hatton, but I dislike mysteries, and most of all I hate deceit.'

'My apologies, ma'am. You needed customers. I mentioned merely that a drive into the country might amuse these bucks, and that Bess's food was better than most. Does that displease you? It seems innocent enough to me.'

'I have learned that nothing is innocent in your actions, sir. There is always an ulterior motive.'

'Dear me! What can it be on this occasion? A delightful skating party? You said yourself that you have enjoyed it.'

'You are impossible!' she said with feeling as she stalked indoors.

Matthew came to her at once. 'Two gentlemen have been asking to see you, ma'am. I've put them in the snug.'

'Very well.' Caught off guard, Sophie was untroubled by this news. The damaged coach must have been repaired and the gentlemen had come to settle their account.

She set aside her bonnet, her tippet and her gloves, straightening her hair as she walked towards the snug. Then she stopped short at the mention of her own name.

'This Mistress Firle? Can you trust her?' a harsh voice enquired.

'It is unnecessary. I don't trust any woman. Sufficient to say that we persuade her to fall in with our plans.'

'I don't like it. You should not have brought me here. This is no part of our agreement.'

'You are happy enough to share in the profits,' his companion observed. 'Remember, no investment is without some risk.'

'Risk? What risk? You said there was none. Certainly I won't risk my neck—'

'You have already done so, my dear sir. There is but one penalty for treason.'

'And you have brought me down here? Our friends won't like it.'

'Our friends will understand the reason for it when I explain. I need you here today to lend a certain air of authenticity to my claim to own the cargo stored here. If I'm not mistaken, Mistress Firle is not a fool. She will need convincing.'

'You are very nice with your dealings with a slip of a girl,' his companion growled. 'If this place had been as empty as you promised, we might have been away by now.'

Sophie heard a sigh of exasperation. 'In broad daylight? Sometimes I think that you don't understand that nature of our business. Secrecy is essential.'

'I know it well. My name must be kept out of this. I may already have been recognised.'

'By whom? Our injured travellers in the parlour? I doubt if they move in our circles.' His sarcastic tone goaded his companion into a furious reply.

'You think yourself mighty clever, don't you, Harward? Don't it strike you as strange that two young women, both widows of Revenue Men, should be living under the same roof?'

'Not in the least. Many of these people know each other. Most probably they sought comfort in each other's company. I am surprised that you recognised Tyler's wife…er…widow. Are you acquainted with her?'

'I met her years ago, at her father's house in Dover. She was a child then, but that face is not easily forgotten.'

'I doubt if she'd remember you, and if she did, what can it signify? Why should she suspect a respectable businessman of dealings in illicit goods? You note that I am describing your activities in the kindest light?'

His companion was unconvinced. 'There are others here. Listen to the commotion! The noise is like to deafen a quiet man—'

'Come now, let us be done with this.' The man known as Harward was losing patience. 'You will not tell me that you fear young bucks, scarce out of leading strings? They frequent this place, merely because it is so close to Brighton.'

Sophie began to breathe more easily. Hatton had been wise to encourage the party of young bloods to visit the inn. In their midst, his own presence would be less conspicuous.

'I hope you may be right. Now, where is this Mistress Firle of yours? I'll do what you require of me. Then I must be away.'

'Leaving others to protect your back?' his companion suggested smoothly.

Sophie judged it time to enter the room before a serious quarrel could result. As she did so, Harward rose to his feet and came towards her with a concerned expression. He made her a deep bow.

'Mistress Firle, you remember me, I trust. Simon Harward, at your service.'

'I do, sir.' Sophie's heart was pounding as she faced the man she feared so much. 'I trust I find you well?'

'Well enough, I thank you, but it is your own health which concerns me. You have recovered from that unfortunate incident? I confess it has been much upon my mind...'

'It is forgotten, but I thank you for your interest, Mr Harward. Will you not present your friend?'

'Ah, yes, I had quite forgot my manners, ma'am. This is Mr Horace Sayles, a merchant and one of those gentlemen who keeps the wheels of commerce turning in the city.'

Sophie found herself under inspection from a pair of eyes which would not have shamed Caligula. Pebble-hard, they fixed her with a basilisk gaze. The man himself was short and squat, almost as broad as he was tall, but she guessed that the expensive coat hid muscle rather than fat.

His bow was perfunctory and he did not speak.

Harward took Sophie's hand and led her to a chair.

'My dear ma'am, pray don't think me forward, but I meant it when I mentioned my concern for you. I know of your sad loss…a tragedy for one so young…but is it wise for you to stay here alone, exposed to such unwelcome attentions as befell you the other day?'

'Sir, I have no choice.' Sophie was very much on her dignity. 'This is my home and also my livelihood. Where else would I go?'

'May I offer the suggestion that you sell the inn? Mr Sayles here might possibly be interested. His property investments are extensive.'

Sophie was silent. Three weeks ago she would have jumped at the chance to sell, but since then she had learned that the inn was not hers to dispose of. She became aware that both men were awaiting her answer.

'I…had not thought of it,' she faltered. 'I have no one to advise me. Will you give me time to consider your proposition?'

Sayles rose to his feet and walked over to the window. His impatience was evident, but Harward's manner did not change.

'Of course, my dear. This is a big decision for you. Naturally, you are wondering why we have approached you quite so soon?' He paused, and Sophie realised that he was weighing his words with care. 'The thing is, Mistress Firle, that we had an arrangement with your late husband. For a consideration he allowed us to store our surplus cargoes in your cellars.'

Sophie managed to look suitably astonished. 'We keep our ales and spirits in the cellars, sir. I have seen nothing else…'

'I don't expect you would,' he said agreeably. 'The entrance is concealed. Your husband insisted that it should be so. There is always the danger of pilfering, as he knew.'

'He said nothing of this to me,' she protested. 'Do you tell me that you have goods there at this moment?'

'We have!' The blue eyes rested earnestly upon her face. 'There is a danger that some of it may perish if it is left too long. Lace, for example, may rot in damp conditions.'

'I wonder that you should have chosen our cellars, Mr Harward. More suitable warehousing might have been found elsewhere.'

'You are quite right.' Harward sighed heavily. 'Sadly, Brighton is so overcrowded that every inch of space is taken. This is one reason why Mr Sayles proposes to buy the inn. There is little point in importing goods if one cannot store them safely.'

Sophie looked at the bland face. This was a clever man. He was so plausible. If Hatton had not warned her, she might have believed his every word.

An exclamation from his friend drew him to the window, but Sophie could not hear the whispered words which passed between them.

'Who is the tall gentleman?' Harward asked in casual tones. 'I think that I may know him.'

Sophie's blood ran cold. Almost paralysed with fright, she forced herself to join him at the window, knowing full well that Hatton must be the object of his interest.

That gentleman was strolling across the stable-yard with Kit settled happily on his shoulders.

'Do you think so, sir?' Her voice was surprisingly calm. 'Mr Hatton has but recently returned from the Peninsular War. You must have known him years ago.'

'A soldier, and one of our brave lads? I must be mistaken, ma'am. What a charming sight, to be sure. The gentleman looks very much at home here…' The keen eyes scanned her face.

Sophie willed herself to blush, but she could manage only a demure expression. 'I refused him then, but now that I am widowed he hopes…that is…' Her voice died away in confusion.

'Most understandable,' Harvard comforted her. 'Am I to wish you happy, ma'am?'

'Oh, no! Not yet! It is too soon. A widow cannot…I mean, I must not offer him encouragement before the year is out.'

'And then?'

'I am not sure, sir. It may be that I shall have no option.'

'On the contrary, my dear there is always an option, if one wishes to take advantage of it.'

Sophie stared at him. 'I don't know what you mean,' she said.

'Let me assure you, ma'am, it is nearly always a mistake to enter into wedlock merely to secure one's future. There are other ways for a sensible woman to earn a comfortable living.'

'Perhaps so, but I do not know of them.'

'Why, it is simple, Mistress Firle. If you decide to stay on here, we could pay you rent for the use of your cellars. We ship only the most valuable of cargoes, so the rent would be correspondingly high. Indeed, we owe you money at this present time.'

He drew out a large roll of notes and laid them upon the table.

Sophie gasped. 'Great heavens! Surely that is far too much?'

'Not at all, my dear. Now, if we might make some arrangements to move the goods?'

Sophie was seized with a spirit of mischief.

'Certainly, Mr Harward. I must imagine that you will wish to arrange for wagons immediately. They can't move when the ground is sodden. Shall we say tomorrow morning?'

For the first time Harward looked non-plussed. Then he recovered himself.

'You are right about the roads,' he agreed. 'I believe we should move whilst this frost holds. Darkness is not ideal for travelling, but we may have rain by morning.'

'Will you show me the entrance to this cellar?' Sophie asked in apparent innocence. 'I find it difficult to believe that it exists when I did not know of it.'

As she had expected, Harward was fully conversant with the layout of the cellars. As she watched, he strode towards the hidden entrance and motioned her inside.

'You see the value of these goods, ma'am? Believe me, we have not overpaid you.'

'Will it not be difficult for you to carry them up the staircase and through the inn?'

'I think not, Mistress Firle. There is another exit some few hundred yards beyond the inn. All that we ask is that you allow one man entry to this cellar. He will unbolt the doors beyond.'

'I see.'

'I felt sure you would. Now you shall not trouble yourself further. Leave the rest to us. We have no wish to disturb your slumbers tonight.'

Sophie found that her hands were trembling. The man must think her a fool. What woman would accept such a cock-and-bull story? It must be clear to anyone of intelligence that this was a smuggling operation.

Sophie fingered the roll of notes in her pocket, and then she understood. Harward was under no illusions. If she had guessed at the truth of the matter, she had been paid to hold her tongue. Whether or not she believed him was not of any importance.

She led the way out of the cellars to find Matthew waiting for her. He was trembling with anxiety.

Sophie frowned a warning at him. At the sight of her companions he looked like a rabbit transfixed by a snake. Strangely, his terror stiffened her own resolve.

'Yes?' she said sharply. 'What is it, Matthew?'

'It's the folk in the parlour, mistress. Their coach has been repaired and they are wishing to be on their way after settling their account.'

'Tell them I'll be with them in a moment.' Sophie turned back to her companions to find Harward gazing thoughtfully at the retreating Matthew.

'Your servant seems to be of a nervous disposition,' he observed.

To her own great relief, Sophie managed a girlish laugh.

'My dear sir, you must know what country people are like. They are suspicious of all strangers.'

'An unfortunate characteristic in his circumstances, ma'am.'

Sophie was on her dignity at once. 'Mr Harward, I cannot run this place alone. Help is not readily available. Both Matthew and his wife are loyal to me.'

Harward was all apologies. 'Pray forgive me, madam. I did not mean to criticise. It is just that…well…one wonders if the man would defend you should the need arise?'

'Now I see what you are about!' Sophie's glance was coy. 'You are trying to frighten me in the hope that I will sell to you…'

She heard a jovial laugh. 'You are too shrewd for me, my dear young lady. Now, are we agreed that you will open the cellar doors tonight?'

Sophie made a pretty show of hesitation. 'I don't know what to say,' she admitted in apparent confusion. 'Oh, dear! You will think me as suspicious as my servant, but do you have some paper to show your title to these goods?'

She heard a snort of anger from his companion.

'No, ma'am.' Harward's look was enough to put a stop to any further demonstration of ill will. 'Your late husband did not think it necessary. We had a gentleman's agreement.'

Gentlemen indeed! Sophie almost choked with indignation.

'Then I suppose I must take your word for it,' she told him grudgingly.

'I cannot blame you for your caution,' Harward continued. 'But consider, Mistress Firle. How could I know of the entrance to the cellar or find the key to the door if we had not used the place before?'

'Of course! I had not thought of that. How foolish you must think me.'

Harward bowed. 'Not at all. Caution is an admirable quality. It must always serve you well.'

Sophie appeared to be satisfied. 'When shall you wish the outer door to be opened?' she asked.

'Shall we say...at any time after six this evening. It will take us some time to arrange for wagons and ponies.'

And it will also be full dark by then and the moon will not be up, Sophie thought to herself. 'Anything else?' she enquired. 'Shall you wish that my servants help you?'

Pure mischief had caused her to ask the question and his answer did not surprise her.

'We should not dream of troubling you or them,' came the smooth reply. 'We have men enough of our own. There is, however, one further matter...'

'Yes, Mr Harward?'

'May I stress the need for discretion? This arrangement with your husband was not known to others...not even to your servants, I believe. We thought it better so. Word gets about in the most curious ways and we do not care to offer a target to any of the lawless bands who roam the countryside. Best to keep all your shutters closed tonight.'

Sophie was staggered by his effrontery, but she kept her countenance.

'Then, gentlemen, if you will excuse me? My customers are waiting.'

Harward made her a deep bow. 'A pleasure to do business with you, Mistress Firle. We shall not bid you goodbye, but merely *au revoir*.' With that he took his companion by the arm and strode away.

Sophie's eyes were sparkling with excitement. Now, at last, she had news for Hatton, but first she must see her customers on their way. She was too absorbed to notice that the partially opened door at the far end of the smug now closed without a sound.

The injured travellers were generous in their thanks, and also with their tips. Sophie tried to hide her impatience for them to be gone. Then she summoned Matthew.

'Will you find Mr Hatton for me?' she asked.

'No need! Matthew came to fetch me when you went into the cellars…' Hatton's expression was a curious mixture of pride and anxiety. 'Are you all right, my dear?'

'Of course I am!' Sophie could not wait to tell him her news. 'You were right! They plan to move the goods tonight.'

'So soon?' Hatton grew thoughtful. 'Matthew said that there were two of them. Who was our friend's companion?'

'Harward introduced him as a Mr Horace Sayles.'

Hatton gave a low whistle of surprise. 'Indeed? Now we are getting somewhere. What could have brought him into the open?'

'He offered to buy the inn.' Sophie gave him a mischievous look. 'I almost sold it to him.'

Hatton chuckled as he looked down at the vivid little face. 'Now you are making game of me,' he accused. 'What did you say to him?'

'I told both gentlemen that it was too serious a decision for a foolish little woman, with no one to advise her.'

She heard a shout of laughter. 'Did they believe you? If so, they can't be much of a judge of character.'

'Why, thank you, Mr Hatton!' Sophie dimpled at him. 'To be honest, I don't know if they believed me, but they made me another offer.'

'And what was that?'

'They wished to make me their associate. You were seen, you know, and they questioned me about you. I explained your lovelorn condition, but Mr Harward was at some pains to assure me that to marry for security alone was always a mistake. There were other ways for a lady to secure her future.'

Hatton's face darkened. 'They insulted you?'

'Of course not!' Sophie was puzzled. Then she understood him. 'Neither gentleman was looking for a companion, sir. They suggested that I continue the so-called "gentleman's agreement" which they had enjoyed before...before...'

'Before Firle was killed?'

Sophie swallowed hard and nodded.

'And what did you say?'

'I did as you suggested and was not too eager to fall in with their plans. I made a number of objections, but Harward was most persuasive. He even gave me this!' She took out the roll of notes and laid it on the table. 'It is a large amount of money. I don't know what to do with it.'

'Keep it! You have earned it!' Hatton was surprisingly abrupt.

'Is something wrong? I thought you'd be pleased.' Sophie's sense of achievement vanished.

'Of course I'm pleased. You have done well. I am only sorry that you had to be the one to deal with them.'

'I'm not!' Her tone was defiant. 'If you must know, I enjoyed it. Oh, I was afraid at first, but it was not so difficult to play the part of a nincompoop.'

'Try not to get a taste for danger, Mistress Firle. These men are ruthless. From what I know of Harward, he is not easily taken in, and nor is Sayles. It may have suited them to appear to believe you.'

'Well, sir, I am glad to hear that you don't believe that I can play the part of a nitwit!' Sophie's tone was acid. She'd been proud of the way she'd played her part, but Hatton had dismissed her efforts out of hand.

'On the contrary...sometimes you play it to perfection, ma'am...and not always when you intend to do so.'

He was teasing her again and Sophie bristled. 'You are the most ungrateful wretch I know,' she cried.

'Am I?' He reached out and took her hands in his. 'Never think that of me. I am in your debt for life.'

The warmth in his voice brought hot colour flooding to her cheeks and she drew her hands away.

'What will you do now?' she said in a low voice.

'I think we must be ready for them. They will be allowed to get away from here. Then we will follow them to London. Sayles and his friends will be anxious to reap the rewards of this consignment after all these weeks. I shall hope to attend their meeting.'

Sophie's hand flew to her mouth. 'Will that not be much too dangerous?'

'It won't be without risk,' he agreed. 'But with any luck we shall catch all our birds in the same trap.'

'Is...is there anything I can do?'

'No, my dear. Your part in this is finished. Just do as they suggested. Say nothing to any of your servants, and keep all the shutters closed tonight.'

Sophie felt deflated. The part she'd played in Hatton's plans now seemed insignificant. His quarry would be caught, then tried and sentenced, and she might never know the outcome.

'You feel, then, that nothing will go wrong?' she asked.

'One can never be sure. There is always the chance of the unexpected...'

Suddenly she was seized with terror. 'Suppose you should lose them?' she cried.

'Then we must try again, but this is a huge consignment, Sophie. Neither men nor wagons will be easy to conceal upon the road.'

This time she did not reprove him for the use of her given name. Indeed, she barely noticed.

'That is not to say that they won't know they are being followed,' she insisted. 'At the first sign of danger Harward and Sayles will disappear. Dear God, they may come back to find out how they were betrayed.'

Hatton rested his hands upon her shoulders and shook her gently. 'Do you suppose that I haven't considered the possibility, my dear? Each of them will have two men to watch him at all times.'

'But they are clever. They could still elude you.' Sophie looked up at him and suddenly she was in his arms, held close against his chest.

'Would I let harm come to you?' Hatton's voice was raw with passion, muffled against her hair.

'Look at me, Sophie! Surely you must know by now…' His mouth came down on hers.

This time she could not doubt him. This was no part played to deceive her servants. His lips were warm against her own, at first gentle, and then insistent, willing her to respond to him.

Sophie melted into the spell of that embrace. Her arms reached up to circle his neck as she gave herself without restraint. Their mutual passion was dizzying in its strength, and she was breathless when he released her.

It was only to hold her away from him as he looked long into her eyes. Then he began to kiss her again, caressing her eyelids and the corners of her mouth with the lightest of a butterfly touch.

Sophie turned her head to find his lips again, but he held her at arm's length.

'Well, now you know, my love!' he told her in mock despair. 'I had hoped to wait until a more suitable time before declaring myself.'

Radiant with happiness, Sophie could not resist the chance to tease him. 'You have not done so, sir. I am at a loss to understand your strange behaviour.'

'Witch!' he tugged at a straying curl. 'What of your own, you shameless hussy? It was unkind in you to lead me on—'

'*I* led *you* on? Why, you wicked wretch! You kissed me without a by-your-leave.'

'So I did. It had escaped my notice, ma'am, that I should ask your permission first. But now I have another question for you. Will you be my wife?'

Too overcome to speak, she held out her hands to him and he saw the tears sparkling on her lashes.

'My dearest love?' he protested as he wiped them away.

'They are tears of happiness,' she assured him.

Chapter Ten

Still uncertain whether to laugh or cry, Sophie looked deep into Hatton's eyes.

'This can't be happening!' she whispered. 'I don't believe it. Am I dreaming, or have I really agreed to become your wife?'

'I hope so, my dear.' Hatton held her closer to his heart. 'Otherwise I shall be deeply shocked. Seated upon my knee, and with your arms about my neck, you are in a most compromising situation.' He chuckled as he nuzzled his lips to her cheek.

Sophie blushed as she struggled to free herself. 'We must be mad!' she cried.

'Of course we are! But love is sweet madness, is it not?' His arm stayed firmly about her waist.

'But I did not think that you...I mean, I had no idea that—?'

'That I cared for you, my darling? Sophie, you must be blind!' He began to laugh. 'There isn't a

231

soul within this place who hasn't been convinced of it for days.'

'But you said that you were play-acting...'

'I lied, my love.'

'Oh! When did you first realise...that it wasn't simply a part of your plan?'

'It was never part of my plan to fall in love with you, and I struggled against it mightily, but to no avail. I was lost from the first moment I saw you, though I did not know it at the time.'

'I thought that you disliked me,' she said in a small voice.

'Then I must be a better actor than I had imagined. I was unsure of you, my darling, and, speaking of dislike, I did not dare to hope that you could ever care for me. I have treated you so ill...' His face grew sombre.

Shyly, Sophie reached up and pressed her lips into the hollow of his neck. 'That isn't true! I didn't understand at first, and that was why I fought you. Now I know that you only did your duty.'

'Drawing a woman...any woman...into danger is a most unpleasant duty. I hated threatening to turn you out of your home, and playing upon your fears for Kit. I'm not proud of my actions.'

'You should be, sir, especially as they must have cost you dear.'

A large hand ruffled her hair. 'Sophie, do you feel that you could unbend sufficiently to call me

Nicholas? It is my given name, you know, and we cannot continue to stand upon formality.'

'I'll try!' The colour flooded her face once more. 'It will seem strange. I know so little about you.'

'Not true! Aside from the fact that I have three cousins, you are well aware that I am an unfeeling, deceitful and arrogant brute. In fact, the ideal husband!'

Laughing, Sophie hid her face in his coat. 'Did I really say all that?' she whispered.

'You did, and more besides. I wonder that I had the temerity to make you an offer. It took some courage, I can tell you.'

'What persuaded you to speak?' she asked in muffled tones.

'Sheer desperation, my love. I'd resisted it so often, believing that you'd laugh me to scorn, but today, when I took you in my arms, I thought there might be hope for me.'

'You know it, Nicholas. When you kissed me…well…I too was lost. Oh, my dear, is this not sheer folly? You have given me no time to think…to consider…'

'What is there to consider? If we love each other, that should be enough. Do you love me, Sophie?'

'I do, with all my heart, but it has come as a shock. I might have suspected, if I'd had any sense at all, but I never thought of it. I missed you dreadfully when you went away, but I told myself that it was because I'd been left without protection.'

'You had my men here,' he protested with a smile.

'It wasn't the same. I needed to see you, to be with you, and to know that you were close at hand.' She gave a rueful sigh. 'In these matters, Kit is wiser than I am myself. He thinks the world of you.'

'I am the luckiest man alive!' Hatton raised her hand to his lips. 'Sophie, this must be our secret for the moment. If Harward were to hear of our betrothal, you might be in danger.'

'How so?' Sophie was puzzled.

'At this present time he believes you to be without protection and vulnerable. With no one to advise you, you have fallen in with all his plans. The prospect of an imminent marriage for you will not suit him in the least.'

'But I'd still allow him to move his cargo,' she objected.

'A husband might not be so gullible.'

'I could promise not to speak of it.'

'You think he would believe you? You must have heard of pillow-talk, my dear. Harward would think it more than likely that you would confide in your beloved. He won't risk it.'

Sophie's eyes widened. 'You believe that he might try to stop me?'

'You know too much, my darling. Let him continue to believe that you have not thought of marriage. All that concerns you is a secure future for yourself and Kit.'

'Are you talking about me?' Kit came into the room and stared. 'Hatton, why do you hug Mama? Has she given you a present?'

'The best present in the world, Kit, but it is a secret. We shall tell you of it in a day or two.'

Kit was too full of his own concerns to object. He walked towards Sophie with his arms stretched out before him. In his upturned hands he held a box.

'I have a present for you, Mama. I made it myself.'

Sophie looked down at the jewel-like object resting in the folds of paper. It was a brightly coloured fishing fly.

'This is truly beautiful,' she exclaimed. 'Did you really make it, Kit? It must have been very difficult.'

'It was,' he admitted. 'Reuben made me do it six times. I nearly gave up, but he said—'

'Yes?' Hatton prompted.

'He said I'd do it in the end, and I did.'

'You did indeed, my darling, and I shall treasure it.'

'It might make a brooch, Mama, or you could wear it in your hat.' Kit climbed on Hatton's knee and dropped a kiss upon his cheek.

'I'd like another one of those,' Hatton told him.

Chubby arms encircled his neck as Kit obliged. Then he looked at his mother. 'I love Hatton,' he said.

'Better than Reuben?' Sophie teased.

Kit's reply required long and careful thought. 'Both the same,' he said at last.

'I see that I am promoted,' Hatton chuckled.

'Then you must take care that you are worthy of your god-like status,' Sophie joined in the joke.

It warmed her heart to see the loving relationship between her son and this stranger who had appeared so unexpectedly in their midst.

Not for the first time she mused on the caprice of fate. Three weeks ago she'd had no idea that Hatton existed. Almost crushed by the blows that life had dealt her she'd felt numb with misery and only half-alive. Now she contemplated her future in a daze of happiness. All her doubts were stilled.

What she had mistaken for dislike had been an unwillingness to commit herself to love for a second time. How she'd fought against it, refusing to see any merit in this man who now possessed her soul.

When had she changed? She couldn't quite decide. She'd even suspected Hatton's kindness to her child, believing that he must have some ulterior motive. It had taken time to convince her that this apparently unfeeling brute had a gentler side to his nature.

Now Kit was playing with the fobs on his watch-chain.

'Could you skate when you were as old as me?' he asked.

'No! I learned later when I went to Holland. The men there race each other along the frozen canals in winter. I wanted to try it.'

'I'd like to see them. Will you take me one day?'

'One day. You have my word on it.'

'Promise?' Kit's face was solemn.

'It's a promise.' Hatton set the child down. 'Sophie, I must go. There is much to do before tonight. We can't risk mistakes. I may not see you for some time.'

Sophie couldn't hide her dismay. So much had been left unsaid. She wanted to assure him of her love once more, to say that he would be always in her thoughts, and to beg him to be careful. She turned to Kit.

'Will you ask Bess if she has some food for us, my pet? Mr Hatton has to leave quite soon. He must not be delayed.'

Kit's face fell. 'Hatton, you *will* come back, won't you?' His lower lip was trembling.

'Nothing is more certain.' Hatton held out his hand to the child. 'Take care of your mother, Kit. I shall be back before you know it.'

'Must you take Reuben too?'

'Yes, but we shan't be gone for long. For the time being you must rely on Bobbo to keep you company.'

Kit's face cleared. Then, humming a little tune, he hopped out of the room on one foot.

Troubled though she was, Sophie was forced to smile.

'That's the sign of a particularly happy day for Kit, my dear.'

'The hopping and the singing? Perhaps I should follow his example. It is certainly a particularly happy day for me.' His expression was quizzical as he looked at her.

'I beg that you will not. There are many fragile objects in this room. I should not care to see them broken.' Sophie's laughter did not reach her eyes. She knew what he was about. The joke was an effort to lift the tension in the air.

Now she wanted to throw herself into his arms and beg him not to leave her. It took all her self-control not to do so. Her throat was dry and she found it difficult to speak, but she managed it at last.

'I was surprised to hear you speak of Bobbo. When did Kit tell you of his imaginary friend?'

'It was at our first meeting. Since then he joins us every day. A difficult chap, this Bobbo! He and I do argue on occasion. He has some curious notions as to what is best for Kit, but between us Reuben and I have Bobbo well in hand.'

Sophie burst into tears.

'What is it, my love?' Tenderly, Hatton took her in his arms. 'Are my jokes as bad as that?'

'Don't!' she sobbed. 'Pray don't make light of what you are about to do. I'm so afraid for you...'

'I shan't be alone, Sophie, and you've seen my bruisers. Don't they give you pause? Personally, I shouldn't care to meet them in a dark alley if they were my enemies.' He slipped a finger beneath her chin and raised her face to his. 'They'd lay down their lives for me, you know, but hopefully that won't be necessary.'

'But you will be careful?' she pleaded.

'Yes!' His ardent gaze brought the colour to her cheeks. 'I have much to live for. Don't trouble your head about me. Now, for your own part, you will remember my instructions?'

Too overcome to speak, she nodded.

'No heroics, mind! Follow Harward's plan to the letter. It will take courage to go into the cellars and open the outer door, but you alone can do it. You may be under observation and Matthew must not be seen to have any knowledge of the store. Everyone must be warned beforehand to keep their shutters closed. They must be blind and deaf to any sound outside the inn in the early hours. We have come too far to risk a mishap now.'

He took Sophie in his arms once more. 'Don't be afraid!' he urged. 'These men need you, Sophie. They have no reason to distrust you. They believe you to be a willing accomplice. You won't be in the slightest danger as long as you follow their instructions. Open the outer door, don't look back, and then go to your room.'

Then his mouth found hers and she melted into his embrace, her arms about his neck.

'Come back to me!' she whispered. 'I couldn't live without you.'

'You worry too much!' He dropped a kiss upon the tip of her nose. 'Take heart, my love. All this will soon be over. Then it will fade from your memory like a bad dream.'

'I pray that you are right.' She clung to him once more in a last embrace. Then she disengaged herself. 'Come,' she said. 'You must eat before you leave. You shall not go away unfed.'

Her smile was uncertain, and, looking at her, Hatton knew that she was trying to bring her courage to the sticking point.

'The sooner I go, the quicker I shall return,' he told her lightly. 'Shall we join the others?'

They found a merry party at the dining-table and Sophie saw to her surprise that Kit was with them, propped up on several cushions to bring him level with his plate.

Any fears she might have had about his normally finicky appetite were soon dispelled. Too absorbed in chatter to quibble, he demolished a bowl of mutton stew almost without noticing.

So much for coaxing him into eating just another mouthful, she thought wryly. Evidently the thing to do was to ignore the problem and leave him to it. Her son was leading a most unusual life. Other children of his age would have been banished to a nursery and warned that they might be seen but not heard at a set time each day.

Well, it would not do for her, no matter how unconventional her treatment of her son might appear to others. These years of childhood were too precious. Kit must feel always that he could come to her and join in whatever life she could offer him.

She looked at Hatton, half-fearing to see a look of disapproval, but he was smiling broadly at Kit.

'You've joined the other men, I see.' He drew out a chair for Sophie. 'Are you keeping them in order?'

'We are thinking of making Kit the president of our club,' the man named Wentworth told him. 'A magician must take first place. Don't you agree?'

'Undoubtedly!' Hatton peered at his plate. 'This stew now. It could be from an ancient recipe. What do you say, Kit? Will it turn us into tadpoles?'

Kit was too convulsed with glee to answer him. It was Wentworth who replied.

'My dear sir, you need not fear to eat the dish. Kit murmured an incantation before we took a bite. Any spell there may have been is broken.'

Hatton looked at the grave face and his shoulders began to shake. He bent his head and began to eat.

Sophie too was trying hard to hide her laughter. At the same time she was warmed by the kindness of the young men about her table. Clearly, they had made it their business to take an interest in her son, and she liked them for it.

Their banter was both witty and entertaining, and gradually she was persuaded to join in. Later she was surprised to find that she too had cleared her plate almost without noticing.

Slowly and imperceptibly her spirits lifted, and by the time they took their leave of her she was able to return their thanks with the assurance that she had enjoyed their company.

Hatton, she noticed with a pang, had decided to leave with them. Throughout the meal she had watched him closely as he spoke to the other men. He'd given no indication that Wentworth and two of the others were his cousins. As far as her servants were concerned the gentlemen were travellers met together in the casual way of customers at any hostelry.

She schooled her own expression to no more than friendliness as she watched the little party ride away. Then she went back to the parlour.

As always the place seemed empty without Hatton. Life was very strange, she mused. Call it fate, or luck, or chance…whatever it was, she could only wonder at the quirk of fortune which had led her to this point in her circumstances. A delay of only half an hour would have caused her to miss the visit of Richard Firle to her father's home all those years ago.

If she hadn't fallen in love with him on sight, she might have married any one of half a dozen suitors for her hand. Somewhere she had read that human beings were no more than playthings of the gods. They had been more than ordinarily capricious in her own case if that were so.

Then she dismissed the thought. Chance might play a part in determining one's future, she decided, but human beings always had a choice. She'd chosen Richard, and it had been a mistake, but now she had been given a second chance to find happiness. She would not let it go.

Her ill-starred marriage had brought her to this place, but without it she would not have had Kit, nor would she have met Hatton. Perhaps in time the gods grew tired of cruelty and decided to relent.

She was still lost in thought when Abby came to find her.

'Will you come to the kitchen, Mistress Firle? Me and Mother...well...we're that worried!'

'What is it, Abby? Everyone enjoyed their meal. No one found fault with it, though mutton stew is not a favourite of mine. Only your mother can make it taste delicious.'

Abby did not answer her question. She shook her head and set off for the kitchen without further comment. There she walked over to her mother's side and both women turned to face their mistress.

Sophie knew at once that there was something sadly wrong.

'Has someone been hurt?' she asked anxiously. 'What is it, Bess? Pray don't keep me in suspense.'

'You'd best sit down,' the woman told her bluntly. 'What I have to say won't please you.'

'Very well. I'm waiting…'

'It's Nancy Tyler, mistress.'

Sophie sighed with relief. 'Is that all? Have you quarrelled with her? If she isn't doing her work, I'll speak to her myself.'

'That isn't all, ma'am. She works too hard if anything. Fair runs herself into the ground, she does. 'Tis the nights, you see.'

'What on earth do you mean? Does Nancy go out at night? She needs no permission to do so…she may like to walk.'

'She don't go out.' Bess's mouth set in a tight line. 'She locks herself in her room.'

'Bess, she is entitled to some privacy. I wonder that you begrudge it to her.'

Bess shook her head. 'You don't understand. Abby, you had best tell the mistress what you saw.'

'I weren't spying, Mistress Firle,' the girl said in her own defence, 'but Nancy's room is next to mine. She talks all night, and I can't sleep.'

Sophie frowned at her. 'Nancy has had a tragic life. No doubt she has bad dreams. Won't you be patient for a while? In time she may not suffer so—'

'She weren't dreaming, ma'am. She were quieter when she came here, but I could hear her clearly. At first I thought she had someone in the room with her…it were like…well, like a conversation with another person.'

'That can't be so,' Sophie protested. 'Nancy has no friends here whom she might ask to visit her.'

'No, ma'am, I know that.' Abby was clearly uncomfortable, but a look from her mother urged her on. 'I didn't know what she were up to, so I…well, I took the knot out of the wall.'

'You did what? Must you speak in riddles, Abby. I don't know what you mean.'

''Tis a loose knot in the wooden panelling.' Bess answered for her daughter. 'It gives a sight of the other room.'

'I wonder that it was not sealed long ago,' Sophie cried in indignation. 'Anyone might have watched the maids if they knew of it.'

Bess avoided Sophie's eye. 'Well, it weren't sealed up,' she said. 'And now, when you hear what Abby has to say, you might think it for the best.'

Sophie felt sickened and disgusted. It did not need Bess to tell her for whose benefit the peephole had remained unsealed. Richard must have watched the girls dressing and undressing as the fancy took him.

'Go on!' she said faintly.

'Well, ma'am, I were that surprised. Nancy had a table laid for two, but there was no one there but her. She were talking to an empty chair as if it were a person, pouring wine and serving food. I thought it were some fancy game of hers, but then she began to cry and hold out her arms...I didn't watch no more.'

'I see. Has this happened more than once?'

''Tis every night now, mistress, and it's getting louder. She shouts and screams and cries and last night...well...she has a pistol. Waving it in the air, she was.'

'You should have told me of this before,' Sophie said sternly. 'I won't have firearms in the house. They could prove a danger to all of us.'

She was at pains to hide her anxiety about Nancy's state of mind. Those conversations seemed likely to be with the girl's dead husband and Sophie felt sick with horror. Clearly, Nancy fancied him to be still alive.

Now she blamed herself for this tragedy. She should have concerned herself far more with Nancy and less with her own problems. Hopefully, it was not too late to bring the girl back to reality. She smiled at Bess and Abby.

'I'm glad you told me. Nancy is in need of help. I'll speak to her today.' She rose as if to go, but Bess stayed her with a gesture.

'I'm sorry, ma'am, but you ain't heard the worst of it. There's more...' She signed to her daughter to go on.

By now the excitable Abby was subdued. 'Nancy has changed, ma'am. Last night the table wasn't laid and she didn't pour the wine. She sat by the fire with a bundle in her arms, and she was singing lullabies. Then she laid the bundle in a drawer, made up like a cot. She seems to think she has a baby now.'

Sophie's blood ran cold. This was a step too far. Nancy sounded seriously unhinged, and it would take someone far better qualified than Sophie to help her. Meantime, she could prove to be a danger to all of them, especially as she knew of Hatton's true identity. She might prove to be the ruin of his plans.

Drawing on all her courage, she made her way to Nancy's room to find the girl engaged in sewing.

'Leave that, Nancy, please!' she said. 'We need to talk.'

'Yes, Sophie?' The great blue eyes looked up at her with guileless innocence.

Sophie did not know where to start. 'Are you sleeping well?' she said lamely.

'I don't sleep! There is no need!' came the startling reply.

'Nancy, we all need to sleep, otherwise we get so tired. Then we begin to imagine things. Suppose we call the doctor. He will give you something to help you.'

'No! I need to keep my wits about me.' Nancy's look was furtive. 'I mustn't lower my guard.'

Sophie adopted a coaxing tone. 'Well, then, won't you come and sit with me? You might help me with my sewing.'

Nancy shook her head. 'I can't do that today. I mustn't leave my baby.' She gestured towards a shapeless bundle lying on blankets in a drawer beside the fire.

Sophie felt close to tears. The bundle bore no resemblance to a child. She swallowed hard.

'You might…you might bring the child with you,' she suggested. Nancy must not be left alone again in her present state of mind.

'No! He's safer here.' Nancy took the bundle in her arms and began to croon a lullaby. 'Poor little one! He cried so hard last night, but he's quiet now.'

Sophie made a desperate effort to hide her alarm. It was clear that Nancy's mind had given way under the pressure of her grief at the loss of both her husband and her unborn child. She tried again.

'Come down to my room,' she urged. 'It's much too cold for you in here. You will take a chill.'

'Do you find it cold?' Nancy began to throw sticks upon the fire, smiling as it blazed. 'There, that's better! We shall be cosy now, won't we, my pet?' She looked down at the shapeless bundle with such tenderness that Sophie felt stricken to the heart.

She forced a smile. 'You are quite right, my dear. It's warmer now. May I come and share your fire with you?'

'If you like, but you won't harm my baby, will you?'

'Of course not, Nancy, I want to help you. Now I must fetch my things. Will you promise not to lock your door against me?'

A look of cunning flickered across the girl's face, but it vanished so quickly that Sophie wondered if she had imagined it. A nod was the only indication that Nancy had heard her.

Sophie was torn between unwillingness to leave her alone and the knowledge that she must summon the doctor without delay. Nancy's condition was beyond the help of a lay person.

Swiftly she ran down to the kitchen to find Matthew talking to his wife and daughter. She saw real anxiety in his eyes.

'How is she?' he asked.

'Nancy is very ill, I believe. Matthew, will you fetch the doctor?'

'I will if I can find him, mistress, but it is getting dark. Sometimes they comes for him at night.'

'They…who are they?' she cried impatiently.

'Why, the…free traders, ma'am.'

'You mean he treats these men? You surprise me. Surely a man in his position should inform the authorities as to their whereabouts?'

'They takes care that he can't do that, ma'am. He's always blindfolded before they leads him away.'

'He could still inform on them. It might be possible to set a trap.'

'He won't do that,' Matthew told her firmly. 'Not if a man is wounded.'

'Indeed!' Sophie was furious. 'A nice distinction, I must say. I wonder if he knows that a deranged mind is the result of the activities of his villainous patients.'

Bess stepped forward then and laid a hand on Sophie's arm. 'Ma'am, you are upset and its not to be wondered at. Matthew will fetch the doctor, as you say...' She jerked her head towards the door, but Matthew hesitated. Then he cast a look of appeal at Sophie.

'Mistress Firle, you will take care? If the girl is as sick as you say, she may be dangerous. Abby tells me that she has a gun... Mayhap you shouldn't be alone with her. We could lock her in her room.'

'I won't do that!' Sophie said with decision. 'Just be as quick as you can. The inn must be secured as soon as possible, with the shutters drawn and the doors bolted.'

Looking at her companions, she realised that these instructions came as no surprise to them. Hatton must have made his wishes clear before he left. Bess looked anxious and clearly Abby was terrified.

'Off you go!' she ordered as Matthew lingered by his womenfolk. 'Ben and his son may sleep indoors tonight.'

A look of gratitude was her reward. In the normal way of things the two men slept above the stables. Now even Abby looked relieved.

'Must I come with you to sit with Nancy?' she asked with some reluctance.

'I think not, Abby, though it is kind of you to offer. Later you may bring us something light for supper...perhaps a little broth? Has Nancy eaten anything today?'

'She ain't been out of her room all day,' Bess told her. 'I thought she must be sick. A girl like that...well, she wears a wedding ring but that's not to say she has a husband. Some man may have got her into trouble...'

'Nancy isn't pregnant, if that is what you're suggesting, Bess. If you must know it, she was widowed and the shock caused her to lose her unborn child.'

Bess flushed. 'We was not to know it,' she said defensively. 'She ain't spoken more than a word or two to any of us.'

'Why didn't you tell me?' Sophie cried. 'You must have sensed that there was something wrong.'

''Tweren't none of our affair if she chose to keep herself to herself. She did her work and that was good enough for me.'

Sophie stifled further reproach, knowing that she was more to blame than her servants. Hatton had accused her of being blind as far as his own feelings were concerned. She had been blind in regard to Nancy too. Now she must try to put things right as far as she was able.

She hurried back to the snug, only to find Nancy wasn't there. She went back upstairs and found Nancy sitting by the fire. Then she noticed that the bundle was still in its makeshift cot tucked up beneath a blanket.

Sophie sighed with relief. Nancy seemed much calmer and her eyes were closed. The girl must be exhausted. Sleep might possibly restore her to a more rational frame of mind, Sophie thought without conviction.

Well aware that she was clutching at straws, she walked over to the window and stared out into the darkness. There was no sign of Matthew yet. Now she prayed that he would find the doctor. Tonight, above any other, she didn't need a sick woman upon her hands.

Too much lay ahead of her. Under other circumstances she would have sat with Nancy through the night, but if she were to play her part in Hatton's plan she would be forced to leave the girl for a time. When the doctor came she would insist upon a sedative for Nancy.

Wearily she reached out to close the shutters, but a voice at her shoulder made her jump.

'Don't!' Nancy cried sharply. 'I must watch for them.'

Startled almost out of her wits by the girl's stealthy approach, Sophie stepped back and collided with her. Then she froze. Nancy's hands were hidden within the folds of her skirt, but there could be no mistaking the fact that she was holding a pistol.

'Please give me that!' Sophie held out a shaking hand for the gun.

The girl seemed not to have heard her. 'They'll come tonight, you know. I listened to them talk…' Her voice was dreamy and her smile struck terror into Sophie's heart.

'Listen to me, Nancy! You are imagining things. A snatch of conversation can be misleading. It could have referred to anything.'

The glittering eyes rested on her with a look of pity. 'You didn't think so, Sophie. You agreed to all they said.'

Sophie stared at her. These flashes of lucidity made the girl's condition all the more frightening. It wouldn't be easy to deceive her, but how could she have known of Harward's plans?

Then she remembered the door at the far end of the snug. It had closed almost imperceptibly as she'd left the room with Harward and his companion. She'd paid no attention. If she'd thought of it at all, she'd have imagined that it had swung to of its own accord. She hadn't considered an eavesdropper.

Now she came to a quick decision. She laid a gentle hand on Nancy's arm. 'Let us sit down,' she said. 'I think we need to talk… I'll leave these shutters open for the moment. Then, if we hear anything untoward, we can look out through the window.'

Nancy appeared to be satisfied by this concession, but her hands remained hidden in her skirts, as Sophie busied herself with building up the fire.

It threw out little warmth as the grate was too small to hold more than a lump or two of coal and a few sticks. Comfort, as Sophie realised to her shame, had not been the first consideration in a servant's bedroom. Looking about her, she saw that it was bleak in the extreme, furnished only with a wooden-slatted bed covered by a thin mattress and a couple of worn blankets. The chair on which she sat had a broken strut and the chest in the corner leaned drunkenly on missing feet.

This miserable abode was where Nancy had been left to cope with her grief. It was little wonder that she had found no solace here.

'I'm sorry that you've been living under these conditions,' Sophie said gently. 'Why did you not tell me, Nancy? We could have made you much more comfortable.'

'I thought you knew. In any case, it did not matter. I had a fire. At my last place the servants were forbidden to take fuel. You could freeze, however sick you were.'

I could have given her a room on the floor below, Sophie thought miserably, though it would have given rise to speculation by the other servants. Nancy's part in Hatton's scheme might have come to light if she'd been treated in a different way.

Sophie thrust aside her troubling regrets. It was important now to gain Nancy's trust, and every minute counted. The hours were passing quickly. It would not be long before she must go into the cellars to do Harward's bidding. She dared not risk the chance that Nancy might follow her.

'If you overheard our conversation, you will know that Mr Harward had an arrangement with my husband,' she said steadily. 'Some of his goods are stored in the cellars beneath the inn. He has asked if he might move this cargo. Is there anything strange in that?'

Nancy laughed in her face. 'Do you think me a fool?' she cried. 'I had not thought you stupid, Sophie. Why the secrecy? Why must they move these goods at night?'

'They are afraid of being ambushed,' Sophie faltered.

'By smugglers?' Nancy was growing hysterical. Her voice had risen to a shriek. Now she caught at Sophie's hands, crushing them in her own so hard that she threatened to break the bones.

'The truth now?' she demanded harshly. 'These men are the smugglers themselves, and you know it.'

Sophie disengaged herself with difficulty. There was little point in attempting to dissemble further.

'I suspect it,' she said carefully. 'But we can't be sure. That is why Mr Hatton intends to watch them—'

She heard a contemptuous laugh. 'His lordship is convinced, if you are not—'

'His lordship?' Sophie stared at her. 'I was speaking of Mr Hatton.'

'So was I? Didn't you know that he was heir to the Earl of Brandon? I thought he must have told you.'

Chapter Eleven

Sophie looked at the girl with pitying eyes. How on earth had Nicholas come to play a part in her strange fancies? Now she was at a loss as to what to say or do. Would it be best to appear to agree with her wild imaginings? There seemed little point in attempts to reason with her, but she could try.

'Perhaps you are thinking of someone else?' she suggested gently. 'What gave you the idea that Mr Hatton is a lord?'

'My father knew the Earl quite well before the old man was injured. They worked together for years to stop the smuggling trade.'

'That may be so, but why do you imagine that Mr Hatton is the Earl's heir?'

'I met him long ago in Kent. He came with Claudine and his father…'

'Claudine? Do you mean Madame Arouet?'

Nancy shrugged. 'I had forgot her other name. Now that the Countess is dead, it's said that she will marry the old Earl. She's been his friend for years.'

Sophie was seized with a feeling of dread. Nancy's story sounded plausible…too plausible…but she'd heard that the deranged could be extremely cunning. There might be some obscure motive behind these ridiculous suggestions, but for the moment Nancy sounded perfectly rational.

'I think you should rest,' she said firmly. 'Won't you lie down upon your bed? Give me your gun. I'll keep it safe for you.'

The faintest of smiles lifted the corners of Nancy's lips.

'You don't believe me, do you?' she challenged.

'I don't know what to believe, and nor, I suspect, do you. Now let us have an end to this nonsense, Nancy. Give me the gun…'

Very slowly, Nancy's hand appeared from within her skirts. As Sophie had guessed, she was holding a serviceable pistol. Sophie reached out to take it from her, but the girl's fingers closed convulsively about the weapon.

'No!' She shook her head. 'I need it. You must ask his lordship if you want one of your own.'

'I shouldn't dream of asking for a gun,' Sophie told her sharply. 'I've never fired a weapon in my life. Have you?'

The girl ignored her.

'Nancy, I think you have forgot. We have men here to protect us if danger threatens, though I think it is most unlikely.'

She heard a low chuckle, and the sound was chilling. 'They'll come tonight, but I'm ready for them. Listen!' She raised the pistol with a steady hand and aimed it at the door.

'No!' Sophie too had heard the approaching footsteps. Now her voice cracked on a high note of panic. 'That will be Abby with your supper. Let me talk to her!'

To her great relief, it was Abby who replied to her whispered question. She had brought the doctor.

'Wait, please!' Sophie was terrified as she turned to face the upraised weapon. Nancy might fire at any man who entered the room. It took all her self-control to speak quietly and persuasively. Her mouth was so dry that she had to swallow several times before the words came out.

'The doctor is here,' she said. 'I hurt my ankle on the pond this morning. It's so painful, Nancy. You won't mind if he looks at it?'

'Is this a trick? These men are clever.'

'It's no trick. Come now, you know the doctor, my dear. He came to Bess when she burned her hand. Don't you remember?'

Nancy nodded. She lowered the gun, but she would not relinquish it. It stayed hidden in the pocket of her skirt.

Very slowly Sophie opened the door. Something in her face must have warned the doctor. He hesitated on the threshold.

'Thank heavens you are here,' Sophie felt that she was babbling. 'My ankle is so badly swollen. Can you give me something for the pain?'

He saw the desperation in her eyes and was quick to understand the reason for it. He didn't look at Nancy as he walked into the room.

'Sit down, Mistress Firle!' he said. 'Let us see if the ankle is broken.' He signalled to Abby to bring the candles closer. Then he placed a chair for Sophie so that he could study her companion whilst pretending to examine the foot.

Nancy turned her head away, but he didn't need to see her face to realise that she was close to breaking point. Her body was as taut as a bowstring.

Sophie gave an artistic wince as she removed her shoe. Then he examined her foot with every appearance of concern.

'Nothing broken, ma'am,' he told her cheerfully. 'But this is a bad case. You must be very careful…' It was the clearest possible warning that Nancy was in a most dangerous state of mind.

Sophie's look was pleading. 'What must I do?' she asked.

'Rest is what is needed here, Mistress Firle. Rest and complete quiet. I'll give you a sedative. You won't find it unpleasant. Taken in a hot drink it is unnoticeable. You will sleep for hours.'

He rose to his feet and turned to Nancy. 'Is this your room?' he asked.

Nancy didn't answer him.

'What a pleasure it is to see a cosy fire,' he continued, apparently untroubled by her rudeness. 'Now, Mistress Firle, I must be on my way. I am called to a sick woman in the village. The poor wretched creature is without a single covering for her bed.'

Sophie understood him at once. 'We have bedding and to spare,' she cried. 'Let me find it for you. Abby, will you stay here to make up the fire again? I shall only be a moment.'

Abby looked about to refuse, but a stern glance from her mistress caused her to think better of it.

Sophie slipped out of the door and drew the doctor away to the far end of the landing.

'She mustn't hear us whispering. Oh, what am I to do? Doctor Hill, she has a gun...'

'I saw it, ma'am. Abby told me what has happened. Nancy's mind has gone, I fear. Without the gun we might have overpowered her, but the risk is now too great. She could fire at random. In any case, we cannot move her at this time of night.'

'This time of night?' Sophie glanced at the clock in the hall below and realised to her horror that in less than an hour she must open the cellar doors.

'Will you give me the sedative?' she asked. 'I'll try to get her to take it at once.'

He opened his bag and thrust the preparation into her hand. 'The doses are made up, but don't give her more than one, ma'am. They are very strong. Too much can be dangerous.' His face was grave. 'Have you no one with you other than the servants? You are taking a serious risk. I think we should move the girl without delay. I'll try to arrange it for tomorrow.'

'Must you?' Sophie's look was pitiful. 'I couldn't bear to think of her confined to a madhouse. With care she may recover...'

He shook his head as he took his leave of her, and she hurried back to Nancy's room.

Abby was standing by the door, and, as Sophie reappeared, she shot out of the room. Sophie called her back again.

'Did I not mention that we'd like some broth? Please bring it up at once.'

Sophie awaited Abby's return with ill-concealed impatience. Time was running out. If Hatton's plan was to succeed she must make her way to the cellars within minutes.

'What took you so long?' she cried as she snatched the tray from her servant's hands.

'The broth wasn't ready, mistress. Mother made it fresh for you.' Abby was startled by the unexpected sharpness in Sophie's tone.

Turning her back on her companions, Sophie slipped the sedative into one of the bowls of steaming liquid.

'Now, Nancy, won't you try to eat?' she coaxed. 'You will feel so much better if you do. Come now, just a sip or two to please me?'

Obediently, Nancy picked up her spoon. Then she cried out as her lips touched the scalding broth. 'It's too hot!' she whispered.

Sophie gave a despairing glance at the clock. If she hurried, she need not be away for more than a few minutes.

'Then let it cool. Abby, do you stay with Nancy. I shall be back at once, but I must see your father.'

Matthew was not far to seek. He was waiting for her by the cellar door.

'Give me the keys,' she demanded, 'then please go up to Nancy's room. You need not enter. Just stay by the door. Abby may have need of you.'

Matthew was torn with indecision, wondering whether Sophie or his daughter would be in the greatest danger.

'Nancy is quieter now,' Sophie comforted. 'I think you need not fear for Abby's safety. This is a precaution.'

'But what of you, ma'am?' he protested. 'Won't you go back upstairs? I will open the cellars. It's no task for a woman.'

'Do as you are bidden!' Sophie snapped. 'You know that this is all arranged.' She looked at his worried face and softened her tone. 'Think about it, Matthew! These men may be waiting by the entrance to the tunnel. They are expecting me, but no one else is supposed to know of their cargo. They might kill you on sight.'

Matthew paled, but he persisted. 'It's too dangerous. Why should they not kill you?'

'They need me. Besides, they think that I'm their ally. Now, Matthew, Mr Hatton has arranged this scheme. Do you believe that he would allow me to put myself in peril of my life?'

'I suppose not, but…well…we can't be certain what they'll do.'

'Nothing is certain in this life.' Sophie spoke with a lightness she was far from feeling. 'Now give me the keys! Do you have the lantern?'

His silence spoke volumes as he obeyed her.

'Remember now, you must not follow me!' Sophie's heart was pounding as she made her way down the cellar steps.

The light from the lantern was of little comfort to her. It served only to emphasise the shadows which closed in on her from either side. Following the single beam, she hurried to the hidden entrance to find that Matthew had already pulled the shelves aside and unlocked the door.

Ahead of her the huge cellar lay in darkness, and she was seized with terror.

She could only hope that Matthew hadn't taken it upon himself to open the doors at the far end of the tunnel, otherwise her unwelcome visitors might already be awaiting her.

She stopped and listened, but there was no sound. Reluctantly, she moved into the tunnel, knowing that she was now beneath the hillside behind the inn. The place was damp and at once she had to fight a sense of claustrophobia. If the walls caved in, she would be buried alive.

Fearfully, she raised the lantern to examine her surroundings. Then she noticed with relief that the passageway was shored up with heavy baulks of timber. Evidently it had been found worthwhile to construct it with great care. These men must make a handsome profit, she thought bitterly, if they could sanction such an outlay. How long had it taken them?

Her hands shook as she examined the bunch of keys that had been hidden behind the shelves. There was no indication as to which of them she needed. The first two would not turn in the lock, and she began to despair. Perhaps the metal had rusted from lack of use over these past months.

In her frustration she kicked angrily at the door. If the third key did not fit, Hatton's plan would be ruined.

To her relief it slid smoothly into the lock. She turned it and pulled at the doors. They swung open as if on oiled hinges.

Sophie peered out into the darkness, holding the lantern high above her head. She could see nothing outside the pool of light. She listened in silence, but nothing stirred in the blackness. What had she expected? Wagons, ponies, groups of men? Possibly they were hidden in the copse of trees.

Well, she had played her part. It was over, much to her relief. She turned away. Then she screamed aloud as a figure appeared beside her, and she almost dropped the lantern.

'No, don't raise it!' a conversational voice advised.

Sophie knew at once that it was Harward. Furious with him for giving her such a fright she disobeyed his order, thrusting the lantern towards him. Then she quailed.

In that shadowy light the sharp planes of his features were thrown into relief, giving him a predatory look. His smile did nothing to reassure her. He resembled nothing so much as a savage wolf, his lips curled into a snarl.

Now he took the lantern from her hand and set it on the ground.

'You have been fortunate tonight, my dear,' he observed. 'You did not follow orders, Mistress Firle. That was a mistake...'

'I...I don't know what you mean.' Sophie's voice was little more than a croak.

'Were you not advised to keep your premises locked, with shutters closed and your servants in their beds?'

'I did as you told me.'

'Then how is it that one of your men was allowed to ride into the village this evening?'

'Matthew? He went to fetch the doctor. One of my girls was taken ill.' Sophie's teeth were chattering with fright.

There was a silence. Then Harward bowed. 'Fortunately, ma'am, we know the doctor. It is, perhaps, as well…'

Suddenly, Sophie lost her temper. 'You have been spying on us?' she accused.

'Just a sensible precaution, Mistress Firle. We could not risk betrayal.'

'To one of your so-called bandits?' In her fury, Sophie threw caution to the winds. 'Do you imagine I believe that cock-and-bull story?'

'I never did.' Harward observed mildly. 'I don't regard you as a fool. You know quite well what we are about.'

Sophie tried to recover her position. 'It does not signify to me,' she said. 'I am looking for security, Mr Harward. You have promised me that.'

'And I'll keep my word.'

'Well, then, I shall leave you to go about your business. It is dark enough, God knows. You will be undisturbed this night.'

She heard a low laugh. 'You underestimate me, ma'am. We did not intend to move tonight. We needed to be sure of you. Had your servant visited anyone other than the doctor…well…we might have wondered if you were indeed a friend.'

Sophie shuddered. Matthew had come so close to death that night. She was thankful that her voice was steady when she spoke again.

'I trust that you are satisfied,' she said in haughty tones. 'Let me remind you, sir, that I am taking all the risks here. If this cargo is discovered on my premises I face imprisonment, transportation, or even death. I want it moved without delay.'

'Of course you do, and so do we. Shall we say tomorrow evening, then?'

'Certainly! That is, I suppose, unless I have need for a further visit from the doctor…'

'Ah, now you are offended.' Harward sounded regretful. 'I am sorry for it, ma'am, but you must understand that a degree of caution is as much in your interest as in our own.'

Sophie nodded stiffly.

'Then may I suggest that you lock the door behind me? Until tomorrow, then?' With an exquisite bow Harward turned and disappeared into the darkness.

Breathing hard, Sophie closed the heavy door, slamming home the bolts and turning the key in the lock. Then she hurried back along the tunnel and through the cellars, bruising her ankles on crates and boxes in her haste.

She found Matthew waiting for her.

'Didn't I tell you to look out for Abby?' she cried. 'She might have had need of you.'

Matthew shook his head. 'My girl is in no danger, ma'am. Nancy is asleep.'

'Thank heavens for that!' Sophie's sense of relief was overwhelming. Nancy must have drunk the broth containing the sedative. She questioned Abby at once.

'She ain't eaten much of it,' the girl informed her, indicating the half-empty bowl. 'She wanted to wait for you. I set the dishes beside the fire to keep them warm.'

Sophie was in a quandary. Had Nancy taken enough of the sedative to quieten her for hours, or would it be best to persuade her to finish off the broth? Nancy stirred then and Sophie decided on the latter course.

'I'm sorry I was so long, my dear. I was looking forward to sharing this meal with you. See, Abby has kept our food warm. Won't you try a little more?' She picked up her own bowl.

Rather to her surprise, Nancy made no objection. She took the proffered dish and sipped slowly at the contents.

Sophie decided on a little encouragement. Food was the last thing on her mind, but Nancy was regarding her intently, so she began to eat with apparent relish.

'Abby, you need not wait to clear away,' she said. 'It is very late. Do you go to bed. The dishes can wait until morning.'

Nancy had stopped eating.

'Finish it up,' Sophie urged. 'See, my own bowl is almost empty.'

Nancy picked up her spoon again, much to Sophie's relief. Aside from the necessary sedative, the broth would do her good. Heaven alone knew when she had last eaten. Now, with food inside her and a roaring fire to warm her through, the girl should fall into a sound sleep.

'Won't you lie down upon your bed?' she suggested. 'I'll help you to undress.'

Nancy baulked at the suggestion. 'May I not sit here by the fire?' she whispered.

'Of course you may!' Sophie was determined to avoid a confrontation. 'I thought only that you would be more comfortable…'

Nancy smiled, gazing at the leaping flames as if she were in a trance-like state. Then she turned her head and Sophie was startled by the look of triumph in her eyes.

Something was wrong. Sophie attempted to get to her feet, but her limbs would not support her. Overcome by an appalling sense of lassitude, she tried to move her leaden body.

'Sit down!' Firm hands pushed her back into her chair. 'You shouldn't have tried to drug me, Sophie. I watched you through the mirror.'

'It was only to help you sleep…' Sophie could barely recognise her own voice. Her words were slurred and now the smiling face above her seemed to be changing, dissolving into a whirling mist.

'What have you done to me?' she whispered.

'I changed my bowl for yours. Now *you* will sleep. I couldn't let you stop me, Sophie…I know what I must do.'

'Oh, please! You must not. You could ruin—!' Sophie closed her eyes and fell into darkness.

When she awoke it was to find herself in her own bed, with Hatton at her side. His face was grim.

'Nicholas?' She reached out a hand to him. 'What are doing here?'

'Thank God!' He gathered her to him with a groan. 'I thought she might have poisoned you.'

'It was only a sleeping draught,' she said with some difficulty. She still felt heavy-eyed and lethargic. 'She changed the dishes, giving hers to me.'

'I should have listened to you.' Hatton was filled with self-reproach. 'I had no idea that she was so close to breaking point.'

'Nor had I. I knew she was disturbed, but I didn't realise how badly until Abby told me that she'd been holding conversations with her dead husband. Worst of all, she believed she had a child…' Two large tears rolled slowly down Sophie's cheeks.

Hatton kissed them away. 'Don't worry!' he soothed. 'When we find her she shall have the best of care—'

'*When* you find her? Oh, no! Do you tell me that she is gone?'

'She won't have gone far. Her quarry is here. I thank heavens that you kept her close last evening, else all might have been lost. Can you tell me what went wrong?'

'I sent Matthew for the doctor,' Sophie told him miserably. 'It didn't occur to me that the inn might have been watched. He was followed. They suspected betrayal, you see. It was only when he came back with the doctor that they trusted me again.'

'So that was why they didn't move the goods last night?'

'No! They had no intention of doing so. Harward is a careful man. He wanted to be sure of me.' She heard a sharp intake of breath.

'You mean you actually spoke to him last night?'

'He was waiting for me by the entrance to the tunnel.'

Hatton held her close. 'I should never have let you take such risks.' His face was muffled against her hair. 'Can you ever forgive me?'

'There was no risk,' she answered lightly. 'He even apologised when I flew at him—'

'You flew at him?' he echoed in disbelief. 'Sophie, why must you take such chances? Were you not afraid?'

'I was terrified at first,' she told him frankly. 'But then he made me angry. He looked so smug...so sure that he had me in his power. I didn't take kindly to his threats, especially when he spoke of Matthew.' She shuddered. 'I hadn't realised that he would watch the inn so closely. If Matthew had gone anywhere other than to the doctor's house, they would have killed him.'

'Matthew was in no danger,' Hatton told her. 'We were watching too. He was followed by one of my men both into the village and back again.'

'Then you were close at hand? I wish I'd known it.'

Hatton kissed her gently. 'You are the most precious thing in life to me, my darling. Would I leave you before our enemies are gone from here?'

Sophie rested her head against his chest. 'I'm so glad,' she whispered. 'Yesterday was one of the worst days of my life. Oh, Nicholas, I needed you so badly. I didn't know what to do, with Nancy half-demented. I tried to reason with her, but it was useless. She has a gun, you know.'

'Yes, Matthew told me.' Hatton's face was sombre. 'We must find her quickly. She could be in great danger.'

'You didn't see her leave the inn?'

'No, my dear, but it was dark, and we were some little distance away, hiding in the woods.'

Sophie thought for a moment. 'She wouldn't go far, I think. She knows now that Harward gives the orders and must have been responsible for her husband's death. He is her target. I am certain of it.'

'I wonder. She has had other opportunities to kill him, Sophie.'

'I think she wanted to be sure. I didn't know it at the time, but she was listening when Harward and his friend made their proposition to me. Then, as you know, they went away before she could take action.'

'We must find her. This could mean the ruin of all our plans. She could remove our only lead with a single shot. Have you any idea where she could be?'

'I don't know.' Sophie thought hard. 'It is full daylight now. You might search the outbuildings…'

'That has been done.' He hesitated. 'You must not think me unsympathetic to her plight, my darling. I can scarce imagine what she must have suffered in these last few months. I am not thinking only of our present operation, but Nancy is a danger to herself as well as others.'

Sophie held his hand against her cheek. 'I don't think you hard, my love, and if you had seen her yesterday…well, I hope never to witness such a tragedy again.'

'It must have been very bad.' Hatton held her closer.

'It was horrendous. Perhaps I shouldn't have sent for Dr Hill, but I felt that Nancy needed some expert help. She wouldn't allow me to take the pistol from her. All I could think of was the sedative. It didn't occur to me that she could be so cunning.

She watched me through the mirror when I slipped it into the bowl of broth.'

'You have little experience of madness, Sophie. I have met with it only once myself. The most frightening aspects are these sudden flashes of apparent lucidity. They put everyone off guard, but the dementia is always there.'

'She wasn't violent,' Sophie said defensively.

'That was because she saw a simpler way of outwitting you. Thank God that you didn't attempt to restrain her by force. I dare not think what might have happened.'

'Doctor Hill advised against it, and she did seem quieter after he had gone. She was still rambling, of course. She even mentioned you...'

The arms about her tightened. 'How was that?'

'Oh, she had some wild idea that she had met you long ago, with Madame Arouet. It must have been a childish fancy. The Earl of Brandon was part of this strange dream. She said that you were his heir.'

Sophie did not know what she had expected. Perhaps some further words of sympathy for the demented girl, or even an expression of surprise. She heard none of these.

Hatton stiffened, and as she looked up at him her heart turned over.

'What is it?' she asked quickly. 'Why should this nonsense trouble you? Oh, I've been so foolish. I should not have told you of these crazy fancies.'

Hatton was silent for so long that Sophie was seized with dread. He had grown very pale.

'They are not fancies,' he said at last. 'Nancy told you the truth.'

'No!' she cried. 'I won't believe it! Could you not trust me enough to reveal your true identity? You said you loved me. You even asked me to become your wife. Tell me it isn't true!'

'It's true,' he answered stubbornly. 'How could I tell you, Sophie? I had several reasons for keeping my identity a secret. My father is known to be the scourge of the smugglers. His name is known to every villain in the land. Would they overlook the sudden appearance of his son on this part of the coast?'

Sophie turned her head away. 'You deceived me,' she said coldly. 'Did you think that I, who loved you, would be likely to betray you? I was the one person you might have taken into your confidence.'

Hatton's face grew harsh. 'I thought I had explained,' he said. 'Anyone can be forced into betrayal. With a knife at Kit's throat would you have given me away?'

Her face gave him his answer, but she refused to be mollified.

'I was never questioned, Nicholas. There was no question of betrayal.'

'We could not be sure of that.'

Sophie disengaged herself from his embrace. 'You said that there were other reasons,' she challenged. 'Will you go on? I'd like to know exactly why and when you decided to continue in this deception.'

Hatton put his head in his hands. 'Does it matter, Sophie? You say you love me. Isn't that enough?'

Sophie stared at him. 'Of course it matters,' she replied. 'When I was a girl I married a man whose life was based upon deception, whether it was concerned with money or...or other women. I can't allow it to happen to me again.'

'I should have told you, my darling.' Hatton's face was a study in misery. 'But I wanted to be sure that you loved me for myself alone.'

'I see.' Sophie might have turned to stone. 'You felt that the prospect of wealth and a title might have persuaded me into marriage, however much I disliked you?'

Hatton did not reply.

'I suppose it is understandable.' Now Sophie's tone was cutting. 'You must have been the catch of several London Seasons. How many matchmaking mamas have you managed to fend off, to say nothing of their hopeful daughters? It has given you a biased impression of the female sex.'

Again he said nothing.

'Will you please go now?' she said in a high, clear voice. 'We can have nothing more to say to each other. I was mistaken in you and, clearly, you do not know me at all.'

Hatton attempted to take her hands. 'Don't send me away like this,' he pleaded. 'I love you, Sophie, and I thought you loved me.'

'I thought so too, but now it is over. I won't be misled again. Now you had best find Nancy. Harward intends to move his cargo tonight. You won't wish for anything to go wrong.'

'Don't you mean anything else?' His look was ghastly. 'Sophie, please! I beg you to reconsider—'

'No!' She would not look at him. 'There is nothing more to say.'

Chapter Twelve

Hatton went without another word, leaving Sophie numb with misery. Happiness had come so close, only to be snatched away again.

She had loved Nicholas with all her heart, and she'd trusted him implicitly, only to be deceived once more.

Had she been unreasonable? She thought not. She could understand his reasoning in part. Harward would have found no difficulty in forcing her to betray her lover's true identity if his suspicions had been aroused. A threat to Kit would have been enough. Then his carefully planned operation would have failed, with dire consequences for her country.

Worse, Nicholas would have been murdered out of hand, as others had been before him. As for herself and Kit? She understood Harward well enough to know that he would leave no witnesses. No one able to identify him would be left alive. He would not hesitate to order a wholesale massacre. Betrayal would not have saved her.

She found that she was shaking with terror, but she made a supreme effort to regain her composure. What was done was done. She could not unsay the words which had hurt her lover so deeply. Nor did she wish to do so. Her own common sense told her that he had been right to hide his identity when they first met.

What she could not forgive was his assumption that the prospect of wealth and a title would influence her decision to accept his offer of marriage.

How could she have been so mistaken in him? Clearly, he didn't know her at all. A moment's thought would have reminded him that her first marriage had been to a penniless Revenue Officer. Then, she had not hesitated to put love before possessions.

But Nicholas knew that the scars of that marriage were not yet completely healed. Perhaps he had believed that she would not care to repeat the experiment. The man is a fool, she thought with a spurt of anger. Surely he could have trusted her enough to believe that she loved him for himself alone.

A little worm of doubt assailed her. Others had not done so. For years he had been the target of every match-making mama in London. He spoke of them with cold contempt, knowing the reasons for their overtures.

Sophie felt very cold. Now she found that she was rocking back and forth, rubbing her arms in an effort to restore some warmth to her icy limbs. She needed to think and her thoughts were not encouraging.

Was she behaving like some silly schoolgirl? She'd already admitted to herself that in some respects his decision to use an assumed name had been the right one. Why could she not accept it?

She knew the answer well enough. She'd lived with deceit for too many years ever to wish to become a victim again, but she might have forgiven even that, once she knew a valid reason for it.

What had shocked her to the core was the feeling that she and Nicholas were strangers to each other. She'd believed that they had grown so close, but his doubting her integrity had killed that belief.

She could not know it, but he too was regretting his explanations to her. What demon had persuaded him to tell her of that final reason for hiding his identity? He'd known at once that it was a mistake. He'd seen the closed expression on her face, and who could wonder at it?

Even to suggest that wealth and a title would sway a woman of character such as Sophie was an unforgivable insult. Well, it served him right. At the last, his pride had been his undoing. He'd wanted only to be honest with her. Instead, he'd driven her away.

Now he cursed himself. For a time it had been sensible to conceal his identity from her, if only to ensure that his plans would not be put in danger.

Now, when his quarry was almost in the trap, he should have trusted her.

She had loved him enough to agree to become his wife, knowing almost nothing about him, he thought in anguish. Today, when she'd accepted him, he should have revealed that final secret. At this stage, no harm could come to her. Instead, she'd been forced to learn it from another. The agony of his loss was almost too much to bear.

Then Matthew entered the room.

'Have you found Nancy?' Hatton asked.

'No, sir. The men have searched the outbuildings and the wood, but there's no sign of her.'

'And indoors?'

Matthew shook his head. 'She could be anywhere. There are places enough to hide.'

Hatton nodded his agreement. The inn had been used for years by the smuggling fraternity. Even he did not know the full extent of the alterations which he suspected had been made to the building. If the rooms were measured against each other and compared with the walls outside he would have wagered on discrepancies in those measurements. A man might disappear within the walls simply by pressing a certain section of the wooden panelling to give access to the space behind.

'Nancy may have found such a place,' he ordered. 'She cannot stay concealed for long, so you must continue to keep watch. It's important that we find her.'

'And if we do?'

'I think you should pass the word that no one must attempt to take her on their own. She has a gun, as you well know, and at this present time she can't be held responsible for her actions. An accident now would mean disaster.'

'So what must we do, sir?'

'Go on looking. If you find her, keep her under observation. We mustn't lose her again. I must away for a short time, but I'll return as soon as possible.'

Hatton picked up his gloves and his riding crop, flung his many-caped coat about his shoulders, and set off for the stables.

Seated by the window of her bedchamber, Sophie watched him ride away. She felt that her heart was breaking. Was this the last that she would ever see of him? Without him her future seemed bleak indeed, but it had been her own decision. She would not, could not, change her mind. Fighting the overwhelming urge to open the window and call him back to her, she turned away.

As she made her way down the stairs she became aware that the atmosphere within the inn had changed. There was a curious air of tension about the place.

With every sense alert she walked into the kitchen to find her fears confirmed. Bess and her daughter were very pale. Neither looked as if they had slept, and their eyes were haunted.

Sophie sank into a chair. 'Bess, I'd like some chocolate, if you please, and I think I might eat a roll.'

Bess looked startled by this apparent return to normality, but she bestirred herself to do Sophie's bidding. Then she flung her apron over her head and began to wail. Abby looked about to do the same.

'Stop that at once!' Sophie ordered. 'What good will it serve? I had thought better of you.'

Beth's wails changed to gasping sobs. 'We thought she'd murdered you,' she whimpered. 'When Mr Hatton could not rouse you we thought you must be poisoned, ma'am.'

'What nonsense! Where would Nancy find the means to poison me? She hasn't left the inn.'

'There are certain plants—'

'None of which can be found in winter, especially with snow upon the ground. Now, do be sensible, Bess. All that happened was that Nancy gave me the sedative intended for herself. It was a sleeping draught.'

'Wicked creature! I don't know how she durst do that.'

'Nancy's mind is sick. You know that well enough. Now, tell me exactly what happened yesterday. I have no recollection of it. At what hour did you find me?'

'Mistress, it was late. We'd none of us closed our eyes. What with the orders to keep the shutters closed, and all the men on edge, we were afeared.

It must have been in the early hours when Mr Hatton came to find you. He looked that worried…'

Sophie eyed her servant coolly. Hatton's worry was not for her, she imagined, but for the failure of his plans. At that hour he would have expected to be on his way to London, following Harward to his destination.

'What then?' she demanded.

'Well, ma'am, he was like a man demented. He looked ready to kill us all for leaving you alone with Nancy, especially when he heard about the pistol.'

'I hope you told him that it was my decision.'

'He wouldn't listen!' Abby began to weep again. 'I thought that he would strike me. He said…he said…'

'Never mind what he said!' Sophie answered briskly. 'I have not suffered any harm. Now, listen to me carefully. Have you any idea where we might find Nancy?'

Both women shook their heads.

'I doubt if she'll be out of doors,' Sophie considered. 'In this weather she would freeze to death.'

Abby could not repress a scream. 'Oh, Mistress Firle, don't say that she's still here?' She turned to her mother. 'I won't stay!' she cried in panic. 'I want to go back to the village. My aunt will take me in.'

'Abby, you are a fool!' Sophie did not trouble to hide her anger. 'You are in no danger. Has Nancy ever tried to harm you?'

Wild-eyed with terror though she was, Abby shook her head.

'She had opportunity enough,' Sophie continued calmly. 'She could have threatened you with the pistol, or even knocked you on the head, but she did neither.'

'You say that, ma'am, begging your pardon, but my girl did not try to cross her.' Bess came at once to her daughter's defence.

'Nor will she do so now. Good heavens, Bess, I'm not asking either of you to stand up to Nancy. All I ask is that you tell me if you catch sight of her.'

Bess was growing calmer. Now she nodded her agreement. 'Mr Hatton said the same, even to the men. Even so, ma'am, we can't stay. I said as much to Matthew. We'd like to leave as soon as it's convenient.'

'It's never likely to be convenient,' Sophie told her in despair. 'Oh, Bess, I had such faith in you! You and Matthew have supported me even in the worst of times. Will you leave me now?'

'I'm sorry, ma'am!' Bess was adamant. 'I know that you promised us a share whenever you came to sell the inn, but our lives are more important than the money.'

'You are in no danger,' Sophie cried. 'Mr Hatton must have told you—'

'We don't believe him, ma'am. Things are happening here which none of us can understand. The gentleman may be powerful, but maybe he ain't a match for those agin him.'

Sophie was silent. She could no longer argue. For one thing, she had been deceiving these good people for the past few weeks. If the inn was not hers to sell, she could not give them a share of the proceeds.

She'd placed her faith in Hatton. He would not see them destitute, but now that she had broken with him she could no longer ask him for any favours on behalf of her servants.

Her shoulders drooped. 'You must do as you think best,' she said at last. 'Meantime, Bess, I suppose that we must think about provisions?'

Bess would not meet her eyes. 'We've enough and to spare for the present, ma'am. The men must be fed, but I doubt if we'll get any passing trade.'

She was wrong. At noon the door to the inn flew open and a noisy group of customers trooped indoors.

Sophie recognised them at once. The skating party had returned, with Hatton's cousins among them.

With an effort, she forced a smile. 'Do you skate again today?' she asked.

'No, ma'am.' The young man known as Wentworth bowed politely and gave her an engaging grin. 'Today we have brought some other of our friends. We are in search of sustenance…'

'Oh, dear! My cook may be at a pass to feed you all. You are eight in number, are you not? Let us see what we can do…'

Sophie hurried back into the kitchen. 'Bess, must we give them bread and cheese?' she asked.

'No, ma'am!' Bess was on her mettle at once. 'In this weather that won't do. The young gentlemen will be cold and hungry.' She thought for a moment. 'Give me an hour, Mistress Firle. They may pass the time with their wine or ale. Then we'll give them something for their bellies.'

She was as good as her word. Within the hour the company was sitting at table with expectant faces and Sophie was amused to see that Kit was among them, seated on a pile of cushions. He smiled at her, and then returned to a serious discussion with one of his companions on the merits of different fishing flies.

Bess had excelled herself, perhaps ashamed of her decision to abandon Sophie in her hour of need. A creamy leek and potato soup was accompanied by crusty bread. It vanished like snow in summer. This was followed by a dish of trout cooked in wine and butter.

Sophie had been surprised. 'How did you keep this fish?' she asked Bess. 'We could not have bought it recently.'

'It was packed in ice, ma'am, and then stored in the cellar. As long as the ice don't melt, it won't go off.'

Bess busied herself with the final touches to the dish, pounding up a mixture of herbs, capers, anchovy fillets and garlic with mustard and the juice of lemons. Then she mixed together butter and flour. Removing the trout from the baking dish, she heated up the remaining liquor and added the flour and butter paste. When it thickened she threw in the herb mixture and poured it over the fish.

Up to this moment Sophie believed that she had lost her appetite, but the delicious aroma was tempting. At Wentworth's insistence she sat down beside him and tasted a mouthful of the dish.

'You must pray that the Prince never visits you, ma'am,' he told her with a smile. 'Most certainly he would try to take your cook away.'

'You are very kind, sir. Bess will be delighted by that compliment. I must hope that your appetite is not flagging. You are to have ham braised in Madeira wine to follow.'

'Splendid!' Wentworth looked about him. 'Yet we are your only customers, Mistress Firle. Why is that? With food such as you provide I had thought that your tables would be filled each day.'

'We had been closed for several weeks,' Sophie told him briefly. Though Hatton had claimed to be his cousin, the young man did not appear to have been taken into his confidence. Was that claim yet another attempt to deceive her?

She could be sure of nothing, except that the very ground beneath her feet seemed to shift with every hour that passed.

Then Hatton entered the room, nodding an acknowledgement to the assembled company. As he took a vacant chair, Kit slid down from his high perch and climbed upon his knee.

The tiny gesture of affection was too much for Sophie. With a muttered excuse she rose to seek the sanctuary of the snug. Once there, she gazed out at the winter landscape with unseeing eyes, aware only of the anguish in her heart, and the ruin of all her hopes and dreams.

She and Nicholas could have been so happy, especially as Kit adored him so. Then his arms were round her, his cheek resting against her hair. She must have left the door ajar as she hadn't heard his quiet approach.

For one unguarded moment she melted into his embrace, enveloped in the animal magnetism that was so particularly his own. Then she stiffened and pulled away.

'My darling, won't you reconsider?' he pleaded. 'Say that you forgive me…'

Sophie turned to face him, aware that the agony in his eyes must match her own. 'There is nothing to forgive,' she told him quietly. 'We were mistaken in each other, that is all.'

'Will you throw away our happiness because of a few words spoken in haste?'

'I hope I should not be so foolish,' she said with dignity. Suddenly she felt very calm. 'Let me try to make you understand. I have had time to think, and I believe that events have overtaken us. We have been thrown together in unusual circumstances. Perhaps it is no wonder that we have fallen victim to illusion.'

'That isn't true!' he groaned.

'Isn't it? Have we not each seen in the other some ideal, to be found only in a world of fantasy? I don't know you, Nicholas. Everything has happened much too fast. Even now, I do not know your name.'

'There, at least, I did not lie to you,' he muttered. 'My given names are Crispin Nicholas. I am the Viscount Hatton.'

'I thank you for your honesty.' Sophie's face was grave. 'I can only wish you well, my lord.' She held out her hand. 'Let us not part in anger. I must thank you for many kindnesses.'

'I don't want your thanks!' he cried in desperation. 'Sophie, I want your love. Don't tell me that it is too late.' He reached out his arms to draw her to him, but she moved away.

'Must you make this so painful?' she whispered as she moved towards the door. Her words were a mistake. She knew it when he stayed her with a hand upon her arm. Then he looked deep into her eyes.

'Would it be painful if you didn't love me still?' he asked.

Gently she disengaged herself. 'I won't lie to you, my dear. I hadn't thought to know such pain, but I shall learn to live with it. We should never suit, you know.' With that she hurried back to the dining-room to join the others.

As they entered the room together, Wentworth's gaze flickered from one face to the other. Then, without comment, he addressed himself to his meal once more.

Hatton took Kit upon his knee. 'Will you do something for me?' he asked easily.

'Of course I will.' The child beamed up at him.

'Then find Reuben and the other men. Tell them I wish to see them on a matter of importance.'

He waited until Kit had skipped away. Then he rapped on the table for silence.

'We go tonight,' he said.

'You are sure this time?' Wentworth turned to face him.

'I think it certain that our quarry will wait no longer. These are careful men. The inn has been under close observation. It was unfortunate that Matthew rode out to fetch the doctor yesterday, but no harm was done. They didn't intend to move their cargo until they could be sure that Mistress Firle had not betrayed them.'

Wentworth glanced at Sophie with admiration in his eyes. 'I salute your courage, ma'am. You have played no small part in this.' He looked across at Hatton. 'Cousin, is there no alternative? Surely someone else could open the outer door tonight. Mistress Firle has done enough. Must we ask more of her?'

'The choice is hers.' Hatton kept his brooding gaze fixed firmly on the table. Duty demanded that he should insist upon her participation, but he could not ask her to put herself in danger once again, even though it meant that all his plans might fail.

Sophie made the decision for him. 'I shall open the door,' she announced. 'I am in no danger, Mr Wentworth. The leader of these men believes that I am his willing accomplice, motivated only by a greed for gold. He judges others by his own desires.'

Wentworth smiled at her. Then he turned back to Hatton. 'What of the girl?' he asked. 'I take it that Nancy has not been found?'

'Not yet. My greatest fear is that she will appear from hiding and take action on her own, but I have ordered certain measures. All the servants will keep watch indoors, especially on this floor. She won't be allowed to gain the doors.' His face was grim.

'Nicholas, you will not harm her?' Sophie asked in dismay.

'She must be restrained, ma'am.' He would go no further and Sophie was reduced to silence.

Looking round the table at the circle of eager faces, she was forced to admit that he'd been clever.

Now she understood the reason for the frequent visits of this party of apparently carefree young bucks. Hatton would use only men that he could trust, and who better than his own flesh and blood.

But there were so few of them, she thought in anguish—even with Reuben and his bruisers added to their number they would be less than a dozen. She thought again of the silent crowd of smugglers who had trooped into the inn on the day she had first met Harward. There must have been thirty or more and she had no doubt that they were well able to call upon others.

Hatton sensed her disquiet. 'Don't worry!' he soothed. 'We are not planning on a pitched battle. We intend to follow them to London. We believe they unload on this side of the river. Hopefully, their backers will be waiting for them.'

'There are not enough of you!' she cried. 'You cannot fight a mob of murderous ruffians!'

'We shall have support,' he comforted. 'At Southwark others will join us when we give the signal. It is all arranged.'

'Oh, you will take care?' she breathed.

It was Wentworth who took her hand. 'Believe me, ma'am, we all value our worthless hides,' he told her with a twinkle. 'We shall proceed with the utmost caution.'

A general shout of amusement greeted this remark, and Hatton felt obliged to explain it.

'My cousin is not noted for his caution,' he said gravely. 'On this occasion I am hoping that he will follow his instructions.'

Wentworth gave him a mock salute. 'Certainly, my lord! I shall follow them to the letter. Who am I to question the orders of my superior officer?'

The conversation deteriorated quickly into a bout of chaffing which threatened to develop into horse-play.

Sophie looked in wonder at the laughing party. Within hours these gay young men would be putting their very lives in danger. That prospect seemed to be the last thing on their minds.

She turned to Hatton. 'You are sure that Nancy is still within these walls?' she asked.

'She must be, Sophie. Most certainly she did not leave the inn last night. We should have seen her.'

'So you were watching too?'

'Naturally. We were hidden in the woods.'

'You were sure you were not seen?' she asked anxiously.

'I'm certain of it. Harward would not have planned to move the goods tonight if he's suspected a trap.'

'I wish it were all over,' she whispered. 'How I hate that tunnel! It is so dark and dank.'

Hatton took her hand in his. 'No one will blame you in the least if you feel that you can't go on,' he told her gently. 'We all admire your bravery.'

'Brave? I don't feel brave at all,' she admitted.

'Then, Sophie, you must not feel obliged—'

She stopped him with a look. 'I want to draw back, but I can't,' she told him. 'We've come too far to give up now. If I didn't open those doors tonight I could never forgive myself for my cowardice.'

The look in his eyes was reward enough for her. 'Then we must try to match your courage,' he told her very softly. 'Sophie, I still intend to try to win you. Will you give me leave to see you again?'

She was about to answer him when the hubbub in the room was stilled. All eyes rested upon the gentleman standing in the doorway. Dressed in the height of fashion, he presented a striking figure, though not in his first youth.

Sophie repressed an inward groan as she sank down in her chair. Even Hatton's massive figure could not hide her from the searching gaze which scanned the room. This was all she needed. Urged on, no doubt, by her own father, Sir William Curtis had come to call.

He came towards her at once, ignoring the assembled company.

'There you are, my dear!' he said in jovial tones. 'And quite as lovely as ever, if I may be permitted to say so.'

With hands outstretched he drew her to her feet and slipped a proprietorial arm about her waist. Then, with total disregard for her evident distaste, he kissed her full upon the lips.

Sophie was strongly tempted to box his ears. When she was under her father's protection he would not have dared to take such a liberty. Now, apparently, he regarded her as fair game. She was wise enough to school her expression into one of complaisance. At the first sign of her displeasure this unwelcome visitor would have found himself run through by one of the gentlemen who now looked their surprise at this unexpected turn of events.

Hatton looked like thunder.

'Sir William, allow me to make these gentlemen known to you,' she said hastily. His bow was perfunctory to the point of insolence until she came to Hatton.

'The Viscount Hatton, do you say?' Sir William pursed his lips. 'I had not heard that you were returned from the Peninsula, my lord—'

'How should you?' Hatton's reply was curt. 'We are not acquainted, sir. Nor are we like to be.'

It was a sharp set-down, and Sir William crimsoned. He seemed about to retort, but a strange glint in his lordship's eye warned him against it. Clearly, the gentleman was spoiling for a fight.

Sir William turned his back. The younger man was of an athletic build. Doubtless he was able to give a good account of himself in a bout of fisti-cuffs, and he himself had no desire for a bloody nose.

Then his eye fell upon Kit. The child had run his errand. Now he was standing close to Hatton.

'I told them, sir,' he whispered. 'They are waiting for you.'

'Sophie, is this your son?' Sir William asked. 'The boy is not unlike you.'

'Yes, this is Kit.'

'I see. Come here, my lad! Let's have a look at you!' He advanced towards the child, but Kit retreated behind Hatton.

'Disobedient? Hmm! The lad lacks discipline. Your father was right. He should be sent away to school—'

'He's only five!' Sophie exclaimed in anger. She might have said more, but Hatton forestalled her.

He bent down, picked up Kit and set the child upon his shoulder. Then, without a backward glance, he walked out of the room.

Sir William did not trouble to hide his rage. 'Upon my word!' he blustered. 'There would appear to be no limit to the insolence of some members of the *ton*. Strange company you keep, my dear! The man is a perfect lout!'

Sophie heard the scrape of a chair, and peering round Sir William's bulky figure she saw Wentworth advancing towards them with a pur-poseful tread. She caught his eye and shook her head. This was no time for a private fight. She caught at her companion's sleeve.

'We need to speak in private,' she insisted. 'Have you a message from my father?'

Sir William looked at the circle of hostile faces, and made no objection to being led away. Sophie took him into the snug and closed the door, though she was careful to keep her hand upon the latch.

'You wish to be private with me?' her companion leered. 'Let me tell you, Sophie, your father hopes that we shall make a match of it. Then he will be happy to receive you again.' He walked towards her with arms outstretched.

'Keep your distance, sir!' she cried. 'I have not the least wish to be private with you. If you must know it, I have just saved your skin. My friends do not care to see me offered insult.'

Curtis stared at her. 'Insult?' he echoed. 'How have I insulted you? I came to make you an offer.'

'You may keep your offer to yourself. You have just behaved as if you owned me. I have never offered you encouragement, even as a girl. In my father's house you would not have dared to take such liberties with my person, or to use my given name without permission.'

'Ah, but matters are different now, I think.' He gave her a crafty smile. 'You have no protector, unless, of course, you have allowed the estimable Viscount to bed you. He seems very much at home here.'

'If you think that, I wonder that you should consider offering for me,' Sophie gritted out the words. She was too angry to say more.

'I don't mind another man's leavings,' he informed her. 'In certain matters experience is of much value. Pray don't pretend that you cannot understand me. You are no longer an innocent girl.'

Sophie looked long and hard at him until his eyes fell before her own. The years had not been kind to her former suitor, and dissipation had taken its toll. He was now grossly fat, his bulk confirmed to some extent by stays. She could hear them creaking as he moved. She stared at the loose-lipped mouth and the little pig-like eyes. Even now they glittered with lust.

'I am sorry that you have come so far upon a fruitless errand,' she said at last. 'I should warn you, sir, that the roads about this place are not safe after dusk. You had best leave now.'

To her horror he advanced upon her once again. 'Still teasing me, my dear? It will be a pleasure to tame you.'

'Don't touch me!' Sophie made as if to open the door. 'Lay a hand on me and my friends will give you the thrashing of your life.'

He was forced to believe her then, and his face grew dark with rage. Bending towards her, he whispered such a stream of filth into her ear that she was nauseated. He left her in no doubt as to what he would like to do to her if the opportunity arose.

Her hand flew to her mouth. 'Vile!' she cried. 'How vile you are! You have always disgusted me. Now I know that I was right.'

She flung the door wide and ran to join the others.

Hatton had returned. When he saw her face, he tried to brush past her in pursuit of her tormentor.

'No!' she whispered. 'Let him go! He taints the air I breathe.'

'He won't come back?'

'No, he won't come back.'

Hatton's expression did not change. 'You are un-harmed, I hope?'

'Yes, my lord. He did not dare to press his suit much further.' In spite of her ordeal, Sophie's eyes began to twinkle. 'You were extremely rude to him, you know. I think your manner frightened him.'

'What a toad! I should have horsewhipped him.' He took her hand and kissed it. 'We must leave you now, my dear, but will you give me an answer?'

'To what?'

He looked at her in despair. 'Have you forgot so soon? When our friend arrived you were about to give me leave to return to you.'

'I can think of no way of stopping you from re-turning to this inn,' she said demurely. 'It is, after all, your own property.'

'And you?'

She would not answer him, but he gave a joyous laugh. Then, at his signal, the others left the room.

Hatton gathered Sophie to him. Slipping a finger beneath her chin, he raised her face to his. Then his mouth came down upon her own in a dizzying kiss which left her breathless.

'I shall return to claim you,' he promised. 'I won't take no for an answer.' Then he was gone, with a last injunction to follow his instructions to the letter, and to take no chances. 'I love you more than life,' he told her. 'Take great care, my dear. We shall be close by.'

Sophie glanced at the clock. It was already growing dark and in her mind's eye she could see that hateful tunnel beneath the inn. She sent for Matthew.

'Do you think we might light the staircase leading to the cellar, and possibly the wine cellar itself?' she asked.

He shook his head. 'The lights would be seen from the tunnel, ma'am. The doors ain't that good a fit.' His face was a picture of apprehension. 'Will this be the end of it tonight?' he asked. 'Me and Bess…well…we can't take much more of this.'

'It will be over very soon,' she soothed. 'Then, perhaps, you will change your mind about leaving me?'

He looked uncomfortable. 'It ain't our wish, ma'am, but we ain't keen to lose our lives.'

'I know, but I think that we may put our trust in Mr Hatton, don't you?'

He gave her a look of reluctant acquiescence. 'I'd best go,' he said. 'We ain't found Nancy yet.'

That was a worry which haunted Sophie in the hours that followed. Then, as the clock struck midnight, she made her way into the cellars. She'd be fine if she didn't think of what might lie beyond the outer door.

When at last she flung it open she sighed with relief. In the cellars and even in the tunnel she had sensed another presence close upon her heels. She'd swung round once or twice, holding her lantern high, but there was silence. She was being fanciful. Her nerves were playing tricks upon her.

Then Harward stepped into the circle of light.

'You don't need me now,' she told him hurriedly. 'I had best get back.'

He didn't answer her. He was looking beyond her, and something in his face alerted Sophie to danger. She swung round and gasped. Nancy stood behind her with her pistol trained upon the smuggler's head.

'Stand aside, Sophie,' the girl ordered. 'You are in my line of fire. This is the man who killed my husband. Now I'll send him to the fires of hell.'

Before she could utter a word of protest, Sophie was seized from behind. Using her as a shield, Harward drew his pistol and fired it in one swift movement, shooting Nancy through the heart. She fell without a sound.

Chapter Thirteen

Faint with horror, Sophie slumped against her captor, but Harward thrust her to one side, pinning her against the wall of the tunnel with an outstretched arm. Then he motioned his men forward.

'Get rid of that!' he ordered, pointing to the prone figure lying at his feet.

Sophie closed her eyes as two of the men seized Nancy's arms and dragged her away.

'What must we do with her?'

'There's a lake, I believe, or you might bury her, but be quick about it. We can't afford to waste much time.'

'The lake is frozen, mester, and the ground… well…it's too hard to dig—'

'For God's sake!' Harward cried impatiently. 'Must I do all your thinking for you? You'd best hide the body in the woods, then, and cover it with brushwood.'

'And this one?' The man gestured towards Sophie. 'You can't leave her here. She could get you hanged.'

'So she could!'

There was a long silence and Sophie closed her eyes as she waited for the shot which would end her life. She could think only of her son.

Now she prayed with all her heart that Hatton would take care of him.

Then Harward came to a decision. 'There's no hurry!' he announced. 'We'll take her with us. She may prove to be a useful bargaining counter if aught goes wrong.'

Sophie's entire body was shaking, but she found her voice at last.

'You…you said that we were partners…' Her voice was unrecognisable, even to her. 'Why must you treat me so?'

Harward took her arm and dragged her back along the tunnel until they reached the cellar. Making his way past the groups of men already at work upon the cargo, he drew her to one side.

'You must not take me for a fool, my dear.' His expression was almost kindly. 'You have been careless, Mistress Firle, and that I cannot tolerate. Your servant might have killed me.'

'She was sick. I told you of it yesterday. That was why we sent for Dr Hill. Then she disappeared. Believe me, we have tried to find her.'

'Apparently, with singular lack of success,' he drawled. 'Well, it is no matter, since the girl is dead…'

'There was no need to kill her,' Sophie whispered. 'You might have shot her in the arm—'

She heard a low laugh. 'Dear me! What a sentimentalist you are! Alas, it is as I feared! You have no stomach for this business.'

'At least I can use my head!' she cried. 'What have you gained by this…this murder?'

'Only a certain degree of satisfaction. I had not allowed for this unfortunate incident. Now it must change our plans, which does not please me.'

'I don't see why it need change anything,' she told him in despair.

'Don't you, Mistress Firle? You surprise me, since you have claimed to be able to use your head.'

Sophie looked at him. He was smiling, but the smile did not reach his eyes. They were as hard as sea-washed pebbles.

'Perhaps I should explain, since you seem unable to understand me. I no longer trust you, madam. Are you about to assure me that you will overlook this unfortunate occurrence? That you will find some reason for the disappearance of your servant? That our partnership will continue in an amicable fashion? I think not, my dear. I can see it in your face.'

'Won't you give me time to think about it? It has been a shock to me…' Sophie was playing for time, but even as she spoke she knew that her pleas were useless.

'Don't waste your breath!' Harward turned away. 'We cannot use this place again. Now you will go back with us. I suspect that we may have need of you. Every instinct tells me that here is something havey-cavey about this business.'

Sophie was close to breaking point. She caught at Harward's sleeve. 'I won't!' she shrieked. 'You shall not take me from my son.'

For answer he signalled to the nearest man, and Sophie shrank away. She knew the creature by the ugly weal which disfigured the left side of his face. This was the man who had attacked her and received a beating for his pains.

Sophie screamed aloud. Then a fist connected with the point of her jaw and she fell into darkness.

When she came round it was to find herself beneath a pile of packages. Her head was pounding, and her jaw was so painful that she thought it must be broken.

So much for Hatton's assurances, she thought bitterly. Surely he'd heard the shot which had killed Nancy? The sound must have carried clearly in the still night air. Then she recalled that the tunnel was deep underground. The earth must have muffled the gunfire.

But he and his men were keeping watch. He'd told her so himself. Perhaps they hadn't been close enough to see her being carried to this cart. One bundle would look much like another.

She shifted her position slightly in an effort to ease her aching limbs. Then she realised that her hands and feet had been securely bound. Harward was taking no chances. If she escaped, he must know that it would be all up with him.

She groaned as the cart rumbled over a patch of stony ground. Before their journey was over the violent shocks were likely to break every bone in her body. It could not matter now, she thought in despair. She was being taken to her death. Harward would never let her go, knowing that her testimony could convict him of murder.

The tears rolled down her cheeks as she thought of Kit. The child would have no one now.

'Hush up!' a gruff voice mumbled. 'I don't want to be told to knock you out again...'

'Why not, you pig?' She recognised the voice at once as that of the man with the scar across his face.

'I could have hit you harder, ma'am. And 'twas me as wrapped you in the blanket and settled you on these soft bundles.'

'Am I supposed to be grateful to you?'

'You might well be. I left your brooch in the cellar, so's they'd know as we'd taken you.'

Sophie was silent. She was thinking hard. The man sounded almost apologetic, but she didn't allow herself to hope. He was an unlikely ally.

'Why did you do that?' she asked at last.

'I owes you one. Yon Mester Harward would have blinded me, if you hadn't stopped him.'

'Will you release me?' she whispered.

'No, ma'am, I can't do that. He'd kill me for sure.'

'Then will you loosen my bonds? They are much too tight.'

'Aye! Give us your hands!' He hugged at the ropes which bound her.

Sophie repressed a cry of pain as her circulation was restored. 'And my feet?'

Again he loosened her bonds. 'Don't let on if he comes back,' he warned. 'There's many another as will be glad to take my place in the cart and you know what that could mean.'

Sophie shuddered. Harward might consider that rape was no more than suitable repayment for her failure at the inn.

Now she resolved to try to make a friend of her companion.

'Why do you stay with him?' she asked. 'You know that you risk imprisonment and transportation, and even, in the worst case, death?'

'Ain't got no choice, ma'am. There's no work for such as we. The fishing's gone, and mining too. My bairns had empty bellies…'

'You do this for your children?' Sophie warmed towards the man.

'Yes, ma'am.' He seemed to be struggling for words. 'That night…when I came at you…well, I'm sorry for it. I'd taken too much drink.'

'You have already made amends,' she told him. 'Do you know where we are going?'

'Lunnon, Mistress Firle. But I don't know where...I ain't been this way afore.'

'So this is your first run...your first attempt at smuggling goods?'

'Aye, and it's like to be my last. I hadn't reckoned on murder.'

'Poor Nancy!' Sophie's voice broke on a sob. 'It was a wicked thing to do.'

'Yes, ma'am.' Her companion did not argue.

'What is your name?' she asked.

'It's Walter, Mistress Firle, but they call me Wat.'

'Well then, Wat, how long will it be before we reach the city?'

'They wuz reckonin' on many hours, with maybe a stop or two along the way.'

'Will you stay by me?' Sophie was clutching at straws. Wat was her only hope of rescue.

'If I can. You'd best get some sleep.' It was clear that the conversation was at an end.

Sophie didn't argue further. The man had taken a fearful chance in leaving her brooch behind, and also in loosening her bonds, in spite of his fear of Harward. She must not antagonise him. Wat had given her one small glimmer of hope. Later she would speak to him again.

She burrowed deeper among the oiled silk bags. It was bitterly cold and the rising wind was merciless. It sought out every crack in the wooden sides of the wagon, but at least the packages gave her some protection.

Her head still ached, and her jaw was tender, but at least the shaking which had rocked the whole of her body had stopped. She tried to take deep breaths, willing herself to be calm.

As long as Harward thought she might be useful to him, she was in no immediate danger, but if Nicholas tried to rush the wagons in a bid to rescue her, Harward would despatch her out of hand. She was too dangerous a witness to be left alive to send him to the gallows.

She wondered if Nancy's body had been found. The pool of blood at the entrance to the tunnel was clear evidence that someone had been killed or injured.

Now she prayed that in his agony of mind her lover would do nothing foolish. She'd had no time to count the numbers of men within the cellar, but they could not be less than fifty. Others had awaited them outside, loading the wagons and holding the heads of the ponies.

With every mile that passed, others came to join them. She'd heard the whispered greetings and she marvelled at their disregard of danger. A band as large as this could not pass through the Sussex countryside unnoticed, even at night. Perhaps their strength was such that no one dared attack them.

She tried to comfort herself with the thought that Nicholas too was expecting reinforcements, but not until they reached the outskirts of the capital. That might be too late for her, especially if he lost their trail.

She didn't know London well, and she had no wish to know it better. On her rare visits she'd been appalled by the stench of refuse mixed with the horse droppings which littered the streets. She and her mother had carried pomanders, but even at the time she'd wondered if those small bags of aromatic herbs were of much use as a guard against infection.

Then there was the noise. How her ears had rung with the clanging bells of the muffin-men and the pie-sellers and the shouts of the beggars who pressed in upon their carriage.

She tried to remember if they'd passed through Southwark. She knew that it was south of the river and that it was an insalubrious area. Her mother had pulled down the leather curtains to shield her from the gaze of the blowsy strumpets who called from every window. It had seemed to Sophie to be a warren of narrow streets and alleyways.

Here, she guessed, the band of smugglers might break up, making their way to their destination in small groups, so as not to attract attention. Other than the Bow Street Runners, there was no organised force of men to halt them, but the authorities in the city could call upon the Militia or the Dragoons. Harward would know this well enough, and he would take no chances.

Then a thought occurred to her. Suppose her enemy had decided to use decoys? Some of the wagons might not carry contraband. How would Nicholas know which ones to follow?

If only she could think of a way to help him. Careful to make no sound, she began to tear at the lace upon her petticoat. She might be able to thrust a part of it through one of the gaps in the sides of the wagon. It would flutter in the wind.

She had got no further with this plan when the vehicles drew to a halt. Then she heard Harward's voice. He was speaking to one of his companions.

'I'd best check on her,' he announced. 'If I'm not mistaken, our little Mistress Firle has a quick mind. She may be plotting mischief at this moment.'

'What can she do?' a deep voice growled. 'She's bound tight, but if you like I'll take Wat's place to keep an eye on her.'

Sophie heard a low laugh of amusement. 'That won't be necessary,' Harward said. 'I chose my man with care. Wat, above anyone, has no love for her.'

'Don't stir!' the man beside her warned. 'Pretend to be asleep.'

Sophie was happy to obey him. She froze as the covering of the wagon was drawn back, and a light illuminated the interior.

Harward studied her prone figure for what seemed an eternity.

'You must have hit her harder than I thought,' he said with satisfaction. 'Well done, Wat! Don't take any chances with her. She caused you a severe beating.'

The covering was drawn back, and Sophie was plunged into darkness once more.

'Aye!' the man beside her muttered beneath his breath. 'But she ain't the one who gave me a scar I'll carry till I die.'

Sophie waited until the wagons began to roll once more. Then she spoke to her companion. 'Thank you!' she said quietly.

His only reply was a grunt.

'How many children do you have, Wat?' she asked. 'Won't you tell me their names?'

'What do you want to know for?' He sounded surly, but she guessed correctly that any encounter with Harward terrified him.

'I thought it would pass the time if we spoke of them. I have a young son of my own.'

'I seen 'im,' he offered. 'Bright little lad he is, an' all. You should never 'ave taken up wi' Mester Harward, ma'am. Didn't you know the danger?'

'I had no choice,' she told him. 'He isn't the easiest person to refuse.'

'That's true!' he said with feeling. 'Well, what's done is done. There's no use crying over spilt milk.'

'You were going to tell me about your children.'

The man's voice softened. 'There's Em'ly, and my little Amy. My lad is the youngest. 'E's just a babe.'

Sophie couldn't hide her dismay. 'Oh, Wat, you asked why I had put myself in danger. What of you?'

'I told you, ma'am. Did you ever 'ear your child crying wi' 'unger? I couldn't stand it no more…'

'But, Wat, suppose that you were taken? What would happen to them then?'

'They'd starve!' came the grim reply. 'Don't worry, I won't be taken…'

A silence fell between them.

Then, greatly daring, Sophie spoke again. 'There may be another way,' she said cautiously. 'If you were to help me, I could speak out for you. I have powerful friends.'

'They wouldn't be no use to a dead man. I can't do it, ma'am. You wouldn't get six paces afore 'e shot you down, an' me as well.'

'He's going to kill me, anyway. You know that, don't you?'

'Don't talk like that,' he muttered. 'You be useful to 'im, Mistress Firle.'

'For how long?'

When he did not reply, she turned away and closed her eyes. Now that it seemed that her last hope was gone, she tried to help herself. She tore at the lace again, and the stitches gave at last, leaving a length of the fabric in her hand. Now she was in a quandary. Did she dare to use it?

Men were trudging along beside the wagon. She could hear their muttered conversation. A single glimpse of her signal would be enough to bring Harward back. He was on edge already. She'd heard it in his voice, beneath the smooth attempt at a confident tone. He'd realise at once that someone must be following. For all she knew he might halt to arrange an ambush. Either way, it would be the end for both herself and Wat.

She must think of something, but her brain refused to function. All she could see in her mind's eye was the image of Nicholas, with Kit upon his knee, laughing and secure in their mutual affection.

What a fool she'd been. Nicholas loved her truly. In her heart she'd known it all along. Why, then, had she sent him away with some trumped-up charge of an insult to her character? She knew the answer. It was cowardice. After her experience with Richard, she'd been unwilling to trust any man. Her heart had pulled her one way, and her head another.

A sob escaped her lips. She'd seized upon the first excuse to avoid another commitment. Now her darling would never know the depth of her regret. She'd left him without a word of love, and it was too late now to make amends.

'Now, ma'am, don't 'ee take on.' Wat's tone was kindly. 'I ain't said that I won't 'elp 'ee, if I can see my way to it.'

'You've just told me that I can't escape,' she told him in despair.

'Not 'ere, ma'am, and not at this particular minute, but there's a ways to go. They'll be that busy when we reaches Lunnon… Maybe we'll see a chance…'

Sophie reached out for his hand. 'I won't forget your kindness, whatever happens, Wat.'

'T'weren't nothing, ma'am. As I told you, I don't 'old wi' murder.'

The next few hours seemed endless, but as they reached the outskirts of the capital the roads were better. Soon they were rattling over cobblestones, and Sophie knew that they must be near their destination.

'Now don't you go a-doin' nothin' stupid,' her companion warned. 'Leave it to me to take a look about.'

Sophie was aware that they had slowed down almost to a crawl, and there was something else. The wind had died away and the noise from the street seemed to be curiously muffled.

She raised herself a little and tried to move her limbs. Stiff from many hours of lying bound in the bottom of the wagon, she could scarcely move. How long had their journey taken? Surely it must be daylight?

'Where are we?' she whispered. 'Can you see anything?'

Her companion seemed to be enveloped in a haze of yellow mist. Now he loosened the covering at the rear of the wagon and peered out. She heard a muttered exclamation.

'Danged if I can see a thing. In this fog you couldn't find your hand in front of your face.'

Hope flared high in Sophie's breast. 'This may be our chance,' she urged. 'Come with me, Wat! We could slip away without being seen. I'll make sure that you don't suffer for your part in this.'

'Where would we go, ma'am? I ain't been 'ere afore, but I 'eard tell that the streets ain't safe, especially in these fogs. We'd be knocked on the 'ead and robbed for sure.'

Sophie coughed as the acrid vapour caught at her throat. Her eyes were streaming, and she found it difficult to breathe, but still she tried to persuade him.

'That may be better than what may lie ahead of us. Harward cannot allow me to live. You know that as well as I do myself, but won't you think of what may happen to you?'

Wat didn't answer her.

'Suppose the Runners are waiting for you?' she continued. 'There's always the danger of a trap.'

'Mester Harward will see 'em off. There's too many of us for they Redbreasts.'

'But not too many to fight off a company of Militia, or a troop of Dragoons. Do you want to sit in the dock at Newgate, with your coffin in front of you, listening to a person preaching a last sermon, before they take you out and hang you?'

She heard a sharp intake of breath, but Wat had hesitated just too long. Fog billowed into the wagon as Harward raised the covering at the back.

'Awake, my dear?' he enquired. 'I thought I heard you coughing. This fog is so unpleasant, is it not, but it is quite a feature of the London scene. I confess that I enjoy my trips into the country.'

'I'm sure you do,' she told him bitterly. 'They must show a handsome profit.'

'Oh, they do, my dear! They do! Bear up, Mistress Firle. We are almost at our destination. We shall have you safe indoors before too long.'

Sophie was silent, but despair engulfed her. If Wat had acted quickly they might have escaped into the fog. She'd welcomed it at first, but now it was her enemy. Even if her rescuers were close at hand they would find it almost impossible to follow the different groups of smugglers as they made their way towards the river.

They were now close to the Thames. Sophie could hear the hollow boom of the warnings from the mass of shipping which thronged the busy waterway.

She guessed that they were making for one of the warehouses which lined the river banks. Then the wagon stopped. At some prearranged signal great doors swung open upon their hinges and they moved inside, out of the all-pervasive choking mist.

The thud of the closing doors sounded to Sophie like a death knell, but she was given no time to think. Rough hands reached out for her and dragged her from the wagon. Then Harward produced a wicked-looking knife and sliced through the ropes which bound her feet. She held out her hands, but he shook his head.

'Not yet, I think! Now come with me!'

As he took her arm she tried to move, but her legs would not support her. She heard an exclamation of impatience, and then she was flung over the shoulder of one of his companions.

At the head of a flight of steps, Harward led the way into a well-furnished room. Sophie was surprised. It might have been the setting for a business meeting. Then she realised that that was exactly what it was.

Half a dozen men were seated around a long mahogany table. As she was thrust into a chair, they looked up in astonishment.

'What's this then, Harward?' one of the men enquired. 'Have you taken leave of your senses?'

'No, sir! I have an excellent reason for bringing this woman here…'

For the first time in their acquaintance, Sophie detected a note of deference in his voice and she looked at his questioner with interest. This was clearly a man of substance, as were his companions.

'Well, man, out with it! What has gone wrong now?'

'A minor incident, my lord. Unfortunate, but necessary. The lady was a witness.'

'Another killing! Will you never learn? The last one caused a serious delay in realising our profits, or had that escaped your notice?'

Harward flushed. 'We had no choice. None of you gentlemen would care to be the victim of a blackmailer, I fancy.'

He had courage in speaking as he did, as Sophie quickly realised. The men around the table were unaccustomed to being threatened. Their expressions were murderous.

Then one of the others spoke. 'We don't quarrel with your methods, Harward, but we do object to inefficiency. If aught else goes wrong we may have to look elsewhere for co-operation...'

Harward had regained his composure. Now he bowed. 'You will not find it necessary, my dear sir. The goods have been retrieved and it is a large consignment. Shall we get down to business?' He moved to take a seat at the table, but one of his companions stayed him with an upraised hand.

'What of the woman?' he demanded.

'Why, sir, she presents no problem. You need not fear that she will speak.'

Sophie lifted her head and looked at them, but none of the men would meet her eyes. They knew Harward's intention as well as she did herself.

'I don't like it!' One face at least was twisted in distaste. 'Is there no other way?'

'We could let her go, of course.' Harward glanced at Sophie and she shuddered. He looked like some predatory animal, tensing for the kill. 'But remember, gentlemen, she has seen you, and the lady is no fool. Given the opportunity, she will be happy to destroy you.'

'This girl?' The speaker sounded incredulous. 'Offer her money, man! That should silence her!'

Harward took his time, anxious that his next words should carry maximum effect.

'This, gentlemen, is Mistress Richard Firle!' he said.

For Sophie, the silence which followed this statement could only be interpreted as a death sentence. Each of them had been party to the killing of her husband, if not in fact, certainly in their acquiescence. Her fate was sealed.

'Why bring her here?' one of the men enquired. 'You are not infallible, Harward, as we know to our cost. If she should chance to escape, all our lives are forfeit.'

'I think not!' Harward looked at her as a cat might look at an injured mouse. He was toying with her before the kill. 'I believe that she will serve another purpose.'

'We've had enough of your mysteries, man!' an irritated voice announced. 'As for myself, I have no time to waste. We've struggled here through the worst of the weather. Forget the woman! She has naught to do with us.'

'On the contrary, sir, you may find that her presence here will prove to be invaluable. We may not have long to wait...' With great deliberation he drew out his pistol and laid it on the table.

Sophie closed her eyes. Was he planning to murder her here, in front of his companions? She wouldn't put it past him. It would implicate them all—a useful consideration for a man like Harward.

'Spare us the melodrama!' the previous speaker snapped. 'Save your posturings for those who will appreciate them. We have no need of weapons here, though I don't doubt that you flourish them among your men. Kindly remember where you are!'

Harward reddened at the contemptuous tone. It goaded him into a sharp reply. 'Does the thought of violence trouble you, my lord? Perhaps you should consider more carefully exactly what is involved in these operations which bring you so much profit. My hands may be dirty, but your own are none too clean.'

Sophie heard the scrape of a chair, and she opened a cautious eye. One of the men was on his feet, his face a mask of anger.

'Damn your insolence, you dog! You will keep a civil tongue in the presence of your betters. Have you forgotten who I am?'

'No, I have not forgotten you...any of you...' Harward's gaze rested on each man in turn. 'My betters, you say? Tell me, who is more at fault—the man who kills when necessary, or the traitor whose gold has brought about the deaths of many thousands of his own countrymen?'

There was an ominous silence, but Sophie could sense the tension in the still figures of the men who sat around the table. An explosion of some kind seemed imminent, and as she watched, Harward laid a careless hand upon his pistol.

'I suggest that you mind your own manners, gentlemen,' he continued. 'Let me assure you that we sink or swim together.'

A murmur of rage greeted his words. It was left to one of the older men to save the situation.

'Gentlemen! Gentlemen!' he pleaded. 'Where is the sense in quarrelling among ourselves? We are wasting time. Now let us forget our differences. Perhaps our friend here will give us an account of the profits we have made. It was the usual fifty per cent, I hope.'

Harward thrust the pistol into his capacious pocket. Then he bowed, and when he spoke it was in a more agreeable tone. He'd made his point. He had them in his power and they knew it. He was tempted to inform them that those who ride the wind must reap the whirlwind, but he thought better of it. If ever he decided to give up the dangerous occupation of free trading, each of these men would provide him with a handsome income for the rest of his life. They had delivered themselves into his hands. The late Richard Firle was not the only one who had considered the possibilities of blackmail.

He drew out a chair and sat down at the table. 'We have taken the usual profits,' he informed them. 'As always, they are returned to you in the form of goods.'

'Most satisfactory!' The peacemaker beamed his approval. 'We should be able to increase that profit by half as much again if we choose our markets carefully.' He nodded at Harward. 'Will you give me a hand, sir?'

He reached beneath the table and, with Harward's help, lifted up a strongbox. As he raised the lid, Sophie stared, wide-eyed. The box was filled with golden guineas.

'This is the next consignment,' the older man announced. 'Let us hope that in future we meet with no further difficulties such as those we experienced on this last occasion.' He lifted out a small leather sack and pushed it across the table. 'Perhaps you would care to count your share, Mr Harward?' he suggested.

'Not at all, my dear sir! I trust you implicitly.' Harward's tone was ironic as he laid his hand upon the sack. Then, quite suddenly, he motioned the others to silence and jerked his head towards the door.

Sophie's heart was pounding as she followed the direction of his gaze. Then she cried out as Hatton stepped into the room.

'Welcome, my lord!' Harward murmured smoothly. 'We have been expecting you. Gentlemen, pray allow me to introduce our visitor! The Viscount Hatton is the son of the Earl of Brandon.'

The panic on the faces of his companions was unmistakable, but Harward appeared to be enjoying the situation. 'How right I was!' he observed. 'I was persuaded that the presence of the lady must bring you to us.'

Hatton did not answer him, though he kept his enemy firmly in his sights as he moved to Sophie's side. His pistol did not waver.

'Can you stand?' he asked her briefly.

Sophie could hear the emotion in his voice. She knew then that he had not expected to find her still alive.

She nodded, too overcome to speak. Mutely, she held out her bound hands.

'My apologies, Mistress Firle!' Harward rose and walked towards her. 'An oversight on my part! Pray allow me to release you.' Something flickered behind his eyes, and Sophie saw it.

'Take care!' she cried. 'He has a gun!'

Her warning came too late. Harward had moved with cat-like speed. His pistol was already in his hand as he reached her side. Then the cold metal of the barrel was pressed against her temple.

'Drop your gun, my lord!' he advised. 'If you have any doubts that I will shoot, the lady will confirm it, won't you, my dear?' He wound his free hand into her hair, dragging back her head. 'Tell him!' he ordered savagely.

'He killed Nancy,' she whispered. 'I saw him do it.'

'I don't doubt it!' Hatton's tone was cool. 'Don't compound your crime, sir. You can't escape. Your men are already taken.'

Harward did not trouble to hide his amusement. 'Do you tell me that your little band has overcome a hundred men?'

'Not at all! We had the help of a company of Militia, the Dragoons and a number of the Bow Street Runners.'

'You lie, damn you!' Harward snarled.

'If you don't believe me, why not call for help?'

Sophie saw the uncertainty on her captor's face. 'Stand up!' he ordered. With the pistol still pressed firmly to her head, Harward dragged her to the doorway. Then he called down the stairs. No one answered him.

Then there was a movement around the table.

'This criminal is unknown to us, my lord,' one of the men observed. 'He broke in here and tried to hold us up.'

Hatton smiled at the speaker. 'He disturbed your business meeting?'

There was a quick chorus of agreement. 'We have no connection with him,' another speaker said. 'Whatever he may tell you, he has not the slightest shred of proof.'

Hatton shook his head. 'You disappoint me, gentlemen. I fear you are a band of innocents. When we search this room, as we intend to do, the evidence will be found. You have underestimated your accomplice. If I am not much mistaken, his records will be sure to implicate you. He is not the man to miss an opportunity.'

Sophie heard an ugly laugh. 'You have the matter to rights, sir. Allow me to direct your attention to the desk in the far corner of this room. There you will find the evidence you need.'

He dragged Sophie away from the door. Then, as all eyes turned in the direction of his pointing finger, he opened a massive cupboard just behind him. He pulled her inside and turned the key in the lock.

Chapter Fourteen

Sophie screamed aloud, but he struck her sharply across the mouth.

'Be quiet, or it will be the worse for you!' He reached above his head for a tinder box and lit a lantern, ignoring the pounding on the other side of the door.

Well aware that Hatton would not fire for fear of hitting Sophie, her captor showed no sign of undue haste. He lifted the lantern high to illuminate a steep flight of steps.

'Down here!' he ordered.

'I can't! I'll fall! Please let me go! Won't you leave me here? I can only delay you—'

'You could also save my life. Hold out your hands!' He seized the end of the rope which bound her and untied it. 'Down you go, and be quick about it. Hold on to the rail! If you fall you are likely to break your neck.'

He pushed her ahead of him down the wooden staircase.

Terrified though she was, Sophie was trying to think of some way of escape. If he'd gone first she might have pushed him down herself. She might even have managed to unlock the door for her rescuers before he recovered enough to fire, but he'd been aware of that. He'd thrown the key far into the darkness.

Fearfully, she continued to descend the stairs, unsure of her footing. They must be very near the river. She could smell the stench and she recalled that the Thames had been described to her as an open sewer running through the heart of London.

It was very quiet. She paused and listened, but the pounding from above her had stopped. Nicholas must be trying to find some other way of reaching her, but he would be too late. She and her captor had reached a long passageway with a door at the far end.

Harward unlocked it and pushed her through. They seemed to be standing on some kind of jetty.

Sophie was seized with a feeling of despair. Who could find her here? The fog which billowed all around her was thicker than ever. It hung like some evil miasma over the swirling waters of the river.

She had no cloak and she was shivering uncontrollably in that all-enveloping vapour. The acrid mist was choking her and her eyes were streaming.

Her companion looked about him with every sign of satisfaction. 'My luck holds!' he announced. 'I couldn't have wished for better than this. We shall not be followed.'

He raised the lantern above his head and whistled low. Then she understood.

This man was a survivor. He left nothing to chance. He would escape by water—a plan which must have been always in his mind if anything should go wrong. And he would leave no witness to his villainy.

She looked about her wildly, but there was no chance of escape. If she ran he would fire before she could disappear into the fog. She looked down at the swirling waters. Could she jump?

Harward read her mind with ease. 'I don't advise it,' he said almost kindly. 'In the unlikely event that you were rescued, you would not survive. That water is a flowing stream of poison. Look!' He gestured towards the bank and a floating mass of jetsam caught beneath the jetty.

Sophie's hand flew to her mouth. The bloated carcasses of animals bobbed about below her. Worse, a human hand was pointing skywards from a shapeless bundle of clothing. The sight of the corpse destroyed the last remnants of her self-control.

'Let me go!' she pleaded pitifully. 'You can have no further need of me—'

'Patience, my dear! Let us not be too hasty. Must you rush upon your death?'

'So you do intend to kill me?'

'Naturally! What else can I do? I take it that you have no wish to share my future life? Your passion for the estimable Viscount would rule that out, I think.' He was peering into the mist, and for the first time she detected a slight note of impatience. He whistled again, and this time it was piercing.

Sophie knew that she must keep him talking. 'When did you first suspect him?' she asked quietly.

'I never trusted the gentleman, my dear, even before I knew his true identity. He seemed to me to have the habit of command. Even allowing for your undoubted charms, I felt it unlikely that such a man would spend his time at an isolated country inn unless he had some other purpose.'

'You said that you trusted me.'

'Ah, yes, but I could not be sure, even of you. I did not know of your feelings then, my dear. I doubt if you knew of them yourself.'

Sophie did not answer him.

'It is all so unfortunate.' He sighed. 'I offered you great wealth. It didn't take me long to realise that it was not enough. So typical of a woman!'

'You don't think highly of our sex?' she challenged.

'No, Mistress Firle, I don't. Women are a mystery to me. They are capricious, governed by emotion, and often oblivious to danger where their loved ones are concerned.'

'I take that as a compliment,' she snapped.

'It is not intended as such. Great heavens, woman, did you think me blind? Your face gave you away when I was forced to shoot your unfortunate friend. I knew then that you would not forgive me.'

'Do you blame me?'

'No! I had expected as much...' He paused and peered into the mist. 'Ah!' he exclaimed. 'Here comes our salvation!' He waved the lantern as a skiff appeared beside the jetty.

Sophie closed her eyes. Would he shoot her on the spot, or was she to be knocked on the head and consigned to the murky waters of the river?

Harward appeared to hesitate. Then, evidently fearing that a shot might be heard, he motioned her forward.

Sophie could do no other than obey him. There were only two oarsmen in the skiff, and one of them, she saw to her surprise, was Wat. So he had betrayed her at the last, in an effort to save his skin.

'Well done, Wat!' her companion called. 'You shall have the pleasure of seeing to the lady.'

Sophie's eyes were upon the other figure in the boat. Could she be mistaken? The man was hooded, muffled to the ears, perhaps against the fog, but beneath his coat she saw the glint of metal.

Slowly, she began to climb down the rungs of the ladder which rested above the little craft. Firm hands caught her and sat her in the bow.

Harward had dropped his guard. Sure of his companions, he turned his back on them as he came down the ladder.

'Stay where you are!' Wat's companion threw back his hood and Sophie gave a cry.

With his pistol aimed steadily at Harward's heart, Nicholas drew her to him. 'It's over!' he told her quietly. 'They are taken to a man!'

'No! Don't give me over to the law!' Harward was pleading for his life. 'I meant no harm to Mistress Firle. I would have released her.'

'That isn't true!' Sophie told him coldly. 'You told me not an hour ago that you would kill me.'

'I didn't mean it! I was trying to frighten you! I will testify, my lord. You shall have your men.'

'I have them already. You, above anyone, will not escape your fate. You will hang for murder, sir.'

'No!' With lightning speed, Harward slipped a small pistol from his sleeve, but he was given no time to aim the weapon. Nicholas fired, and the shot took him in the shoulder. With a despairing cry, he lost his footing, and tumbled overboard. The water closed above his head, and he was gone.

Sophie gasped in horror. Then, sobbing with relief, she threw herself into Hatton's arms.

'I thought you'd never come!' she cried. 'Is it really over?'

'It is, my darling.' Too overcome with emotion to say more, Hatton enveloped her in the warm folds of his cloak. Then, holding her against his heart, he signalled to Wat, and the skiff drew away from the jetty.

Within minutes they were ashore, to be welcomed by a cheering crowd, and there was Wentworth, smiling as he came towards them.

'Ma'am, you must give up my cousin,' he advised. 'He is much too fond of drama. He has a positive passion for a last-minute rescue! My nerves will not stand it!'

'Nor will mine!' Hatton told him grimly. Picking up Sophie in his arms as if she weighed no more than a leaf, he shouldered his way through the crowd to the waiting carriage.

'My father is here?' he asked.

'At the town house, together with my parents, and my uncle Perry. You have quite a reception awaiting you.' Wentworth swung himself up beside the driver and gave the man the office.

Sophie threw both her arms around her lover's neck. 'I thought I'd never see you again,' she whispered. 'Oh, my love, I've had such bitter thoughts. I sent you away without a word of love, and you might never have known how much I regretted it.'

He kissed her then, with such tenderness that all her doubts were banished.

'I don't deserve you,' he said very quietly. 'You speak of regrets, my dear one. I can't begin to tell you how I felt when we found Nancy's body. I was so sure that you...that you...' He could not go on.

'You didn't hear the shot?'

'No, but remember that you were well inside the tunnel. The walls must have deadened the sound. Had we heard it we should not have waited.'

'They were too many for you at the time. You did well to wait until we reached this place.'

'Did we? I went through the tortures of the damned wondering what had happened to you.'

'You did not find my brooch?'

'We did. That was when we suspected that they might have taken you hostage. It was the first small glimmer of hope, but I'll never forgive myself for exposing you to so much danger.'

'Don't blame yourself, my love.' Sophie pressed her lips into the hollow of his neck. 'Your plan would have worked except for Nancy. We could not have known that she would reappear at just that moment.'

'She too weighs heavily upon my conscience, Sophie. I should have listened to you. You sensed from the first that something was amiss.'

'But, Nicholas, we had no idea that her mind had given way completely. Poor Nancy! I shall always wonder if she might have been restored to health.'

'I doubt it, my love. Matthew almost caught her. She'd been hiding within the panelling of the walls. Unfortunately, he turned his back on her and she felled him with the butt end of his pistol.'

Sophie nestled in the shelter of his arms. 'What will happen now?' she asked. 'Those men around the table? Were they the ones you wanted?'

'Some of them. We have the names of others, many of them in high places. Harward kept the most detailed records of all his transactions. I suspect that he was planning blackmail as an easier way to riches than the smuggling trade.'

'I'm glad you've caught them. They have much to answer for, especially Harward…'

'The others are just as guilty. This was a dirty business and they knew it. They may have turned a blind eye to his methods, but in the search for profits they condoned them, if only by doing so.' Hatton took her hands in his and kissed each of them in turn. 'It is thanks to your bravery that we caught them.'

'I didn't feel very brave,' she told him with a shaky laugh. 'I was terrified. Oh, my love, I could think only of you and Kit. When it seemed as if…as if it was the end for me, I prayed that you would care for him.'

'How could you doubt it! Even when we have children of our own, Kit will always have his own special place in our hearts.'

Sophie looked up at him. 'May we go back to the inn today?' she pleaded. 'I long to see him. We have not been separated for so long before.'

'You will see him sooner than you think. I left orders for Reuben to bring him up to London. My family wishes to meet both of you.'

Sophie did not answer him.

'What is it, my love?' he asked. 'They are sure to love you as I do.'

'I hope so, but…well…'

'Well, what?'

'Oh, Nicholas, just look at me!'

'That is no hardship. I can't take my eyes off you.'

'No, be sensible! What will they think of me? My gown is torn and crumpled and I am…well… unwashed…'

Hatton shook his head. 'Women never cease to astonish me,' he answered solemnly. 'Not an hour ago you were in the most appalling danger. Now your *toilette* is uppermost in your mind. Must we shop in Bond Street? I know of an excellent mantua-maker…'

She heard the laughter in his voice. 'Now you are making may-game of me,' she reproached. 'I cannot think that your relatives will welcome someone as grubby and unkempt as I feel at this moment.'

'You are beautiful, my darling!' Hatton lifted her face to his and kissed her tenderly. 'A lifetime won't be long enough for me to convince you of it.'

Sophie sighed with content. 'I can't believe that we have our lives ahead of us, especially as we came so close to losing them. Now I feel that every day will have a special meaning for us. I'd given up hope, you know, when I was standing on the jetty…'

Hatton shuddered. 'I should have spared you so much suffering. If only we had realised...if we'd seen them putting you into the wagon...but there was so much confusion as they loaded the cargo, with men and ponies milling about. They took good care to hide you.'

'I knew nothing of it at the time,' she confessed. 'I must have been unconscious for some time after Wat was told to hit me.'

'Wat hit you?' Hatton stiffened. 'I'll make it my business to settle accounts with him.'

'Oh, no, please don't! He tried to help me. It was he who left the brooch for you to find, and he loosened my bonds as best he could. He planned to help me get away. It was only when I saw him in the skiff that I thought he had betrayed me.'

'I don't understand the man.' Hatton frowned. 'We feared to lose the wagons in the fog, and we didn't know which of them to follow. Some were decoys, as I'm sure you guessed. Then we saw a length of lace trailing from one of them. I thought you might have tried to signal to us.'

'I intended to, but Harward watched so carefully that I dared not risk it. Wat must have seized his opportunity, but he took a dreadful chance.'

'Why did he try to help you? There can be no doubt that he was one of Harward's band.'

'Wat is a fisherman, my dear. He was forced into smuggling as the only way to feed his children, but he didn't hold with murder.'

'He could have slipped away and left you to your fate.'

'He felt he owed me his life. Didn't you see the scar upon his face? At the very least, Harward might have blinded him. I couldn't bear to watch that beating. I made Harward stop.'

'I see.' Hatton grew thoughtful. 'Then that explains his actions when we entered the warehouse. He called a warning to us, and told me where you were. When we entered that room I thought that you were safe. I should have been prepared for trickery.'

'Harward was clever,' Sophie mused. 'Who could have guessed that such an innocent-looking cupboard was his escape route? He must have prepared it months ago. I was so frightened, Nicholas, I thought that you would never find me by the river.'

Hatton held her close. 'We might never have done so had it not been for Wat. Harward trusted him, believing that he, above any of the others, had good reason to hate you. He told us of the skiff. It was the simplest of matters to take the place of the second man.'

Sophie cupped his face in her hands and kissed him again and again. 'Let us not speak of it again,' she whispered. 'But, my darling, what will happen to Wat? We owe him so much. He risked his life for me, you know. I could not bear to think of him transported…or worse…'

'Nor could I, my love. It will not happen. Wat's bravery will be recognised.' Hatton looked at his betrothed and smiled. 'His future is in your hands. Shall you care to employ him in some way? There are cottages enough on my estate, quite large enough for Wat and his family.'

Sophie kissed him again. 'Then I may offer him a living? Nothing would please me more…'

'I'm hoping that a great many things will please you more!' Hatton kissed her ear as the carriage drew to a halt.

She was still blushing as he led her up the steps of the family townhouse in Brook Street. Any anxieties she might have had were quite forgotten as a small figure rushed towards her and threw himself into her arms.

'Mama! Mama! Reuben has been teaching me how to tool along, and take corners to an inch!'

'Has he, my darling?' Sophie clutched her son. 'How are you, Kit? Were you well wrapped up?' It was an inadequate greeting, but she was very close to tears, remembering how she had feared never to see her son again.

'Of course!' Kit dismissed the enquiry with some impatience. 'Mama, you are squashing me again!'

Sophie relinquished her hold on the child and rose to her feet as a slender woman walked towards her.

'Mistress Firle, I am Prudence Wentworth. You must be very tired. Won't you allow me to show you to your room? You may care to rest before you meet the family.'

Sophie gave her a grateful look. 'I thank you, ma'am. I am more in need of hot water than a rest, I believe. You must excuse my appearance…'

Prudence laughed. 'My dear, you may believe that the men of this family care much more for spirit than for the niceties of an elegant *toilette*. Even so, a change of clothing will not present a problem. You and I are much of a height, I think.'

She led Sophie up the curving staircase and into a well-appointed chamber. A maid was already in attendance, presiding over a steaming bath which stood before the fire.

A number of gowns were laid across the bed, and Prudence eyed them critically.

'I hope you will find something to your liking, Sophie. I may call you Sophie, may I not? My sons have spoken of you so warmly that I feel I know you already.'

'Mr Wentworth is your son, ma'am?'

'Thomas is the eldest of my boys. All three of them have the highest admiration for you.'

'You are very kind.'

'No! It is no more than the truth. But your bath is getting cold. Is Bess to help you, or do you prefer your privacy?'

'I shall manage without help, ma'am, I thank you.'

Prudence motioned to the girl to leave them. 'Good!' she said. 'I have long suspected that we ladies are not nearly as helpless as our maids would have us believe. Perhaps if I were to unfasten you at the back…?'

Sophie turned obediently, but Prudence was not done. 'Do please call me by my given name,' she pleaded. 'It may not describe me very well—in fact, it has amused my husband famously ever since we met. He feels that Prudence is hardly my outstanding trait of character. I threatened to change it, but he would not hear of it.'

Sophie saw the twinkle in the eyes which met her own, and she warmed to this warm-hearted woman who was still so lovely, although, with three grown sons, she must be in her middle years.

'Call me if you need me, Sophie. I shall be in the dressing-room next door, looking out some under-things for you.'

She was as good as her word, leaving Sophie to revel in the luxury of slipping into the scented water. The warmth was soothing, but she had no desire to rest. She bathed quickly and was drying herself by the fire when Prudence returned at her call.

'I'll leave you now…' her companion laid a pile of snowy underclothes upon the bed '…choose whatever you wish, my dear. Claudine assures me that any of these gowns will fit you.'

'Madame Arouet is here?' Sophie was beginning to feel nervous. As young Wentworth had predicted, there must be quite a crowd awaiting her below.

'She is, but you must not let that trouble you. I shan't allow the family to descend upon you in a horde. First you must meet your prospective father-in-law, but even that may be delayed if you should wish it. Are you quite sure that you don't prefer to rest?'

'I couldn't!' Sophie told her frankly. 'I feel that this is all a dream. I want to convince myself that it is happening and that there is no longer any danger.'

Prudence laid a comforting hand upon her arm. 'I know the feeling, Sophie. My own adventures as a girl almost matched your own. I'll tell you about them sometime. Now, let me fasten this gown for you. The blue is a good choice. It will suit you to perfection.' She waited by the window as Sophie slipped into a petticoat and drawers of the finest cambric, then her deft fingers dealt with the rows of tiny buttons as Sophie arranged the matching fichu of the garment over her bosom.

Prudence spun her around. 'You'll do!' she said drily. 'If Nicholas doesn't long to eat you alive, my nephew is not the man I think him!'

Sophie cast a nervous look at her reflection in the mirror and could scarcely recognise herself. Suddenly she felt more confident. In her borrowed plumage she would not disgrace her love. The blue gown fitted her to perfection.

'Prudence, I have you to thank for this,' she said shyly. 'I feel like a new woman.'

'But not *too* changed, I hope,' Prudence cried in mock dismay. 'Nicholas won't forgive me if he cannot recognise his love...though there is little danger of that, I think. My dear, won't you take a little refreshment? You must be very hungry. Let me send Bess to you with a tray.'

Sophie shook her head. 'If you don't mind, I'd prefer to go down now.'

Prudence didn't argue. She guessed rightly that Sophie was feeling nervous at the prospect of meeting the old Earl, and wished to get the ordeal over with as soon as possible.

'Very well!' she said. 'His lordship won't eat you, Sophie. You've taken a great worry from his mind. He'd begun to wonder if his heir would ever wed.'

'I hope he will approve of me...'

'How could he not do so? Besides, your little Kit has been an excellent ambassador. I haven't seen the Earl so entertained for years.'

'I hope Kit has behaved himself. He is no respecter of persons, as I'm sure you have discovered.'

'It is that happy, open quality which has endeared him to all of us, my dear. Kit and the Earl have been closeted together for a full hour this morning. The Lord alone knows what plans they've hatched.' Prudence began to chuckle. 'Come on, let us go down to them.'

She took Sophie's hand and they moved to the head of the great staircase. Then, even as they began to descend, Nicholas strode across the hall below.

'Your love is impatient for you, I see.' Prudence prepared to slip away. 'Go to him, my dear. You have all my wishes for your future happiness.' She turned and whisked away along the landing.

Sophie did not see her go. Her gaze was fixed on Hatton. She had a curious sensation of floating towards him in some kind of dream.

He stopped her before she reached the hall. 'Stay there for just a moment!' he begged. 'I shall remember you all my life just as you look now.'

Sophie blushed, but she did as he asked, though she felt disposed to tease. 'I am in borrowed plumage,' she smiled. 'Your aunt has been very kind.'

'In borrowed plumage or your own, you are the most beautiful woman I have ever seen.' His look was so ardent that she blushed again. Then he took her in his arms and kissed her with an overwhelming passion which took her breath away.

At last she was forced to protest. 'Nicholas, the servants!' she whispered. 'They will think this most unseemly.'

He held her away from him and gazed into her eyes. 'Look about you!' he suggested.

Sophie glanced about the hall. She could see no footmen, and even the porter's chair was deserted.

'Don't you sense the air of celebration?' he chuckled. 'If I am not mistaken, they are gathered below to drink a health to us.'

She looked at his laughing face. The air of strain had gone, and happiness had smoothed the worried lines upon his face. She reached up to caress his cheek. 'You look like an eager boy,' she told him fondly. 'They must have guessed our secret just from your expression.'

'Certainly my father did so. Come and meet him, Sophie. He cannot rise to greet you, but you will understand...' He took her hand and led her into the study.

Any doubts which Sophie might have felt were dispelled as she looked at the scene which greeted her. Kit was seated on the Earl's knee, with an arm about the old man's neck.

'His lordship can't get up,' he told his mother instantly. 'He was injured when he fought the smugglers.'

'That is my claim to fame,' a deep voice remarked. 'It seems to find favour with your son. How are you, my dear? I hear we have much to thank you for.'

Sophie curtsied low, reassured by the kindly tone. 'I was somewhat overtaken by events, my lord.'

'Even so, you showed great courage, and Kit is proud of his mama, are you not, my boy?'

'Yes, sir. Hatton says that she is...she is a pearl of great price.'

'Well, we must all abide by what Hatton says,' the Earl agreed solemnly. 'Bless me, I had no idea that I had produced such a marvel of perfection.'

'He can skate backwards, too,' Kit offered.

'Astonishing! I am overcome! Such godlike perfection!'

'It pales beside the qualities of my coachman, Reuben, I assure you, Father. Now, Kit, the girls are waiting for you. They've challenged you to a game of spillikins. Let me take you to them.' He stretched out his hand and Kit went with him willingly.

The Earl of Brandon looked at Sophie. 'I had not thought to see my son so happy, my dear. I am most deeply in your debt.'

'I love him,' Sophie said simply. 'Kit does not think more highly of him than I do myself. My worry was that you might find this match unsuitable.'

'Why so?'

'I am a widow and I have a son. When Nicholas met me I was running an inn. It was not the most auspicious of backgrounds, my lord.'

'I think you have forgot to mention certain other matters. My son loves you, Sophie, and not only for your beauty, though you are indeed a lovely woman. I had begun to think that he would never wed. In fact, I have been guilty of trying to pressure him into marriage. I didn't understand that he was looking for something which he has found only in you, and that, my dear, is a strength of character which he can admire.'

Sophie looked up at him with brimming eyes. She could not have wished for a nobler tribute. On an impulse she stretched out both her hands to him.

'That's right!' The old man took her hands in his. 'Now give me a kiss, my dear. Let me welcome you to our family.'

Hatton returned to find them deep in conversation. When his father held out his hand, he shook it heartily.

'Congratulations!' Brandon said. 'You are the luckiest man alive, I think!'

'I think so too!' Hatton's eyes devoured his love. 'Sophie, when shall we be wed? It could be tomorrow if you wish it. I can get a special licence.'

The Earl of Brandon shook his head as he looked at the two lovers. 'See what you have undertaken, Sophie! My son has not the least idea that ladies need time to buy a trousseau and to invite their friends to share their happiness in an elaborate ceremony!'

Sophie clutched Hatton's hand. 'I don't care about such things,' she whispered. 'If you wish it, Nicholas, it shall be tomorrow.'

His look was reward enough for her, but now the old Earl chuckled. 'My boy, you are likely to be far too much indulged,' he teased. 'Sophie, take care that you don't always let him have his own way.'

Hatton slipped an arm about his love. 'My darling won't do that. Father, you have no idea! She can be the most difficult woman in the world.'

Sophie's laughing protests died upon her lips as Prudence entered the room accompanied by Claudine Arouet.

The little Frenchwoman's eyes were twinkling as she looked at Nicholas. 'So you have won your lady, my dear? I guessed that this would be the outcome from the first.'

Sophie blushed and shook her head, but Madame came to kiss her. 'It is good!' she said quietly. 'You are well matched, I think. Allow me to wish you every happiness.'

Prudence added her own congratulations. 'Shall you wish to dine with the family this evening?' she asked with her usual frankness. 'If you wish it, Sophie, I will send a tray up to your room. You must be exhausted.'

'I should be,' Sophie admitted. 'But I'm not. I'll be happy to dine with you tonight.' It was true. She had never felt more alive. Now she wanted to savour every moment. It had taken a brush with death to convince her that nothing was more precious than life itself. And that future life would be filled with happiness, she knew. Nothing mattered now except the love which would encompass Kit and herself.

That evening they dined at an unfashionably early hour, but the gaiety could not have been surpassed at the table of the Prince Regent himself. Any doubts which Sophie might have had about her welcome were soon dispelled as one toast followed another to her future happiness.

She smiled as she looked about her, unfolding like a flower in the sun as the warmth of the family's affection flowed towards her. How alike they were—these Wentworth men with their dark colouring and their massive build! The Earl, his brother Sebastian, her own Nicholas and Sebastian's sons resembled each other so strongly. Beside them, their women-folk looked fragile, but Sophie was undeceived. Both Claudine Arouet and Prudence had overcome hardship in the past. That much she had learned from Nicholas.

Then the Earl of Brandon raised a hand for silence. 'My son has set us a good example,' he announced with a twinkle. 'Claudine, have I your permission to let the family into our secret?'

For answer, the little Frenchwoman took his hand in hers.

Sebastian laughed. 'Brother, let us guess,' he teased. 'Claudine has agreed to become your wife?'

Prudence looked at her husband in mock indignation. 'You have spoiled the surprise!' she said.

A murmur of amusement rippled around the table. The Earl looked at the circle of laughing faces and threw up his hands in a gesture of resignation. 'What a family!' he said. 'Never try to keep a secret in this household, Sophie! You won't succeed, I can assure you.'

His news was the signal for another round of toasts and congratulations. Then Prudence rose and led the ladies from the room, leaving the men to their port.

Sophie hesitated in the hall. 'Prudence, will you excuse me for a moment?' she asked. 'I must look in on Kit. He is a restless sleeper. By now, his coverings will be thrown aside.'

She hurried up the staircase. Kit was settled in the dressing-room which adjoined her own bed-chamber, and, to her relief, he appeared to be sound asleep. For once, his blankets were undisturbed.

As she bent to kiss him, a pair of chubby arms slipped about her neck. 'I was pretending!' he announced. 'I like it here, Mama, don't you?'

'I do, my pet!'

'I'm glad to hear it!' A large hand rested lightly on her shoulder and Sophie turned to find Hatton by her side.

'I was playing possum,' Kit informed his friend.

'What on earth is a possum?' Sophie asked.

'It is a small animal which lives in the colonies. Possums hide from danger, but they also sleep for hours and hours and hours, don't they, Kit?'

'I expect so.' Obediently, Kit closed his eyes, but as Sophie and her lover left the room they heard a happy sigh. 'I love Hatton,' the small voice whispered. 'Do you love him too?'

'I do, my darling!' Sophie lifted her face to look deep into the eyes of her betrothed. What she saw there convinced her of a love beyond her wildest dreams. With a little cry of happiness she melted into his arms.

* * * * *